SECRET BRIDE

SECRET BRIDE

SHAROL LOUISE

FIVE STAR

A part of Gale, Cengage Learning

Detroit • New York • San Francisco • New Haven, Conn • Waterville, Maine • London

GALE
CENGAGE Learning™

Set in 11 pt. Plantin.
Printed on permanent paper.

LIBRARY OF CONGRESS CATALOGING-IN-PUBLICATION DATA

Louise, Sharol.
  Secret bride / by Louise Sharol. — 1st ed.
    p. cm.
  ISBN-13: 978-1-59414-718-0 (hardcover : alk. paper)
  ISBN-10: 1-59414-718-3 (hardcover : alk. paper)
  1. Grandsons—Fiction. 2. Grandmothers—Fiction. 3. Fiancees—Fiction. 4. Fiances—Fiction. 5. Family secrets—Fiction. 6. Imposters and imposture—Fiction. 7. Country life—England—Fiction. I. Title.
  PS3612.O82S425 2009
  813'.6—dc22   2008039746

First Edition. First Printing: January 2009.
Published in 2009 in conjunction with Tekno Books.

Printed in the United States of America
1 2 3 4 5 6 7 12 11 10 09 08

To Lynette Alison Young: my #1 fan club,
my friend, my daughter
And to Tomás, life partner *extraordinaire*

ACKNOWLEDGMENTS

I gratefully acknowledge my special seven, who made this journey possible:

Pat Mack
Linda Hoversland
Mary Nicholson
Susi Cradduck
Kaitlyn Elizabeth Moore
Megan Nicole Moore
Susan Elizabeth Groves
And my patient editor, Alice Duncan

CHAPTER ONE

London, 1794

"I have to find a fiancée."

"Did you lose one?" Myles spoke around his pipe stem as his friend joined him.

"I'm quite serious." Damion Templeton, Viscount Woodhurst, took a seat opposite Myles Grisham, fourth Earl of Cantwell, and signaled for a bottle of hock. "And I've only got about a fortnight to find her." He shrugged out of his coat, which was efficiently retrieved and whisked away by one of the club's footmen.

"Two weeks? More than enough time for a well-heeled lad like you to reel one in. Hmm . . . if you had my good looks as well, I'd have wagered one." Lord Cantwell sat forward in anticipation of an entertaining tale. "Why two?"

"My grandmother arrives for a visit in a fortnight."

Myles took the pipe from his mouth and poked the air for effect. "Isn't this the granddame who has been insisting for the past six years that it's time for you to marry?"

"That would be the same grandmother, yes."

"Then why should this year be any different from the other years you've chosen to ignore her?"

"That's what's odd." Damion paused when the drinks and rummers were delivered. Contemplating his glass, he rubbed a thumb over the cut crystal facets. "This time, she *isn't* demanding. In fact, she promises she shall not even broach the subject of marriage. Says she's coming simply to visit, and we needn't discuss it." He took a huge swallow and looked solemnly at his friend's smiling face. "She's dying, Cantwell."

His friend's smile dropped upside down. "I'm so sorry. When did you learn?"

"Just today." Damion dug into a vest pocket and waved a folded sheet of paper. "In a blasted letter." He jammed it back with a sigh of frustration. "I immediately sent off a letter to my parents, asking why I'm hearing it from Grandmother, and not from them."

"May I?" Myles held out a well-manicured hand.

Damion retrieved the note and watched as his friend unfolded it gently.

Myles glanced at the first line, then turned it over, noting the Posthorn watermark. "Woodhurst, is this the correct letter?" He read the salutation aloud:

"Dear Edmund"

His eyes snapped to his friend's face. "Who is Edmund? I'm already confused."

Damion laughed, a sad sound. *"I'm* Edmund."

"Should I have guessed that? I've only known you . . . what? Fifteen years?" Myles returned his perusal to the paper, as if the explanation would appear between the lines.

"I suppose I've never mentioned it. It's quite typical of Grandmother." Damion rubbed a hand through his hair. "When I was born, Father wanted me named after his brother Damion. My grandmother insisted they name me after her father: Edmund. Did I mention my grandmother is stubborn? She's called me Edmund my entire life. We've given up."

"Ah." Myles hardly heard; his attention had returned to the letter:

I sit here thinking about how tentative life is, and decided to pick up pen and write you. I've had bad news recently. Sad news. And it made me realize how short and precious our time together is. Death is an inconsiderate visitor, you see; no warning.

I know I nag you terribly about getting married, but you'll be delighted to know I'm not sending this letter to nag you, Grandson. I promise. I'll be leaving soon, and it makes me think how I shall miss you. I should very much like to see you while I may, dear boy.

Please don't go to any extra effort for my sake, but do say you shall accept a visit from me. I plan on arriving in a little more than two weeks, on St. George's Day, unless I hear otherwise from you."

Love and Rgds.
Your Grandmother

"She's dying, yet she's coming to visit you. Should she be traveling?"

"Exactly my reaction," Damion said. "I began a note, suggesting I come to her instead, but . . . I suspect she is coming for the memories. She's long given up the manor at Fern Crest, but she loves that part of the country, and always insists our longer visits should take place there. My youngest memories are of Fern Crest Hall, when she and Grandfather were in residence there." He stared at those remembrances in his glass, swirling the clear liquid without taking a drink. "He's gone. It's been many years. Though it's now *my* home, still I see the two of them in every corner. They were always laughing, appeared to delight in one another's company. So in love . . . At their age, if you can imagine."

Myles looked away in embarrassment, leaving Damion to his thoughts, before asking, "I wonder why she didn't wait to tell you her sad news until she arrived to visit? I mean, why put this kind of news in a letter?"

Damion shrugged. "Don't know. I suppose I was too upset to wonder at it myself."

"You're close to her, then, Woodhurst?"

He nodded. "Very. She may pester me once a year to marry, but she's a grand woman. The best grandmother a man could have." He drank a silent salute.

"But I'm still missing something. She told you she's not going to badger you about marriage. So why are you looking for a wife?"

"Think of it, Cantwell. Wouldn't that make her happy?" Damion cocked his head to the side as he eyed his best friend. "Isn't that the least I can do for her?"

Myles stared at Damion as if he had a fever. "Well . . . I'm sure it would please *her*. But what about you? You said you'd not marry until the perfect woman came along." His head jerked slightly, in realization. "Ah, I see now: you wanted a love match—the same as your grandparents had." He shook his head. "Yet you're willing to marry the first woman you stumble across in the next two weeks? That doesn't make sense."

"It's only a fiancée, Cantwell!" Damion laughed. "It's not as if I'm going to marry the chit."

Myles started. "Woodhurst, I hate to shock you, but that's what a fiancée is—someone you promise to marry."

"Don't be dense. I'm not about to marry. I'm simply going to make Grandmother *think* I'm marrying. If I set the engagement period long enough, then after Grandmother . . . departs this earth, we cry off the engagement."

"That's cold. But smart." Myles nodded. "However, there is one sticky detail. What lady of our acquaintance will go along with a scheme such as that?"

"Ah, there's the rub, which is why I sought you out."

"Sorry. I'm not on the market for marriage. Especially not to you."

Damion kicked his friend's boot from where he sat. "That's all right then, as you're not my type. So . . ." He grabbed several pasties in his large hand from a passing waiter's tray, "How do I go about finding a fiancée in the next week or two?"

"Do you wish to run through the list of this season's eligible young debutantes?"

"No, I think your initial observation is right. No proper lady looking for a husband on the mart is likely to go along with this sham."

Myles's eyes widened. "You're not thinking of an *improper* lady, are you?"

"Good God, Cantwell, I'm not going to introduce my grandmother to a member of the demimonde . . . though that might be fun." He grinned mischievously.

"Then I confess you've lost me."

"I was, of course, thinking about a respectable lady. So, no ladies of our circle, you think?"

"I certainly believe the ladies of our circle would not only refuse to go along with this scheme, but their papas would not be amused either."

"Then . . ." Damion eyed his friend speculatively. "What about a shopkeeper?"

Myles shook his head. "Have you met any shopkeepers who speak like a lady? That's not been my experience."

"Don't think of a flower-cart Nelly. What if our shopkeeper were to work in a bookshop? Wouldn't she be well-read?"

"Well-read is not well-spoken."

"If you and I rack our brains, Cantwell, I know we can find a solution. Think, man."

Both men sank further into the plush armchairs, seemingly hypnotized by the fire.

Damion straightened. "Milliners? They cater to ladies of quality. They have to be able to hobnob."

Myles took a thoughtful draw of his pipe. "Yes. But I hear the really good ones are French. How would your grandmother feel about a French granddaughter-in-law?"

Damion visibly shuddered. "Scratch that." He refilled their glasses.

Two refills later, Myles said, "Perhaps Chloe would be willing to go along with this. Has your grandmother met my sister? Chloe's a good sport and loves getting into mischief."

"No. Much as I think she'd be perfect for the part, I expect my parents will most likely make an appearance at Fern Crest as well, and they know Lady Chloe and your parents too well. I need them to believe in this sham engagement, as they'd never be able to keep a secret from Grandmother."

"What did you say?" asked Myles.

"I said my parents have already met Lady Chloe."

"No. Before that."

"I said your sister would have been perfect for the part."

Myles snapped his fingers. "Precisely. For—the—part," he repeated slowly. "You need someone who can play—a part." He spread his hands as a magician would, the solution obvious by his upturned palms.

"An actress!" Damion sat up swiftly. "Why didn't I think of that? An actress will be able to mimic a lady's tone."

"And mannerisms."

"And she can dress the part."

"And act the part, if she's paid well." Myles shrugged. "It's just another play to her."

"You, Cantwell, are a genius. What theatres would you recommend I visit? For a classier type of actress?"

"Let's ask Chloe. She's up on all of that."

"I'd certainly appreciate it. It would save me some precious time." Damion rose, signaling to a footman for his coat. "That's resolved, then. I'm off to the estate, to begin preparations for

Grandmother's visit. I should return in a few days. As soon as I'm back in town, I'll get in touch, and hopefully Lady Chloe will have some good leads for us."

Myles stood, sucked on his pipe. "You know, you may need Chloe yet. Won't your fiancée require a lady in attendance during her visit?"

"I wasn't planning on staffing—" Damion colored. "Oh, I see. Yes, I suppose I must also conjure up a pretend companion for the fiancée. At least until Grandmother is settled in, or until my mother arrives."

"Well, be sure to think these nettling details through. You may also need gowns for this fiancée. And a carriage for shuttling her and Chloe from Town to Fern Crest. And . . . maybe some props . . . Musical instruments? Sewing baskets? Books on etiquette? That sort of thing."

"Egad. What a lot of work it is harboring a fiancée." Damion looked tired.

"A *pretend* fiancée," confirmed Myles. "From what I observe, the real ones are even more annoying and expensive. And that's nothing compared to what a wife should demand!"

"I'll take your word on it. It's not something I plan to find out for myself." Damion shrugged into his coat. "I do like this plan. It sounds natural: the two ladies visit my home, so that my fiancée can get to know my grandmother, before she—so that my grandmother can get to know the young lady. It will please Grandmother to have her there."

"And, very properly chaperoned by my sister—"

"Will she do it?"

"Chloe? For *you*? She'll be thrilled."

"You *what?*" Lady Chloe Grisham's screech could be heard in the next townhouse. "How dare you make a commitment for me to do something so foolish, so inane!"

"Calm down, little sister. It's for Woodhurst. I thought you worshipped the ground he walked upon."

"If he wants to ask *me* to be his wife, I'll seriously consider a sojourn in the country. But I'll be scoured if I'll play companion to some other woman who's got her hooks in him."

Myles tucked his chin into his chest in surprise. "You? Interested in Woodhurst? Seriously?"

Chloe blushed. "Of course not. It was a jest. Besides, one of my good friends is still enamored of him. How could I be interested when she plans to have him for herself? Drat. She's going to be devastated."

"Really? Who is it?"

"Oh, no. I'm not going to give you that ammunition to hand over to Lord Woodhurst."

"Hmm. Well, don't get any ideas yourself, as I'd never allow it."

She put her hands on her hips and scowled at her brother. "Why ever not?"

"You don't know him as well as I do, Chloe. He's a rake. I wouldn't want my sister to marry someone such as he."

"He's considered the catch of the Season. Besides, I thought he was your best friend."

"He is. What does that have to do with his suitability as my sister's husband?"

Chloe frowned as if doubting her brother's sanity.

"Anyway, I can't believe we're having this discussion," said Myles. "Because we need you to only *pretend* to be a companion."

"What are you saying?"

"There is no real fiancée."

Chloe's expression went from despair to hope. "He's not truly engaged?"

"It's a sham engagement." Myles eyed his sister sternly. "You mustn't let on. It's to fool his grandmother and his parents. And it's only for a short while. Then they'll cry off."

She looked to be considering it.

Her brother played his trump card. "Just think. You'll be at his manor for a few weeks, escorting this lady as she visits with Woodhurst and his grandmother every day. You'll have lots of information to pass along to your 'friend.' " He studied her skeptically, hoping she was not the one who carried a tendre for Woodhurst.

Chloe smiled evilly. "This might be fun. Perhaps I'll even make him realize he does want a proper fiancée." She was already scheming.

"No scheming. I can see in your eyes when you're scheming."

Chloe looked at her brother, all innocence in her wide eyes. "Not me, Myles. I'm going to be the perfect, feminine companion."

She practically floated from the room, rehearsing already.

What have I done? wondered Myles.

CHAPTER TWO

Widpole Manor Boarding School, outside Fern Glenn Village

"What on Earth are you doing on that wall?"

Tommy wiped a runny nose on his shoulder. His eyes were wet and swollen.

"Tommy, I want you to come down this instant."

"I . . . I can't, Miss Adams." He swiped at his eyes with one hand; the other tightly gripped the stones on top of the wall.

"How did you get up there?"

"I climbed the tree. That tree." He swiftly lifted a hand, just long enough to point to the oak tree whose roots threatened to lift the wall. Then he slammed his hand back down to grasp the capstone. "And the branch bent and was touching the wall, so I climbed over to here. But now I can't get back." He looked accusingly at the oak tree.

Miss Alix Adams huffed noisily, puffing out her cheeks. "All right." She looked back toward the school's mansion. "Let me get Mister Trombley. He'll bring a ladder out here and—"

"No!" Tommy had a look of sheer horror. "No, Miss Adams. Please. He'll cane me for sure."

"But I don't know if I can pull a ladder over here by myself. I don't even know where he keeps them."

"Please don't let him know, Miss Adams." Tommy looked down at her, and then down at the ground. "Never mind. I'll jump." He squeezed his eyes shut, and clung more tightly to the wall. "I can do it."

18

"Tommy, what if I hold out my arms? You drop down and I'll catch you."

He shook his head stubbornly. "I'm too heavy for you."

"What if I were to climb the tree, and bend the branch, like you did? Will you be able to pull yourself back onto the tree?"

"Maybe."

Alix reached up to the lowest branch of the oak tree. She wrapped both hands over the limb, and willed herself off the ground. Her body didn't move, though she was sure she was pulling.

She stuck a foot out, her sole against the rough bark, two hands on the limb overhead. She tried walking up the tree trunk. But her other foot never left the ground, and her left foot slipped against the bark.

"I can't believe this."

"What? What's wrong, Miss Adams?"

"I can't do it. How odd."

"Why is it odd?"

She made a rude sound of disgust. "Tommy, when I was your age, I was the fastest tree climber at Widpole Manor. I could climb *any* tree."

"Mistress Puddin says it's not polite to boast."

"I'm not boasting. I'm telling the truth. There's a difference."

"Hmm," said the young boy, not sounding convinced. "Maybe your body got too old."

"That's ridiculous!" She grabbed the branch by curling both hands behind it, her wrists facing toward her, and attempted to chin herself. She came three inches off the ground. "I'm not old," she asserted with disbelief.

"Maybe you've gained weight?"

She dropped her fists to her waist and turned to face the young truant. "And maybe you'd prefer that Mister Trombley come out and find you on the wall?"

Tommy giggled at the idle threat.

"Tommy, I'm going to find that ladder. It must be in the shed. Don't move until I get back."

It was easier than she'd suspected. The shed wasn't locked, and four ladders hung along the wall to the right of the door. She took the smallest, as it would be the lightest to carry. She hoped it would be long enough. Holding it in the center of its length, she walked as quickly as she could while struggling with its awkward balance.

"I'm back, Tommy lad."

"We'd best hurry, Miss Adams. The sun looks to be setting."

"Yes. If we're not in for dinner they'll be looking for us." She edged the ladder close to the wall. "It's not very stable. The ground's too uneven, what with these oak roots." Leaning the ladder against the stone wall, she wedged its feet against some sturdy roots. Soon she stood on the rung closest to the top of the ladder and could just touch the top of the wall. "Can you drop down to me, Tommy?"

"I'm afraid to let go!"

"Hold on. I've another idea." She descended the rungs hurriedly, and moved the ladder over two feet. "Stay still. I'm going to try something else."

She climbed again, and this time made it to the top rung, leaning her hands against the stone wall for balance. Her head peered over the top of the wall. Locking her elbows on the capstone, she swung a leg up and pulled herself onto the wall, straddling one leg over each side, her dress billowing out as if she were riding a horse.

She inched toward Tommy, whose eyes were still closed.

"Open your eyes, Tommy. Can you see me?" She waited until he squinted.

His eyes flew open. "Blimey! You're on the wall."

"Yes," she said with a cocky grin. "You see, I can still climb."

She looked down at the road that ran along the wall, following it with her eyes until it curved to the west, toward town. "What a grand view. I'd forgotten how it was to sit here and think about escaping into the world."

"Miss? Shouldn't we be getting back?"

"Yes. Tommy, here's what I want you to do. Scoot over toward me." She touched his hand. "Just scoot, as you see me doing." She scooted six inches backwards.

He scooted a bit forward.

"Good boy. That's it. Now . . ." She scooted her bottom back another foot away from him. "Come about another foot, and you'll be above the ladder."

He looked down and started shivering.

"No, don't look down yet, Tommy. Focus on my eyes."

He edged closer, and soon was close enough for her to pull him into her arms. He hugged her fiercely.

"Listen, here's what we're going to do. I'm going to take your hands." She demonstrated. "And I'm going to let you slide down to the ladder. It will be easy."

He shook his head.

"I promise I won't let go of your hands until you tell me you can feel the top step. It's not far at all. And then, it will be a snap to scramble down the rungs. It will be fun."

He shook his head again, but she pretended not to notice.

"Lie down on your stomach. Here we go. I'm holding you." She helped maneuver him until his feet were dangling just above the ladder. She had to swing a leg back so that her stomach was on the top of the wall, and her legs on the opposite side of the wall as Tommy's.

They were both so intent on the task that Alix never heard the rider approaching, the horse's hooves muffled by wet leaves upon the lane.

She had no idea he stopped to admire the derriere and legs

dangling on the lane's side of the wall.

"See how I have a tight hold on your hands?" She leaned down close to Tommy's head. "Do you feel the top step yet?"

"No." He sounded about to cry.

"That's all right, because I'm still holding your hands tight. I'm going to lower you just a tiny bit farther."

He tightened his hold, his eyes closed as tightly as his hands clenching hers.

"Feel with your toes. Any ladder yet?"

"N-n-no."

"This should do it. A little lower we go," said Alix. She heard the hard toes of Tommy's shoes knock on the wood. "Do you feel it yet?"

"Yes. Yes, Miss Adams, I do!"

"Take your time. I won't let go until you tell me you've got your balance, Tommy." She leaned farther down, afraid her arms would tire before he was securely on the ladder.

Just as she worried she could no longer hold his weight, her load suddenly lightened.

"I'm on the ladder, Miss! I'm standing on the top step."

"That's grand! Don't let go of my hands just yet. I want you to take one hand away, and put it against the wall. Hold it there for balance and try climbing down one rung. Can you do that?"

"I'm fine now! I can do the rest by myself." Tommy unexpectedly pulled his hands from her grasp.

Alix's weight fell backwards and she lost her balance on the wall. She stifled a scream as she grabbed unsuccessfully at the stones along the top, and toppled off the wall and down to the road.

"Miss Adams! Are you all right? I don't see you!"

She didn't want the boy to be frightened. If she had to, she could run around the property to the side delivery gate. There was a chance it would be locked after dusk, but Tommy had to get back to the mansion—with haste. The consequences would be worse for him than for her if they were late to dinner.

"I'm fine!" she called. "I . . . I thought I'd pick a few flowers for my room while I'm here. There are some lovely bluebells on this side, along the road. But Tommy, you must run back for dinner, before they find you're still outside. Don't tell them I'm here. I'll be in shortly, I promise."

"I'll wait for you."

"No! You mustn't let Mr. Trombley find you out on the grounds after dusk. I won't get in trouble, but you will. Go quickly. Hurry!"

"I'm going," he called, his voice already fading. Her words must have hit home, frightening him enough to send him on his way. "And . . . thank you. Don't delay too long, Miss Adams!"

She cupped her hands around her mouth. "You're welcome, Tommy. And I won't. Now run!"

She looked at her hands, covered with dirt, and began brushing them together roughly. Then she shook out her skirt. "Hell's bones," she muttered.

"May I be of assistance?"

Alix spun around and almost screamed. "Who are you? And what are you doing here?"

The stranger leisurely turned in the saddle and looked down the lane behind him, and then to the long curving length of the empty avenue ahead. "I'm riding. I beg your pardon if I'm trespassing, but I was under the impression this was a public road."

She narrowed her eyes. "It is, and I think you know that. I meant—what are you doing spying on me?"

"You? No, I was much more interested in the lovely bluebells along the side of the road." He looked pointedly at her feet.

Alix looked down to see the moldy remains of brown leaves from last autumn and the scruffy grass . . . nothing else. She blushed. "I only told him that so he would think I wanted to stay on this side of the wall."

"You're escaping, then?"

"No, that's ridiculous. Why would I wish to escape?"

"Don't all orphans dream of escaping?"

She looked at him, wondering if he read minds. "Who said I'm an orphan? Besides, this is not an orphanage. It's a boarding school. And I'm not a student." Her chin rose an inch. "I'm a teacher here."

"Really?" His tone implied disbelief. "You look too young to be a teacher."

"And you look too old to be teasing young ladies." She turned to study the wall, dismissing him. "You may go now. I need to return to the school."

She waited to hear the clop of hooves continue along the road, but all was silent. She peered over her shoulder. "Why are you still here?"

"How are you planning on getting back up?"

"I . . . I don't know. Perhaps I'll go around to the gate."

"As I recall," he said, "there's no gate along this wall. You've got a long walk ahead of you."

"And that's none of your affair." She concentrated on the gray stones of the wall, her back to him.

"Would you care for a ride?"

"No." Three seconds later she added, begrudgingly, "Thank you, anyway."

"I could place you atop my horse, and we can sidle next to the wall."

"No." She said it firmly, did not even turn around. Did not bother to add, "Thank you."

"All right, then." He jumped down from his horse.

Alix spun to face him, her eyes wide. "What—what are you doing?" She tried to keep her voice even. They were alone, no one in sight along the road.

"What do you think I'm doing?" he said, not without annoyance. "I'm going to assist you up the wall."

"Don't you touch me!" She backed away from him until she felt the round stones of the wall digging into her back.

He held up both hands, palms toward her in surrender. "I won't. I give you my word, I'm not going to grab you by the waist and toss you up." He looked at her slim waist, and muttered, "As appealing as that might be." Stepping next to the wall, he leaned against it and laced the fingers of both hands together. "Here. I'll make a stirrup with my hands, and you use it to step up and grab the wall." He leaned forward; his hands dangled about knee height.

Ten seconds later he looked up at her from under the dark hair that fell across his forehead. "Well? Come on, then."

Alix looked both ways to be sure no one watched them. She slowly stepped up against the wall, and hesitantly she put one hand on the wall and a toe in his cupped hands.

"Put your other hand on my shoulder," he ordered.

She touched his shoulder, then recoiled.

"I'm not going to remain bowed all day, madam." His voice was impatient.

Alix put one hand firmly on his shoulder, the other against the wall, and pushed up from the ground, one foot stable in his hands. He straightened slightly, just enough so that she could reach the top of the wall.

"I can touch the top. Just a bit higher, if you would."

He stood, pushing her foot upwards until she could again straddle the wall.

Alix spied the ladder and scooted toward it, one eye warily on the man who stood by the wall watching her. "Thank you. You may leave now."

He stood with hands on hips.

"Shoo," she said hopefully, her voice rising as if it were a question.

"Shoo?" He laughed.

She eased herself from the wall to the ladder, until the rung was solid beneath her toes. She peeked over the top of the wall at her rescuer one last time. Finally, she felt safe. She'd slip back to the dining hall, and no one would know she'd been gone. And there'd be no reason for the stranger to tell anyone. Besides, he didn't even know her name.

Feeling secure, she ventured a farewell. "Goodbye, sir. And thank you for your help."

"Wait. Shouldn't I introduce myself? Or know your name?" The gentleman had a mesmerizing smile.

She shook her head. "I hardly think that's necessary." She looked toward the mansion. Lights twinkled, and more began to blink on in the evening's deepening dusk. "I really must go." She carefully descended another step, no longer able to see her rescuer.

Yes, it would be best if he didn't know her name, either. She hesitated on a lower step, hidden by the wall, holding her breath until she heard the squeak of leather as he swung back into the saddle.

"Farewell," he called in his deep voice. And then in a higher one, mimicking Tommy's: "And don't delay too long, Miss Adams!"

She almost fell down the last few rungs.

CHAPTER THREE

"I have a few contact names for you." Myles was out of breath as he marched up to where Damion lounged in a comfy corner room of the club, enjoying a small fire and a snifter of brandy.

"Names?"

"For theatres. To find an actress." Myles helped himself to the brandy, filling an empty glass on a side table. "For your fiancée. Chloe was a fount of knowledge. By the way, she's agreed to play companion to your fiancée." He dug inside an inner pocket.

"Oh. Uh, please thank Lady Chloe for me, but I've changed my mind." Damion looked slightly embarrassed. "Not about her playing companion. It's that I've decided an actress won't do as a fiancée."

"Why ever not?" Myles folded his tall frame into the cut velvet chair, sticking long legs toward the fireplace.

"I know we discussed how an actress could dress the part, and act the part. *And* speak the part. But I found a flaw in our logic. An actress wasn't raised to learn proper manners and conventions, and . . ." He waved a hand, dismissing a young lady's many years of practiced learning in one gesture. "All that other. And what if she were to commit some ghastly *faux pas?*"

"That would be entertaining, I suppose." Myles laughed. "I'd hope to be there to see your grandmother's expression. No. Better yet, your parents'. Actually, yours too."

"Well, you'd be the only one laughing, I can promise you."

"Then we're back to where we started? How frustrating."

"No. Not at all. I've been thinking, Cantwell, that we forgot one class of female." He paused theatrically, studying his friend's face. Slowly he revealed each word: "Governesses . . . and . . . teachers."

Myles frowned; then dawning lit his brow. "Ah! Ingenious. Of course. Someone from noble origins, who would be studied in all the finer graces."

"Exactly."

"She could also act the part; talk the part—with no missteps. Well done, Woodhurst. So, where do we look? For our governess or teacher?"

"I'll take care of that." Damion avoided his friend's eyes. "I have a few ideas. More brandy?" He turned to the decanter at his elbow.

"But where will you find a female for hire so quickly? My mother constantly complains that good help takes forever to find. I know! Perhaps my mother or sister could recommend a reputable hiring—"

"No, no. I'm already pursuing it." Damion brushed the idea away with his hand. "Don't give it another thought. Let's have that drink."

CHAPTER FOUR

Damion sat in the school's crowded guest parlor. While empty of visitors, it was stuffed with solid pieces of furniture: sofas, end tables, coffee tables, clusters of chairs. Musty odors arose from the furniture, as if lemon wax and rug beaters hadn't been applied in a quarter of a century.

He glanced down at his boots, then flicked a speck of lint from his velvet cuff. Bored, he continued to survey the room. It was cozy in spite of—because of?—the crowded space. He had expected starkness: a space unadorned and cold, reflecting the dilapidated exterior of the school. Of course, a room such as this was most likely necessary to welcome visiting parents who entertained thoughts of enrolling their children. Sensing a coziness far from home would set their minds at ease—assuming parents had consciences concerning that sort of thing. He wouldn't know, but suspected not.

No large intimidating desk for an administrator to look down from. Instead, small tea tables scattered about the room like errant schoolchildren, each dressed in a delicate doily. No shelves of schoolbooks either. He'd assumed a school should be overflowing with books, each room a library. That's how he remembered his school.

As soon as Headmistress Staunton marched in, Damion realized this woman did not need an imposing desk to announce her authority. He would not have been surprised to hear drum rolls as she strode across the Aubisson carpet, quashing any flowers in its pattern that stood in her way.

"Yes? I am Headmistress Staunton. May I help you, sir?"

Damion rose and bowed. "I am Viscount Woodhurst, Head-mistress."

She eyed him from head to foot. He simmered at her insolence, but bit back any comment.

"You look too young to have a child to enroll, my Lord. Perhaps you are here on behalf of a sibling?" She took a seat facing him. "Sit, please." It was said in a firm monotone, in a voice used to commanding.

He wondered if it were his age that made her think of him as one of her students, to be ordered about. Nevertheless, he sat.

"No, madam. I am not seeking to enroll a student, though this is obviously a fine school." He noted she appeared pleased at the prevarication. "Rather, I am seeking aid from your school for a short period of time."

Her left eye almost closed when she frowned. Her upper body leaned forward, as if to hear better. "I am afraid you will have to explain yourself, Lord Woodhurst."

Damion sighed, and began in honeyed tones. "Headmistress Staunton, I realize this is a most irregular request." He watched her to gauge her reaction. He would start with scenario one: the truth. And why not start out seeking a sympathetic ear? "My grandmother, whom I love, is dying. I only learned this recently. The family is gathering at my estate, Fern Crest Hall. Perhaps you are familiar with it?"

She shook her head. He did not see a sympathetic line anywhere on her face. Perhaps he would go with his second scenario.

"My sister is coming to stay with us during this difficult time. She has two children who will, of course, be arriving with her."

"And her husband?" Her ferret eyes measured him.

"She is a widow." He looked her directly in the eyes as he lied.

"I see." But she said it as if she didn't see; as if she held it against his defenseless sister that her husband had inconsiderately died and left her alone.

Damion bristled defensively for his widowed sister, until he remembered his sister wasn't really widowed . . . Wasn't even married. Hell, he didn't even have a sister. He did not allow himself to smile.

"Two children, you say?"

Good Lord, he had to keep his mind on his story. How many *had* he said? "Yes, two. Two daughters." He quickly guessed the age of the little boy he'd seen on the wall. "Seven and eight years old. Well-behaved children, she assures me."

The woman humphed. Apparently, this was an oxymoron in her dictionary. "I do not board students for short periods of time, Lord Woodhurst."

"Oh, no. We are not looking to have them boarded. The children shall stay with us for the duration of their mother's visit."

She waited. He would not have been surprised if she tapped a toe. Her impatience to remove this visitor was palpable.

"Headmistress Staunton, we do not know how long until . . . how long our grandmother will linger. Even the doctor has not told us with certainty."

Well, at least this was true, as Damion had not spoken to Grandmother's doctor yet. Damion had learned it was always best to insert a kernel of truth in a lie, to make it more believable.

"It could be days," he continued. "Or weeks. But we do not anticipate she will be with us to celebrate Midsummer Day." By the urgency in Grandmother's letter, he doubted she would linger two months.

"I do not mean to be abrupt, my Lord." She rearranged the doily at her side with an irritated snap. "But what does this have to do with the school?"

"My sister requires a governess for the children."

He watched her squinty eyes narrow further.

"Well, be that as it may, our teachers are paid to teach our own students. Exclusively. We do not have unengaged teachers for hire."

Damion nodded reasonably. "I am sure that is because your teachers are impeccable. Or, so they say in the village."

She dipped her head in acknowledgement of what she believed to be true. "Still, I find it unusual for a woman to fret over the lack of a governess for such a short period—a month or two. Especially for female children."

Damn. He should have realized that. He should have said she had two sons. He looked at the headmistress with as much sincerity as he could muster (this was also best when falsifying) as he nodded and said, "I could not agree with you more. My sister is an unusual woman. What is the saying? 'Idle minds?' "

She sniffed and nodded in return. "Quite commendable."

He shifted forward in his chair. Time to cast the fishing rod. "It was suggested to me—"

"By whom?"

He paused and looked up to a corner, studying the cobweb and pretending to look thoughtful. He shook his head. "I wish I could remember. So many persons have declared this school to be excellent. If only I could remember who made that particular suggestion." He shrugged his helplessness.

"You were saying? It was suggested . . ."

"Ah, yes. It was suggested that donations—from benefactors—would always be welcome."

Her eyes changed. He knew the precise moment she made the connection. "Of course," she said, "if it's only for a finite period—a very short period—that you require . . ."

"Of course." He nodded once, with a slight tilt of the head.

"And, uh . . . was a figure perhaps mentioned by this person who advised you?"

His angling had paid off. He reached into the pocket of his jacket. "A generous donation, of course." He held a cheque just out of her reach; tilted it so she could read the figures. "I thought . . . perhaps a draft for this amount?"

Her eyes squinted, and then widened. She looked up at him. "No more than two months, you say?"

"Sadly, no. No more than two months." If Grandmother lingered, Damion would be only too happy to return to the school with another draft. "Much more likely to be one month. Your teacher would return to her duties immediately in that case, although, of course, you would keep the entire donation. She might hardly be missed, wouldn't you think?"

Headmistress Staunton kneaded her thick knuckles. "It is difficult, you realize, to pare the staff at any time of the year. Why, we only recently had a teacher whose illness forced her to—"

"Perhaps this donation could be doubled. Half now, and half when . . . at the end of the time required?"

Her eyes glinted as she eyed the bank note greedily. "I am sure the extra amount would help defray the overworked teachers who must take up her extra students."

And I am sure those overworked teachers will never see a shilling. "Very wise logic."

"I have five teachers currently on staff. I am thinking Miss Eccleston would be a perfect governess for girls that age."

He had not anticipated her naming a choice. But this should not be difficult to manipulate, as they'd already bargained the most important point, that of compensation.

"I . . . I would expect to have the opportunity to interview the lady who will oversee my nieces' education, before relinquishing this draft. I'm sure you would insist upon the same."

She rose eagerly. "I'll send for Miss Eccleston immediately, my Lord."

He held up a hand. "I might save you a little trouble, madam. There was a particular teacher who was mentioned by . . ." Again he furrowed his brow in mock concentration. "Well." He laughed. "I must say I could use a bit of tutoring myself, for memory."

She forced a smile, and her sharp little teeth barely showed between her lips. Tilting her head cooperatively, she blinked agreeably as she enquired, "And which teacher might that be, my Lord?"

"I believe her name was . . . let me think. It was a short name." He stared at the carpet for effect. "Adams! That was it. Miss Adams."

The headmistress reacted as if slapped, her body jerking back. "Miss Adams! Are you quite certain?"

"Perhaps not. There is no Miss Adams at this school?" He made a motion to rise. "Dear me. Perhaps I have the wrong school? Most embarrassing, I—"

"No, no! Do stay, sir." She retook her seat quickly. "We do have a Miss Adams. And this is the only school in the vicinity. I assure you, we are the tiptop school they pointed you to."

"Then . . ."

"It is just that—" Headmistress Staunton turned her head to confirm no one could overhear. She lowered her voice. "To be honest, my Lord, if I were your sister, I should not be happy with Miss Adams."

Damion froze.

He recalled, as he'd already done too many times this week, the impertinent young woman he'd accosted at the wall. She had seemed so proper . . . perhaps a little *too* stiff and proper.

But what could be the headmistress's objections? Seeds of doubt began sprouting around this stranger he thought to plant in his home and present as his fiancée.

"Is she . . . a tippler?" He couldn't help the small frown across his brow.

"Goodness, no!"

"Immoral?"

"Lord Woodhurst! You insult my school—"

"I am so sorry." *Well, at least it couldn't be anything too bad.* "Then . . . can you elaborate on her flaws?"

"She is—" The headmistress sniffed, as if embarrassed to admit one of her teachers was flawed. "—unmanageable."

Oh, was that all? He'd already suspected she was a bit headstrong. Hardly worth mentioning, as he could easily control that.

"And," the woman said, warming up to a passionate topic. "She is overly independent for such a young woman. All of my other teachers are much more biddable. *Any* of them would make a much better governess than Miss Adams, I assure you."

"Still . . ." He looked down at the bank draft. "I came here with that name stenciled upon my brain. May I interview her and decide for myself?"

She shook her head. "I'm afraid you must trust my judgment here. Miss Adams is most unsuitable for the position you require."

"And yet you retain her as an employee?" *Her services must come so cheaply you can't let her go.*

Headmistress Staunton colored as if reading his thoughts. "One hopes to eventually make an impression upon her. She is young." She looked out the window as if she expected to see the young woman hanging upside down from the eaves or taunting her with some other outrageous behavior, and shuddered. "But she is so often a daily challenge to my nerves."

"Perfect." Damion slapped his hands upon his knees.

"Perfect?" She stared at her guest, not without suspicion.

"Yes. If we may assume her being here presents a daily challenge to your nerves, then I trust it will be a relief for you to have her gone. Even if only for a short time. Just think, she will be out of your hair, *and* she will be aiding you further by earning a stipend for the school." He edged the bank draft a bit closer to the headmistress.

She reached a pudgy hand forward, and he sat back, taking his arm and the paper with him. "Assuming she interviews suitably, of course."

"Of course. Would you care to speak to her now?" Her eyes were on the cheque, not on him.

"Yes. And should we reach an agreement, I would feel comfortable leaving this draft with you today. I'll return—with my sister, of course—to retrieve the teacher next week. Seven days from tomorrow."

"Your sister is not yet in residence?"

"No. I . . . informed her I would conduct the interview myself." He saw a cloud of hesitancy in the headmistress's eyes. "Her correspondence directs my full authority—as head of family—to select an appropriate governess for my nieces."

"I see. And surely you realize, Lord Woodhurst, that I shall expect your sister to arrive to escort Miss Adams to your home. I would be remiss in releasing her to the sole company of a gentleman—even one such as yourself."

"Of course. My sister shall be here with me next week, to escort Miss Adams."

"And . . . the draft shall be left with me today? *Before* your sister meets Miss Adams?"

"If I find Miss Adams suitable during our interview, the draft remains with you, regardless of my sister's impression of Miss Adams. Is it that you allude to?"

Headmistress Staunton blushed. "I do not mean to be so blunt, sir. But it would also be remiss on my part not to repeat that you must consider yourself warned about the young Miss Adams."

"Agreed. You shall have my decision—and the draft—within the hour, Headmistress Staunton."

They both stood. By time he finished bowing, her dress was already trailing around the doorjamb.

Damion led Miss Adams out to a simple hewn log bench beneath one of the large maple trees. Movement at the window confirmed the headmistress watched them closely. She'd presented Lord Woodhurst to Miss Adams and allowed him to step outside for a short interview. Damion had insisted on the privacy. He'd decided he would not interview Miss Adams inside, where they could be easily spied upon and overheard.

Aware of the headmistress's watchful eyes, he was careful to stand a good distance away when Miss Adams took a seat.

"Yes? Why did you wish to speak to me?" Her brow wrinkled prettily.

"Miss Adams, I insisted to Headmistress Staunton I wished to interview you in private so we could speak freely without being overheard."

The pretty wrinkle worked in earnest to become a frown. "Privately? I don't understand." Her eyes narrowed. "Did you say something to her about the . . . the incident in the road?"

"No, of course not. This has nothing to do with that chance meeting." *This has everything to do with that chance meeting.* "I told her I am here because my sister requires a governess from this school for a few weeks. That is, for a very short period. No more than two months, I am sure. Headmistress and I agree you will suit, but I requested to interview you privately first."

"And of course, I am given no say in whether I 'suit.' " It

wasn't said rebelliously; more in resignation.

"I do not mean to sound so high-handed," Damion said. "But it will mean a generous contribution to the school. Surely she anticipated you would be willing to assist the school?" At her slight nod of agreement, he continued. "Perhaps the money will buy more books for the children. Or . . . a climbing ladder for young Tommy." He could see she struggled to hide a smile. "But I wish to ask you a few questions before sealing the bargain with the headmistress."

He noted her wary look and wondered what skeletons could possibly pop out of a mild school teacher's closet.

He smiled reassuringly. "And I wished for privacy because . . . Miss Adams, I'd like to be candidly honest with you. This is rather difficult to explain. There are no children, so I don't need a governess, actually."

Her eyes flew open. "I will not be party to illicit—"

"No! No, it's nothing immoral or illegal, I assure you." He held up his hands in honest surrender. "You see, Miss Adams . . . What I need is a fiancée."

Her reaction to this was worse. "I am not in the market to be married. How dare you assume—"

"No, no! I see I am not explaining well. May I start from the beginning? You'll think it quite funny, truly."

She waited without a smile on her face.

Damion placed one foot atop the bench, and placed his hands on his knee, leaning in confidentially. "My grandmother—whom I love dearly—is dying."

"And you think that's funny?" Her voice was incredulous.

He'd anticipated an endearing sigh of sympathy; young ladies always sighed endearingly over death.

"No! No, I love my grandmother very dearly," he said, not without a trace of annoyance. "I'm merely giving you a little background. I recently found out, in a letter from my grandmother, that she is dying."

Her eyes revealed the sympathy she'd withheld, but still she waited coolly for his explanation.

"Her one wish these last years has been that I marry. And I failed her." He sighed deeply. "I received a letter from her telling me she won't be long on this earth, and she wants to come visit me in the country one more time. She promises not to nag me about marrying."

"Oh . . . I'm so sorry." She looked down, her clasped hands resting upon a simple homespun dress.

"I can't let her die unhappy. You can see that, can't you? I decided to let her think I'm engaged. After all, a little lie can't hurt. She won't be with us much longer."

Alix looked up with clouded eyes that matched the overhead sky. "But . . . why me? Aren't there other women of your acquaintance who would be willing to help?"

"That's just it . . . the women I'm acquainted with would expect me to make good on the proposal."

A corner of her mouth turned up. "Perhaps you flatter yourself a little too much?"

He frowned at her skepticism. "Perhaps you do not understand the ways of noblemen's daughters and mamas. But nevertheless, no. I do not plan to test that theory. The women I know come from good families—" he turned red from his collar up. "I'm sorry. I don't mean to say your parents are not of good families . . ."

"My parents are no longer alive. I was orphaned at a young age."

"Then that's perfect—Dear God, I've done it again, haven't I? Of *course* it's not perfect. I'm very sorry for your loss. I simply meant you were . . . unattached? Alone?"

"You make it sound so tragic. Perhaps I'm quite happy being

on my own." He saw the tiny dimple in the stubborn chin she raised.

"Yes, I'm sure you are." He didn't sound convinced. "Regardless, all I need is a woman who is willing to pose as my fiancée while my grandmother arrives for her visit. And you shall be well compromised—compensated! Of course, I meant to say 'compensate.' "

She wrinkled her brow again, the clouds in her eyes darkening.

"And you will have a proper companion, I promise," he added hastily.

"Why would I need a companion when your sister will—Oh, I suppose there is no sister, if there are no children?"

Damion nodded, pleased at her astuteness. He looked around the empty grounds, which were devoid of shrubbery and flower beds. "Wouldn't you welcome a change? Think of it as a holiday from your regular employment."

She followed his gaze, from the few scattered maples to the dandelions sprinkling the sparse grass at their feet. "Well . . . I suppose it would be a change."

"There is one other sticky point."

"I was sure there would be." She arched an auburn eyebrow.

Damion narrowed his eyes at her impertinence, secretly sympathizing more and more with the headmistress. "My parents have also decided to come visit. So we shall have to carry on the charade for my parents as well as my grandmother. But they shan't stay any longer than she."

"And how long will she be staying with you?"

"Until . . . until her death." He found the words difficult to say. "Which we understand is imminent."

She nodded, pink with embarrassment. "So, I . . . I come to your manor. And I will have another female for propriety's sake. Is she a stranger to you as well?"

"Lady Chloe? Hardly. I've known her since she emerged from the schoolroom. Her brother and I are great friends. You'll enjoy her company."

"Wait. Why not ask *her* to be your fiancée, if she's someone you already know?"

"I gave it a thought, but my parents know her. Our families often attend the same functions."

"Ah, I see." Alix brushed at her skirt while she thought, as if she could banish the wrinkles in the serviceable bombazine. "So." She looked up at Damion, her voice all business as she began again. "I come to the manor. Your friend accompanies me as my companion, and—why do I need a companion if your family is there?"

"I plan to get you established before they arrive. Hence, the need for a companion."

She nodded, then tilted her head as a thought occurred to her. "But why not wait until your grandmother arrives, and then bring your fiancée to meet her? If your grandmother were there, would I still need a companion?"

Damion considered. "Where were you, Miss Adams, when Cantwell and I were hatching our plan? Your logic is sound. However, Lady Chloe has already agreed, and I promised the headmistress I'd have a lady with me—she believes it to be my sister—when I arrive to escort you. Besides, Lady Chloe will assist in guiding you in any matters you are unsure of."

She nodded again. "And I pretend to be your fiancée when your family arrives, and until they all . . . depart. Then I return here, to the school. Is that it, my Lord?"

"That's it, madam." He studied her, wondering what thoughts those grey eyes dwelt upon.

She looked at him from under long lashes. "You said I would be compensated. How much are you paying?"

"I didn't mean you personally. I am paying the school for

41

your services." He saw this did not satisfy her question. "I offered Headmistress Staunton fifty pounds. I shouldn't require more than a month of your time. Perhaps two."

"And how much are you offering *me*, Lord Woodhurst?"

He didn't know whether he felt embarrassed or defensive. Perhaps a little of both. "Well, I thought your wages were paid by the school, and if I were to pay the school—"

"I think I should be compensated as well." She straightened her shoulders.

He bit back a muttered epithet, swearing his empathy for the saintly Headmistress Staunton. "And how much would you expect?" He bared his teeth, hoping it appeared as a friendly grin.

"You offered the headmistress fifty pounds." She wouldn't meet his eyes. "Then I . . . I should expect . . . fifty pounds as well?"

He studied her silently, waiting until she looked hopefully up. "One hundred if you can convince my family."

Her face lit. "I can do that."

"Then it is a deal?" He held out a hand, not caring whether or not they were being watched.

"Yes." She took his hand briefly, and dropped it just as quickly.

He would not have been surprised to see a spark jump to the tree, setting the dry bark on fire. Her touch left a warm trace that lingered along his palm.

Chapter Five

In the dining hall, Alix found herself glancing several times at the youngest children's table. How was she going to explain to Elizabeth and the other students that she'd be gone a month or two?

All the children held a special place in her heart, but Elizabeth in particular.

Orphaned at an early age, Elizabeth was one of the charity students taken in by the school. Alix remembered meeting her newest pupil when the little girl arrived two years ago: Elizabeth had trembled like a puppy. Her condition reminded Alix of her own first days at the cold mansion, feeling small, lost, and unwanted. Similar to Elizabeth, she'd been orphaned at an early age. It made her want to pull the little girl protectively into her arms. Alix had decided to speak to the child the moment they left the headmistress's office, to let her know how much they shared in common, to let her know she had a friend at Widpole.

Except that Elizabeth didn't speak.

She did allow Alix to take her hand that first day, although several months later she still hadn't spoken. The village doctor declared the child to be untreatable. One especially cold winter day, while Alix was buttoning up Elizabeth's woolen coat, a tiny little voice said, "My mama and papa gave me this coat."

Alix had stilled in shock, then smiled warmly, willing tears away from her eyes. "It's beautiful, Elizabeth."

· Yes, it would be hard to say goodbye to Elizabeth, even for a short time.

Like young Alix, Elizabeth performed chores to earn her keep at Widpole Manor, but she also benefited from a minimal education. When Alix had been brought to the school, she had been surprised that she was allowed—no, expected—to attend classes with the other students. As she grew older, she considered herself extremely fortunate that Headmistress Staunton had taken the advice of a staff member who recommended Alix be groomed to become a teacher.

That hadn't meant the other students had to accept her. She could still hear Betty Anne's regal voice the first time her young schoolmate had dismissed her with, "You're an orphan." At the time, she thought it was a compliment because she was a better student than Betty Anne. She hadn't heard the disdain accompanying the words.

Typical of Alix, she was at first more interested in how to spell it than in what it meant. After class, she hung back and leafed through the huge musty dictionary that sat open on a table. It was almost too high for her to reach, but she could read the words at the top of the page if she stood on tiptoe. Miss Yarrow was quite proud of that dictionary. You'd think she'd written it herself rather than Mr. Johnson, its author.

Frustrated, she carefully searched "o-a-r" and "o-r-e" but could not find the word.

"May I help you, Alix?"

Alix jumped to find Miss Yarrow at her elbow. "My word is lost, Miss Yarrow. I can't find it. Are *all* the words in the world in here?"

"I'm not sure they are, but let's see if we can find it together. What word are you looking for?"

"Or-phan," Alix said with a child's precise pronunciation.

"Oh." Miss Yarrow's lovely face fell. She put her slim hand

on Alix's head and said, "Where did you hear it, dear?"

"Betty Anne. She said I'm an orphan. Is an orphan a nice person?"

"Humph. Obviously nicer than Betty Anne," said the young teacher.

Alix giggled. "Show me where it is. How do you spell it?"

Miss Yarrow hesitated. "All right. But as we look it up, I want you to remember that words by themselves aren't good or bad. It's people who are nice. Or not so nice. Here. I'll spell it, and you turn the pages. It starts with the letter 'O.' Then comes an 'R.' " She waited patiently while Alix stretched and carefully flipped the pages. "Mm-Hmm. Next letter is 'P.' The 'P' and an 'H' together make the sound of an 'F.' "

"That's a silly spelling, isn't it?" Alix's small pudgy finger found it then. She read exceedingly slowly: "A child de . . . de-ser . . . ted. A child deserted by its mother." Her mouth formed an O and she looked up forlornly at Miss Yarrow. "That's not true. My mama didn't die on purpose."

"No, of course not. Look. It also says a child whose parents have died." Miss Yarrow hugged Alix close to her side. "It wasn't your mother's choice. She misses you, you know."

Alix nodded her head up and down. "I miss her too."

"Well, see, it just means you're special. I'll bet you're the only orphan in my class. And I'll bet nobody else can even spell it. Let's close the dictionary, and see if you can remember how to spell it."

It worked to distract Alix. She snapped the large volume closed, and closed her eyes. "O-R-P-H- . . . U?"

"Try the letter 'A.' "

"A-N."

"Very good. Shall we go to dinner? I expect the bell's about to ring."

They left the room, Alix's hand in her teacher's.

"When I grow up, Miss Yarrow, I'm going to have my own dictionary. And I can look at all the words I want. Every day."

She smiled now, remembering how she'd caressed that book years later when Miss Yarrow left the school's employ. Emma Yarrow gave it to Miss Alix Adams, her good friend, who became a teacher that same year to fill the open position Miss Yarrow left.

"Elizabeth, I'd like to talk to you." Alix sat under the same tree where the gentleman had touched her hand. She did not allow herself to dwell on the memory, which came unbidden often enough as it was.

Elizabeth set the one-armed doll on the bench next to her. The doll was one of the school's communal toys, shared by all. Elizabeth set it as close to her small body as possible, so that no one else should come by and snatch it away. "Yes, Miss Adams?"

Alix touched Elizabeth's soft curls. "I want to tell you about something I'm going to do. For a very short time. I'm going to see someone. You know, like when the teachers go shopping in the village?"

Elizabeth nodded. "Are you going to go shopping?"

"Not exactly. But I'm going to go visit with someone."

"When?" Elizabeth touched the sparse curls that no longer covered the doll's head, mimicking Alix's affectionate touch.

"Quite soon, though I'm not sure exactly what day. My friend will be sending a carriage to pick me up."

Elizabeth sat up. "How exciting! I've never ridden in a carriage before." She instantly sagged. "How long will you be gone?"

"I should only be gone a month. Perhaps two, but I'll return as soon as I can. Another teacher will lead your class until I get back."

Elizabeth's smooth brow creased, matching her downturned mouth. "You won't be in the classroom?"

"No, darling, but I will when I return. I'll be back before you know it."

Elizabeth startled Alix as she grabbed desperately at her sleeve. "Nooo." It was a sobbing wail. "Please don't leave, Miss Adams. Don't leave."

"Elizabeth, stop this," she said gently. "I told you I'll come back. It's only going to be for a short while. Perhaps only thirty days," she added. "And I'll come back just as soon as my friend no longer needs me. I promise."

Elizabeth still clutched Alix's sleeve, wrinkling it in her tiny fist. "No. You won't come back. Please don't go."

"Elizabeth, why the tears? Don't you believe me? Of course I'll come back. I'd never leave you alone."

Elizabeth let go of Alix's dress and wiped dirty hands across her eyes. Her breath came in short intakes as she made an effort to stop crying. "My mommy promised she wouldn't leave me."

Alix's blood turned to ice.

"But she did," Elizabeth said, hiccupping a small sob. "She never came back."

"*I* will." Alix took the little girl's face in her hands, but Elizabeth refused to look at her and stared at her scuffed shoes.

"Look at me, Elizabeth." Alix waited until the small child raised wet eyes to hers. "I *will* be back. I won't leave you forever."

Elizabeth nodded forlornly. She didn't look convinced.

CHAPTER SIX

"Edwyn—Edwyn, I have a letter you must see."

Her husband sucked on his pipe and didn't look up from his newspaper.

"Edwyn. Did you hear me?" CoraLee Templeton, Countess of Nottingdale, sailed into the bright room, her eyes intently perusing a sheet of paper.

"Yes, I did, Cora." His rote answer strummed with a chord of boredom. "Who's it from?" Blue smoke rose from his pipe to swim with the morning sunbeams.

"It's from Damion." She sniffed the air. "Is that a new tobacco?"

"Mm-Hmm." He continued to read the paper.

"I don't think I like it as much as the other." She sniffed twice more.

"What does Damion say? That he couldn't have come to tell us in person? I thought he hated writing letters." He pulled at the margin, spreading the next page open.

"Here. You must see for yourself."

Now he did look up. "Can't you just tell me, Cora?" He rattled his paper to signal his annoyance.

"It's extremely odd." His wife glided over to perch on the arm of his chair. Staring at the paper in her hand, she said, "For some reason, he thinks my mother is dying."

"We all are, dear." But this time Edwyn didn't go back to his paper.

"He says Mother wrote him a letter saying that she doesn't have long on this earth, and that she's coming to pay him a visit before it is too late."

Lord Nottingdale blew a puff of indignant air out his lips. "That's absurd. We just saw your mother last week. She's in the peach of health. Surely she'd have told us."

Lady Nottingdale finally looked up from the letter to her husband. "Exactly. In fact, all she wished to talk about was her excitement of her coming trip to Wales."

"Well, while *that* may not bode well for her sanity, at least we know she's in good physical health."

"Edwyn, perhaps we should go for a visit." She distractedly tapped a manicured fingernail against her front teeth.

"Visit Wales?"

"Very funny, darling. No. To visit Mother. I want to find out what this is about. Would you care to come along?"

He groaned in mutiny. "We both visited your mother recently. Why don't you go along on your own, dear."

She barely heeded his answer; was halfway to the door. "I should be back in time for tea."

"Mm-hmm." He was already hidden again in his paper.

"Elizabeth . . . wake up, darling." Alix whispered close to the child's ear so as not to wake the other sleeping youngsters in the row of dormitory beds.

The tiny girl blinked heavy-lidded eyes twice, then struggled to sit up in bed. Alix was there to cuddle her in waiting arms. Glossy dark curls leaned against Alix's shoulder until Elizabeth pulled away to look up.

"What is it, Miss Adams?" She rubbed her eyes with tiny fists.

"Elizabeth, I need to talk to you about something." Alix leaned down to peer into Elizabeth's sleepy face. "But it has to be our secret. You must promise, dear, not to tell anyone."

Elizabeth's curls nodded obediently as she said in a child's sing-song, "I won't tell anyone, Miss Adams. I'm the best secret keeper."

"I believe you are." Alix smiled as the little girl twined her chubby fingers in Alix's long ones. "We're going to play a game. Would you like that?"

"What kind of a game?"

"A pretending game. I'll bet you're very good at pretending."

"I'm the best pretender too."

Alix laughed softly. "Do you remember what we talked about earlier today, Elizabeth? About my visit to see my friend?"

Elizabeth's lips pouted and clamped shut. She nodded.

"I want to take you with me, Elizabeth."

Elizabeth's tiny mouth made an O.

Alix pulled Elizabeth close so the little girl wouldn't see Alix's tears escaping. "I've decided I'm not going to go without you. I'm taking you with me, or I won't leave Widpole Manor."

"You promise?"

"Yes, I promise. And *I'm* the best promiser," Alix smiled down at the child.

"Will I get to ride in the carriage? Will your friend let me come visit too?"

"I hope so. If my friend says 'no,' then neither one of us will leave the school. But I'm going to have to tell my friend a fib."

"We're not supposed to tell fibs." Elizabeth was instantly somber.

"No, darling. You're right. We're not supposed to tell fibs. But . . . if I told a fib so that you and I could stay together, would that be acceptable? Just one small fib?"

"Oh. Then that's all right, I think. Isn't it?"

"I think so, Elizabeth. I hope so. This fib will need to be our secret."

"What is the secret fib?"

"I am going to tell my friend that you are my sister, and that is why I must care for you and take you with me."

Elizabeth's eyes lit up as if she spied a Christmas tree with toys and sweets bursting from its boughs. "Could I? Could I truly be your sister?"

"Well, you're going to be my *pretend* sister. And you said you're a good pretender, right?" She gently placed her hands on Elizabeth's upper arms, and looked the little girl in the eyes.

"I promise! I'll be the best pretender. Will I still call you Miss Adams if you're my sister?"

"Oh, dear, I hadn't thought about that." Alix bit her lip, already doubting whether this was such a wise idea. "I think you shall call me by my first name while we're playing our game. That's what sisters would do. Don't forget, though, when we come back here . . ." She looked around the bleak room, already dreading their return. ". . . I'll be Miss Adams again. I don't think Headmistress Staunton would be pleased if you were to call me by my first name."

This made Elizabeth giggle. "She would be soooo angry." She looked up with round eyes. "Do you *have* a first name?"

It was Alix's turn to laugh, remembering to keep her voice down. "Yes. I sometimes forget that I do, I'm so used to being Miss Adams."

"What is it?" Elizabeth watched Alix lean close to whisper. But Alix first had to move several springy curls aside. Then she whispered. "Alix."

"Ooh. That's a pretty name, Miss Adams."

"Not as pretty as 'Elizabeth.' "

A dimple indented Elizabeth's left cheek. "When can I start pretending you're my sister? Now?"

"No, dear. Let's make a rule that our game starts after we go out the main gates of Widpole Manor. While we're here inside the school, I must remain your teacher, 'Miss Adams.' When we go outside of the school, I'll be your sister 'Alix.' That might be tomorrow or perhaps the following day."

Elizabeth yawned, but as soon as her lips closed they turned into a smile again.

"You're tired, precious. Go to sleep. I'll rub your back."

"Thank you, Miss Adams." Elizabeth lay on her side and looked up at Alix. "Big sister." She formed the words with her mouth, silently.

"Good night . . . little sister," whispered Alix.

Oh, dear. Was this right, what she was doing? Was she going to hurt Elizabeth, when all she'd wanted was to help the little girl? She couldn't stand the idea of leaving her behind at the school. But . . . what had she done?

The late afternoon sun slanted in as Lady CoraLee Nottingdale came rushing into the dining room on her return and stopped short. "Walter, where is my Lord?"

"In his library, my Lady, but he asked that I summon him for tea upon your arrival. I'll let him know you're here."

"No. Don't bother. I'll go to him myself. And please do serve tea in the library." She rushed back along the hall.

The library door swung open and she swept to her husband's desk.

"Ah, excellent timing, dear. My stomach is telling me it's time for tea." Edwyn set his pen down and rubbed his hands in anticipation.

Lady Nottingdale took a seat facing his desk. She hadn't spoken a word.

"Cora, what's wrong? You're pale, are you feeling all right?"

She nodded mutely.

Lord Nottingdale rose swiftly and came around to his wife. "Cora? Is everything all right? Is it your mother?" He sat in the leather seat next to hers and lifted her hand. "Was Damion correct? About your mother?"

She shook her head. Finally she spoke, in a voice filled with wonder. "He's getting married."

"Damion?"

She nodded.

"Cora, what is this about?"

"Edwyn, I went to see Mother. She said it was all a misunderstanding. She seemed to think it all very funny."

"A misunderstanding? About what? His getting married?"

"No. No, darling. She says she *did* write him a letter. Right after her friend, the Dowager Duchess of Elderberry, died last Tuesday night. Do you remember when we saw Mother, how she was quite distraught about her friend's failing health? She believed the duchess to be dangerously ill at the time. The poor woman died last Tuesday, just after we saw Mother."

"No, can't say that I remember that piece of the conversation." Edwyn had the grace to look sheepish, since he rarely paid attention to what the women chattered on about.

"She says she mentioned to Damion that it had her reflecting on how short our time on earth is. She believes she must have rambled on, and then she told Damion she wanted to come see him. Before she left for Wales." She touched her husband's hand affectionately. "Mother said it made her quite maudlin to think of death and never seeing one's loved ones again." Lady Nottingdale perked up and waved a hand dismissively in the air. "Evidently she decided she would stop to see Damion on her way to Wales."

"Cora, I'm not sure I follow. And this is why he thought she was dying?"

"Evidently, yes. All she could guess was that he misunderstood and thought she was talking about the shortness of her own life. And when she said she must see him before she leaves . . . Well, you can imagine the conclusion he must have drawn."

"Good Lord." Lord Nottingdale couldn't help laughing. He stopped abruptly. "But you mentioned marriage. Damion's marriage. What is that about?"

Lady Nottingdale's eyes sparkled. "You won't believe this." She took both her husband's hands in an exuberant squeeze. "Damion wrote back to Mother and told her he was going to surprise her and make her happy at last. That he was planning on marrying."

"All because he thought she was dying? Shouldn't we write and correct his impression?"

She dropped his hands as if they were hot coals. "Don't you dare!"

"CoraLee—" He used her full name only when displeased. "—you cannot let him continue under this misconception. That is not a valid reason for marriage."

Her ruby lips thinned in displeasure to near invisibility. "Don't you wish to see our son married, Edwyn?"

"But—"

"Ed-wyn!" She drew his name out into two long syllables, half whine, and half exasperation.

Her husband astutely read the threat in his wife's lovely eyes. "I admit it's about time. And overdue, of course, but. . . ." His voice trailed off and he raised a bushy eyebrow. "I suppose *we* cannot be blamed for the misunderstanding. This was all your mother's doing, was it not?"

She nodded her head in the affirmative, holding her breath.

"Well. Why not? We won't perpetrate the error. We'll simply pretend not to know."

She closed her eyes in delight.

"Who is the girl?"

Lady Nottingdale opened her eyes. "What girl?"

"Cora! The girl our son has decided to marry. Don't you care whether she's acceptable?"

"No, Edwyn, I do not." Lady CoraLee's voice was unbudgeably firm. "I do not give a fig whether she has three legs or three eyes. I want grandchildren, Edwyn."

"Well, if they take after their mother, you may soon care whether she has three eyes."

They both chuckled together, and Walter entered with their tea.

"Edwyn, I wish to go for a visit. To Damion's country home, when Mother arrives, to meet his fiancée. May we?" she asked prettily.

"Of course." He patted her arm. "I'd like to as well. Can't wait to meet the mysterious young lady." He raised an eyebrow thoughtfully. "If only to count how many legs our grandchildren will have."

CHAPTER SEVEN

Damion rose as Miss Adams entered the school's best guest parlor. "Are you ready to leave?" he asked.

"No. Not quite." Miss Adams glided into the room and stopped exactly in the center, her hands folded on her skirt. It looked as if she were about to rehearse well-practiced lines. "I'd . . . I'd like a moment of your time."

Damion smiled. "I should think you'll have many moments of my time when we reach Fern Crest Hall." He lightly slapped his gloves against his leg. "I wish to leave immediately, as my grandmother could be arriving at any time. And your chaperone awaits in the carriage."

Miss Adams nodded without meeting his eyes. "There is one small detail I . . . I neglected to tell you, my Lord."

His eyebrow dropped to mirror his frowning mouth. "What kind of a *small* detail are we talking about?"

"I. . . ." Alix swallowed. "There is someone else who must accompany us this morning."

"But I told you, I already arranged for a chaperone."

Alix noted the stern line about his mouth. This was not going to be easy. "This is not a chaperone. This is a . . . little person."

Another impatient slap of gloves against his thigh. "Miss Adams, I am anxious to get on the road, as I've already made clear. A little more conciseness, if you please. What exactly is 'a little person?' "

"A child. My Lord, there is a child I must bring—"

"No. Absolutely n—"

"I've already cleared it with Headmis—"

"No—"

"But you don't understand." Alix looked desperately around to ensure they were alone. She moved closer and put a pleading hand on his arm. "Please, my Lord. The child is mine."

Drat! Why on earth did she say that? She'd meant to say, "my sister"!

She closed her eyes in mortification. Should she correct herself? Her mouth went dry. Instinct told her this man would coldly insist on leaving a mere sister behind. Would he allow her to bring a daughter? She'd hesitated too long; there was no turning back now. She opened her eyes to judge his reaction.

His eyes widened, and he blushed.

"I know I should have told you when we discussed the arrangements." Alix twined her hands against her dress, and looked down. She peeked up at him from beneath her lashes. "But I was afraid you would react like this. She's—she's just a tiny girl. She won't take up any room in the carriage, I assure you."

"My God! What will my family say? How can I pass you off as my fiancée if you already have a child?" His horror increased.

"Shhh! Please, lower your voice." Alix rushed her words. "We mustn't be heard. We'll tell them she's my sister. In fact, *she's* been told she's my sister." *Well, that was almost the truth, now, wasn't it?* "I meant to tell *you* she was my sister. I really don't know why I said otherwise. It was a silly slip of the tongue. I—"

"Stop! Stop your rambling." His voice was a fierce whisper. He ran a hand through his hair. "This is impossible. I haven't time to find someone else."

"I can keep her out of the way, I promise. They'll never even see her. But I can't leave her here." Alix's voice broke, and tears sprang to her eyes. "I can't."

"They'll never even see her? You'll keep her out of the way? That's absurd." He finally lowered his voice. "How old is she, by the way?"

"Six. Almost seven. But just a tiny little thing. You'll barely notice her."

"Miss Adams, I am . . . at a loss." He shook his head. "I haven't time to find another person for the position." With stern censure, he said, "And you obviously banked on that. This is disastrous."

"We'll tell them she's my younger sister," Alix repeated, crossing her fingers behind her back. "*Let's hope she doesn't tell him she's only my student.* It didn't matter, though. She knew if he forbade her to bring Elizabeth, she would renege on their agreement and remain here at the school with the little girl. Assuming the headmistress didn't dismiss her from her position for insubordination, that is. She lifted her chin. "I won't leave without her, my Lord."

He clutched at straws. "Let me think." He paced. "Shall I let them think she's your sister, or shall I admit she's your daughter, and tell them you are a widow? That might cause my mother some grief. My grandmother . . . she'd accept it, if only to be contrary to what my mother says, of course. My father—" He spun around. "Are you?"

"Am I what?"

"In truth, a widow?"

Alix groaned inside. This was getting more complicated than she'd expected. She should have corrected her first lie immediately, and said Elizabeth was her sister. Though that was also a lie. And now Alix must tell another lie. She should say, "Yes, I am a widow." Else, what must he think of her? She hesitated a moment too long, a dark flush showing above her neckline to her scalp.

"Ah. I see."

"No, you don't—"

"Please." He slapped the tan gloves against his thigh with impatience. "Please don't bother explaining to me. We haven't time. Besides, I'm not your judge, madam." But the slight coldness to his tone belied that avowal.

"Up you go . . . is it Miss Elizabeth?" Damion held out a gloved hand to the youngster.

"Yes, sir. I mean, yes, my Lord." Elizabeth looked up hopefully as she stood on the second step. She executed a quick curtsy without falling off the narrow ledge.

"Damion," he corrected warmly. "You are hereby allowed to call me Damion, Miss Elizabeth." He bowed formally, and grinned to see Elizabeth shyly capturing her smile with a small hand.

" 'My Lord' will be most appropriate, Elizabeth," called out Alix, peering around Damion's broad shoulders as she waited to ascend the carriage steps.

Damion turned to Miss Adams as Elizabeth continued to climb into the carriage. "Do you intend to correct me when we are married, madam?" he asked in all seriousness.

She saw the twinkle in his eyes. This was going to be a most fun adventure. "Only when you are wrong, my dearest fiancé."

He laughed and held his hand to assist Miss Adams up the steps. She ducked to enter the carriage, finding the left bench blocked by Elizabeth, who sat close by the door. The right banquette's far corner was occupied by a young lady.

"Elizabeth, please move over," said Alix, aware she was half in and half out of the carriage, and that Lord Woodhurst was definitely not seeing her better half.

Elizabeth looked at the stone-faced young woman on the facing seat, and then at Alix with pleading eyes. "Must I?"

"Elizabeth?" Alix used a stern tone, and the child reluctantly slid over, giving Alix barely enough room to squeeze onto the left seat beside her. Elizabeth immediately sprang back against her side. Realizing this was the first time Elizabeth had been outside Widpole Manor, Alix wrapped an arm around the child. She had a flash of her own coach trip from London, taking her away from where she'd grown up, bringing her to the ominous school. She hugged Elizabeth closer.

Lord Woodhurst climbed in following Miss Adams and took a seat next to the other woman.

"My friend, Lady Chloe Grisham," he said with a palm held toward her. "Lady Chloe, may I present Miss Adams? Miss . . . my apologies, Miss Adams, I just realized I don't know your full name."

"Alix. Alix Adams. And please, Alix is fine, Lady Chloe," she said, nodding to the other woman with a friendly efficiency that would brook no argument.

Chloe nodded coolly, never taking her stare from Alix.

"Please," Damion said into the silence. "Not so formal. You are companions, and will be spending the next few weeks together in my home. Miss Adams, I'm sure she'll wish you to call her Chloe, as I do. Right, Chloe?"

Chloe looked stonily at Lord Woodhurst. Alix thought she detected some slight annoyance.

"Of course . . . Damion." Chloe smiled smugly at her use of his Christian name, glancing back at Miss Adams with feline eyes. She looked as if she'd just enjoyed a sharp tongue-full of cream.

"And this is Miss Elizabeth," he nodded toward the little girl, who cowered as far away from Chloe's infringing skirts as possible. "Miss Elizabeth is Miss Adams's sister." He emphasized the last word while looking at Alix, who barely nodded but could not prevent the warm flush that began as two warm spots upon her cheeks.

Damion tapped the roof with his travelling cane, and they lurched forward.

Alix glanced at Lady Chloe, who stared out the window. *She's beautiful,* Alix thought, as the woman fluffed her skirt, an ivy green damask. Part of it swirled across Damion's boot, and Alix swallowed. Why that should seem such a proprietary, sensual movement, she couldn't say. Chloe looked up at her, as if reading her thoughts. Similar to a cat's, her eyes tilted up at the corners.

Elizabeth inhaled sharply, and everyone turned to the little girl. "Your eyes," she blurted to Chloe. "They're different colors. One is blue, and one is brown."

"Elizabeth!" Alix was shocked the little girl would be so brazen, but Chloe smiled, albeit a smile that did not reach her exotic eyes.

"Yes. It's something men often comment on, don't they, Damion?"

He shrugged. "I'm sure I've never noticed, Chloe. Is it a fact?" He leaned to peer into her face.

"You know it is. Don't be dense. All the men of our acquaintance comment on my eyes." Her lush lips pushed into a sultry pout. "Do you think my eyes are my best feature, Damion?"

Alix watched the woman roll her shoulders toward Damion, thrusting her bosom forward till it pulled tautly at the soft linen blouse. Alix raised her eyebrows, looking forward to his answer.

"I . . . I wouldn't know, Chloe," he said, with a quick glance down and then away. "I daresay I'd never noticed them before. Your eyes, that is," he muttered, his own eyes darting to Miss Adams and then to the passing scenery.

Chloe turned her glance back to Miss Adams. "And what would be your best feature, Miss . . ."

"Alix. Please, I insist you call me by my first name . . . Chloe.

61

Especially as we shall be companions for a spell." She enjoyed using the woman's first name, if only because it seemed Chloe stiffened at the familiarity.

"What is your best feature, Alix?" Chloe repeated. "Other than being named after a man?"

Elizabeth giggled, and Alix wanted to reprimand her but knew it would seem churlish. The coach seemed small and stifling of a sudden.

"I believe it is my manners," Alix said. "I think that good manners are so important. Don't you—Chloe?"

Damion appeared oblivious to the sharpened weapons being unsheathed in the confined space of the coach.

CHAPTER EIGHT

The coach turned down the long hedgerow outlining the manor lane. Alix strained to see their destination, but the windbreak of densely branched cypresses marched alongside, guarding its privacy.

"Damion, what if your grandmother has already arrived?" asked Chloe. "I mean, I hate to be so forward, but . . . her clothes . . ." Chloe's smile was painfully pinched as she glanced at Miss Adams.

He looked blankly and waited for Chloe to continue. "Yes? What about them?"

Alix was annoyed that this woman could make her blush so easily. "I think, my Lord, your friend is trying to say that my clothes are not appropriate." At his frown, Alix placed a hand upon his arm. "She is only trying to be helpful." Realizing she touched him, she quickly removed her hand, turning to the other woman. "Thank you, Lady Chloe. I . . . I didn't think about it. However . . ." She looked down at the dark muslin. ". . . this dress is similar to my other. A teacher has no need of fine clothes."

"Don't apologize, Miss Adams." Damion's warm gaze was reassuring.

"Damion, what are you going to do? You cannot allow your family to see her in those . . ." Chloe waved a hand disdainfully and wrinkled her pretty nose. She didn't bother to finish her sentence.

"What would you recommend, Chloe?" He sounded resigned.

"Send a modiste up from the village. If you can't find one—and I doubt you shall—we'll send to Brighton. That would be closer than London. I can oversee the pattern and fabric selection."

"All right," Damion said, a bit more graciously. "Thank you. I'm in your debt."

Chloe tipped her head to the side, eyeing the man seated next to her. "Poor Damion. You really *do* need a proper wife to look after your household." Chloe leaned across to pat his knee, allowing her hand to linger.

Alix felt ashamed and inadequate. Of course, she should have thought about this when Damion interviewed her. This venture was not going to be as simple—or as fun—as she'd anticipated.

Damion interrupted her thoughts. "Should my grandmother arrive early, Miss Adams, I shall explain that your clothes were misrouted or . . . Well, I'll think of something. Just go along with whatever I tell her." He turned again to Chloe. "How soon can a dressmaker have suitable clothes made ready for Miss Adams?"

"If the modiste can arrive today, we'll have a few essentials made fairly quickly. They can then work additional outfits as time permits, and we should have a proper wardrobe in no time at all."

He nodded, agreeing with this strategy. "Ah, here we are," he said as the coach slowed at the gatehouse.

Alix leaned toward the window in time to see the trees give way to a gated iron entry. A basket handle of stones arched regally across its span, several of the voussoirs carved with a crest that was softened with age and impossible to read.

The loud ticktock of hooves on pavement accompanied them through the gate at a smart pace. She inhaled silently, her eyes sweeping from one wing of the mansion to the other. The welcoming porte cochere softened the heavy stonework and dark quoins at the far edges of the manor. Massive bow windows dominated the ground floor, making miniatures of the dozens of smaller windows above; Alix began counting, but stopped at sixty as they swayed gently to a halt.

Damion alighted the moment the footman set the step, and then handed each lady down from the coach. She waited until everyone had exited the carriage, and hung back to whisper to Damion.

"My Lord, I cannot afford new dresses. If I weren't such a coward I would have said so in the carriage in front of your friend."

"Don't be absurd. I would not allow you to pay for the dresses."

"Could you at least, please, deduct a portion of their cost from the salary we agreed upon?"

"Miss Adams, this is not a partnership. You are my fiancée. Please try to remember that."

With stiff gravity, she said, "I see. You do not consider a fiancée or a wife to be a partner in a marriage. How extremely fortunate this is a temporary position, my Lord."

"And what exactly is that supposed to mean?" he asked, but she put her nose in the air and pretended to be studying the huge mansion as if her very life depended upon its accurate description.

They moved as one toward the wide portico, but Damion stopped and turned so suddenly that Alix bumped into him. "Remember, Miss Adams, if my grandmother has already arrived, just follow my lead. Allow me to do the talking."

Alix tried not to show her annoyance and waited until he'd started forward again, then muttered, "I may be poor, my Lord, but I am not stupid."

Damion stopped again. He let Chloe go on ahead and waited

until Miss Adams came alongside. He hooked his arm in hers, pulling her to his side. "And I can see you are biddable, as well, my delightful fiancée."

Chloe looked at Miss Adams over her shoulder, then at Damion. "Your just desserts, Damion," she said to the air.

"I don't understand *what* he was about." Chloe perched on a satin chair almost the exact shade of her skirt. One knee was crossed over the other, and her leg swung impatiently as she watched the seamstress measure Miss Adams.

"Who? Lord Woodhurst?" Alix began to turn around so she could face Chloe, but stopped when the seamstress tugged her back with a measuring ribbon.

"Yes, of course I mean Lord Woodhurst. This is ridiculous. He should not be bearing this throwaway expense." Chloe's chin rested on a palm, her elbow perched upon her knee. She was twisted into a disgruntled knot of boredom.

Alix blushed. "I . . . I offered to pay for the dresses myself."

Chloe snorted. "You? And how could you afford it? Damion tells me you're penniless . . . an orphan."

Alix looked guiltily toward the modiste, who appeared to be deaf where her clients were concerned. Mortification slid into pique; Alix stiffened. "What else did Lord Woodhurst tell you about me?"

Chloe eyed her speculatively. "Why? Is there more I should know?"

Alix looked down at the ribbon being wound tightly round her waist. "No, there's not much to know about me. I think you summed it up quite well: a penniless orphan. That should do."

"Whatever was he thinking, to try to pass you off as the fiancée of a nobleman? I should have been able to bring any one of several acquaintances at a moment's notice."

The seamstress moved her a quarter turn, and Alix could

only look over her shoulder at Chloe. "I asked him the same—why he did not bring someone of his own circle. I also thought that would have made more sense."

"And?" Chloe stopped swinging her leg. "What did he say?"

Alix chuckled, remembering his frightened expression. "He looked about to faint. Said they would expect a true marital contract from him."

Chloe grunted. "And why not? It's past time he married."

"Why?" Alix was looking down at the modiste's busy hands, and didn't see Chloe's annoyed expression and wrinkled nose.

"Can you be so naive? He has a title to fulfill. It's his duty. But of course, *you* wouldn't know about duty." Chloe lifted her chin from her palm and studied her nails.

Alix smoothed down her skirt, not trusting herself to look Chloe in the eye, not trusting her voice should she answer that comment. Because Alix knew all about duty. About a child getting up at three o'clock in the morning to see to the laundry as the bevy of ladies upstairs were just finishing their business. About laundering sheets and rinsing out the fine stockings and chemises that needed delicate treatment, lest she get her ears boxed. About working in the hot kitchens, her eyes burning and watering from the strong lye soap, her clothes damp and clinging. About serving meals before she could see to her own grumbling, empty stomach. About taking care of her mother as she became steadily more ill until she needed the young girl to sponge bathe her, to hold a cup to her lips as she—

"Are you listening to me, Miss Adams?"

Alix held back a tear. Her righteous anger had twisted into sorrow. And she wouldn't feel sorry for herself. Especially not in front of this lady. "I'm sorry. I must have been daydreaming."

"I said you may leave us." Chloe arched a delicate brow. "You are dismissed."

Alix hated the way Chloe talked to her as if she were a

servant. "Shouldn't we discuss dresses with Mademoiselle Seaton?" Alix eyed the red-faced woman with pins puckered in her mouth.

"No, I shan't need your input." Chloe rose and strolled to the table laden with fabrics. "I shall direct Mademoiselle in the appropriate styles for you. Run along now." Chloe turned her back to Miss Adams and spread out several pattern books Mlle. Seaton had placed on the table.

Alix almost said, "Yes, ma'am," but caught herself in time.

She moved to the lintel, where she stood contemplating several replies, but both women were bent over the fashion plates, already considering her invisible; and so she left.

CHAPTER NINE

Alix stood frozen. This couldn't be her bedroom. There must have been a mistake. She stepped backward into the hall. Yes, it was the second doorway on the left from the top of the stairs.

Entering the sun-drenched sitting room, she spied an adjoining bedroom through an open doorway across the large room. The walls in this first room were painted the palest of peach shades, edged by white cornices and wood trim. Hesitantly she approached the windows. The grounds outside were manicured to within one inch of perfection. The view did not look real; one could have been studying a painting similar to those she'd seen hanging in the special guest parlors at the school.

Peeking into the high-ceilinged bedroom, she was drawn to touch the starchy white eyelet counterpane and matching pillow covers. The bedroom window drew her with splashes of color. The view of the rose gardens from this room made her suck in her breath. This room—her room.

At the school, other teachers had been jealous of the tiny bedroom Alix had to herself, due to her tenure. The wood planks on the floor of that tiny room were rough, leaving splinters in bare feet. The drawers stuck unless she pulled the handles carefully, evenly, with both hands. There was no window.

From this bedroom's window she could see a river winding at the bottom of the hill. And a pond. Three white ducks sailed on the pond. A heron stood at the edge of the reeds.

She left her suite reluctantly, and almost bumped into Damion as she rounded a corner of the hall.

"Is your room to your satisfaction, Miss Adams?"

"Oh, my Lord, I love my room!"

He grinned. "I hoped you would."

"May I explore?"

"The house? Do you mean the rest of the house?" When she nodded he said, "Of course. And perhaps you'd like to take a walk a little later?"

"Outside?" she asked a little breathlessly.

Damion laughed. "Unless you prefer to remain in the circular gallery upstairs, though you may get bored after the seventh glimpse of my ancestors."

"Where may we stroll outdoors? Anywhere? I can see a pond from my window. There were ducks in it. And a blue heron. May we stroll down to visit the ducks at the pond?"

"You want to visit . . . ducks. Yes, that can be arranged." Smiling, he crooked his arm to escort her downstairs. "And perhaps, if the weather cooperates, a picnic or two?"

"Thank you." Alix's eyes lit with a glimmer of awe.

"Good afternoon, ladies." Damion strolled into the lavender parlor where Elizabeth and Miss Adams sat side by side on the settee, sharing a large book with drawings. He gave a brief bow. "Are we ready for a visit to the duck pond after we have our tea?"

Alix remained seated, smiling at Damion as she set aside the book they'd been reading, and Elizabeth jumped up, clapping her hands.

"I would love that, please, my Lord." The little girl executed a curtsy, spreading the skirts of her simple dress, and in the same exuberant motion she spun around to Alix. "How did I do?"

Alix beamed. "That was an excellent curtsy, Elizabeth.

But . . ." She lowered her voice to a loud whisper, softening her words with a smile. ". . . you don't want to spoil it by asking how you did."

Elizabeth's face fell. "Oh. May I try again, then?"

"Try again?" said Alix. "I don't think—"

"Of course you may," said Damion. "I myself was thinking I should like to try my bow again. It didn't feel quite right. Would you mind if we both tried again?"

"Oh, but I thought yours was just right. You looked very hansome," Elizabeth emphasized the word.

"Thank you. Now . . . you stand here." He gently moved Elizabeth to the center of the square cinnamon-brown rug. "And I'll come around the corner, as if I'm just entering." He walked to the door, stepped out, but leaned his upper body back to peek at them. "And do you know *your* part, Miss Adams?"

Alix laughed. "I believe so, my Lord." She stood up and walked over to join Elizabeth.

He ducked out of sight. Alix smiled down at Elizabeth, who covered a giggle with her hand. In ten seconds, when he had still not appeared, Elizabeth crept over to peer out, and they bumped into one another as he swung through the doorway.

"Ah! And whom have we here?" He looked pleased to see Elizabeth, then turned formally to Miss Adams, clearing his throat.

Alix laughed again. "My Lord, may I present my sister, Miss Elizabeth?"

Elizabeth curtsied a perfect curtsy. She didn't turn to Alix this time, but smiled angelically at Damion.

He executed a deep bow. They both spun expectantly to Alix. "Did we both perform correctly this time, Miss Adams?" Damion asked.

"Yes," said Alix, painting a serious face upon her gentle

features. "I think you both may be ready to present to society. Or even to Lord Woodhurst's grandmother."

Damion turned to the little girl. "I agree. Well done, Miss Lizzie."

Elizabeth scowled. "Don't call me that!"

"Elizabeth!" Alix rushed over and put a firm hand on Elizabeth's shoulder. "That is most rude."

"It is fine, Miss Adams. I should not have assumed—"

"It is *not* fine, my Lord."

At the schoolteacher's stern chastisement, he appeared taken aback but did not reply. Alix turned back to Elizabeth, waiting for an apology.

The little girl pursed her lips as she pulled away and looked up at Damion. "But I don't want him too call me that." When he looked at her with wide eyes, she added, "My name is Elizabeth. Miss Adams—I mean Alix—says 'Lizzie' is common."

"Well," he drawled. "If a teacher says so, then it must be so. Miss Elizabeth it shall be."

"Elizabeth," said Alix, "can you think of another way to ask—politely—that Lord Woodhurst call you by your full name?"

Elizabeth ducked her head and nodded it with eyes downcast. She came over to Damion, and taking him by the hand, began to lead him out the door.

"Where are you going?" asked Alix in a surprised voice.

"We're going to try this one more time. Isn't that right, Lord Woodhurst?"

"Yes, Miss-E-liz-a-beth." He enunciated each syllable carefully, which made the young girl smile.

"That sounds funny. I think you also need some practice."

"Elizabeth, please do not be precocious," Alix called out. As Elizabeth came back in to stand in the center of the carpet, Alix said, "And, this is the last time we shall . . . practice. I am sure Lord Woodhurst is a busy man."

Damion had already ducked out of the room. He solemnly strolled in again, one hand in his vest pocket, looking so serious that Elizabeth bubbled with laughter.

"Oh! And who might this enchanting young lady be?" He made his voice unusually deep; his eyebrows flew up in mock surprise. He turned on his heel to face Miss Adams and waited expectantly.

"My Lord." Alix could not suppress a smile. "May I present my sister, Miss Elizabeth?"

Elizabeth's shoulders shook as she tried not to laugh aloud. She curtseyed and stood straight, waiting for Damion to say his lines.

"I am so pleased to meet you." He bowed. "And, may I call you 'Lizzie'?"

In a calmly serious voice, Elizabeth said, "If you please, my Lord, my name is Elizabeth. 'Lizzie' is rather common, don't you think?"

Alix rolled her eyes.

Damion tried not to smile, which emphasized the deep line in his right cheek. "Rather common. Yes, I must agree with you, Miss Elizabeth."

"This is intolerable, Damion. As the senior ranking female in your household, I expected to have the Apricot Bedroom." Chloe's arms were akimbo, hands on hips. She'd trapped Damion as he left the parlor after tea.

"I would have thought my grandmother would be the 'senior ranking female.'" He kept his voice low, but his drawl hid a touch of impatience. "Besides, if Miss Adams is to pose as my fiancée, then I must position her in the forward bedroom."

"And what of your grandmother?"

"Chloe, what is this about? There are a dozen well-appointed guest rooms in the manor, as you well know. My grandmother has one of the finer guest rooms, a *very* fine room. As do you," he added pointedly.

Alix stopped abruptly at the parlor doorway, immediately catching the gist of their discussion. She knew it: the bedroom she'd entered was too beautiful to be true. Her sigh was efficiently captured before she stepped into the hallway. She chastised herself for caring, but her imagination ignored her. How perfect it would be to retire to the soft pastels beckoning in the room after dinner; to awaken and look down upon the pond and the hills dipping toward the valley.

But of course, such luxury was not for the likes of her. She only wished Damion had corrected the mistake earlier, before she'd seen it and fallen in love with the view. And the pond. And the walls. And—"My Lord, please. I'd be happy to exchange guest rooms with Lady Chloe. That room is much too grand . . . for me." She shrugged, smiling to hide her disappointment. "I'm sure I'd have trouble finding my few dresses in its voluminous wardrobe."

"You see, Damion?" Chloe spun back to face him, speaking quickly. "Even she admits the room is overly elegant for a schoolteacher." Sotto voce she added, "It's not what she's used to, Damion. You wouldn't want to make her uncomfortable in a room that size." She turned back to Alix. "Don't you agree, Miss Adams? Surely it's much larger than you're used to."

Alix ducked her head, not wanting any desire to peep through. "Yes, certainly."

"Miss Adams?"

She looked up, surprised at Damion's stern tone. "Yes?"

"You do not care for the room I gave you?" He appeared displeased.

She could not fathom his clouded expression. How should she answer? It was important he not think her ungracious. But equally important he should not think her selfish.

"I . . ." She chose honesty. "I think it is the most beautiful room I have ever seen, my Lord. In my entire life." She looked over at Chloe. "But Lady Chloe is a good friend of your family. I would not want her to be uncomfortable on my account. She is correct. I am not used to anything so . . . so lovely. A small upstairs room would serve me just as well." She made herself nod her reluctant acquiescence.

"There. I told you so," Chloe said. "Miss Adams is probably used to an upper-story room with small dormer windows. Perhaps she would be more comfortable on the nursery level. Or below stairs. In truth, she is just your hired help for the next month or two."

The butler came from the tea parlor, following the footman, who balanced silver utensils and soiled dishes on a tray.

"Excuse me," Chloe addressed the butler, and he paused. "Please let the housekeeper know we wish to switch the room arrangements."

The man looked to Damion before responding.

"Chloe, I don't remember asking you to run my household for me," chided Damion.

"But I thought we were all in agreement." Chloe looked her surprise. "Honestly, Damion." Her voice was soothing, as if speaking to a child. "You truly do need a woman capable of running your household. You shouldn't have to make these day-to-day decisions. I'll be glad to direct your housekeeper on which rooms will be appropriate for all of your . . ." She glanced at Miss Adams. "Guests."

"Sir?" asked Philbin.

"No." Just the one firm word from Damion. Philbin immediately left.

"What do you mean?" whined Chloe.

"I mean 'no,' Chloe. I mean the room arrangements shall be as I originally planned them. I do believe the Rose Room is quite adequate. More than adequate. You will be comfortable there."

"But where shall you put your grandmother? And your parents?" Chloe's lower lip stuck out in a becoming pout.

"Where I put them is truly no concern of yours."

Her eyes narrowed. "I think you're making a mistake, Damion. If you're not careful, you're going to give Miss Adams airs. And won't it be more difficult for her to return to her small room at the school when this farce is over? You know I'm only thinking of her interests."

"Yes, I realize that, Chloe. Your regard for the comfort of others has not gone unnoticed." He glanced toward Miss Adams, who noted the hint of a smile.

Chloe softened visibly at this compliment. Moving closer, she touched his arm. "I am sure *your* bedroom is large enough to share, Damion."

"Ah, but I wouldn't want to give you airs either, Chloe."

Chloe did not see the humor in his remark, and with a shake of her head she flounced off.

"Oh, dear," said Alix, after the woman was out of earshot. "Lady Chloe is right. Where shall you put your grandmother? I fear you've given me the finest room in the house, my Lord."

Damion stepped so close their noses almost touched. "Miss Adams, this grows tiresome. Do you, or do you not, like the room I gave you?"

She opened and closed her mouth. "I told the truth. It *is* the most beautiful room I have ever seen."

"Then, as my fiancée, you have exactly two choices before my grandmother arrives at Fern Crest Hall."

"Yes?"

"One: you may remain in the room where you are." His voice was again stern. "The room *I* chose for you."

"Yes?"

"Or two: as my fiancée, you may move into *my* bedroom."

Alix gasped.

Damion raised an eyebrow in speculation. "We will scandalize my poor grandmother, but I'll tell her you insisted. I daresay she may die of apoplexy earlier than she anticipated, but I'll offer to move up the wedding date."

He moved closer, to Alix's side. She could feel his warm breath stir the curls that fell artfully behind her ear. "Would you prefer that, Miss Adams?"

She stepped back, her cheeks on fire. "I'll stay in my room. Thank you, my Lord."

She curtsied without thinking. Drat! She hadn't meant to do anything so servile. It's just that he confused her when he stood so close.

Alix and Elizabeth held hands, swinging arms as they walked along the path in front of Damion. Alix spied yellow water irises in the pond ahead, amid a striping of brown and green reeds. It was comfortably warm; the dipping sun would hold the cool evening away for another few hours. Every dozen or so steps Elizabeth would spy a rock that she'd declare was the most fascinating she'd discovered so far and it would join the others clacking in her pocket.

"Elizabeth," said Alix, "I meant to ask if you will be comfortable sleeping alone in the big house?"

Elizabeth stopped suddenly. She no longer swung her hand with Alix's, and Damion almost tripped over her.

Alix could not read the little girl's expression, and asked, "Would you prefer to share my room?"

"Must I? I mean, I beg your pardon, but must I, Miss Adams? I mean—" Elizabeth gulped nervously. "Am I supposed to say Miss Alix? Or just Alix?"

"Just Alix, dear." Alix looked her apologies at Damion. "When we are at the school, Elizabeth is required to call me Miss Adams, as the other students do."

"I see: Just Alix," he repeated. "May I also call you Just Alix?" he asked with a studious face.

"No, you may not. You may call me Miss Adams, my Lord."

Elizabeth took her hand again, and said, "I don't want to sound rude . . . Alix. It's just that . . ." Elizabeth went silent, and her face scrunched up like the saddest clown in the circus.

"Elizabeth, why the long face?" I am not saying you must share my room. But it's the most beautiful room—"

"But not as beautiful as mine!"

"No?" Alix smiled at Damion over Elizabeth's head.

"No. I have a *princess* bedroom. It has princess curtains on the window, and a princess bed, and a princess mirror, and—"

Alix laughed. "I see. I can imagine everything you're describing, Elizabeth. You must show me your own room when we return."

They strolled in and out of shade, the trees thinning as they angled down the sloping lawn toward the water. Elizabeth dropped her hand from Alix's and ran on to the wooden bridge that arched across one end of the pond.

"Be careful, dear," Alix called, continuing down to the water's edge, but she no longer watched Elizabeth. Leaning down, she stared at the muddy border teeming with fish and bugs, intrigued by a school of minnows flashing by in the shady shallows. "Oh, my! Look! Look at the little things. They're miniature fish. They're too adorable." She hurried alongside the school of fish flashing in the sunlight, changing direction like a prism hung at the window. The silver phalanx moved beneath the bridge and Alix followed, crossing behind Elizabeth. At the middle of the bridge, she leaned over but couldn't spy the little school. She stood on tiptoes and leaned further still, until she felt Damion's hand upon her elbow.

"Do be careful, Miss Adams. What will I tell my grandmother if my fiancée should drown the first day she's here?"

"Look, Alix," called Elizabeth. "Those white circles floating on the pond. Don't they look like soiled doilies?" Elizabeth made a disgusted face, and ran across the bridge to the other bank. "And look. Do you see the yellow flowers? They're growing right out of the water."

"Their roots are down in the mud where you can't see them." Alix hurried down the wooden rainbow to the other side of the stream. "There's a bog primula. I've only seen them in pictures. I wonder if they have a smell." She stepped carefully down the bank toward the marshy ground and squatted among the grasses, leaning closer to the flowers.

Damion laughed, watching them from the apex of the bridge. "Miss Adams, you're determined to go swimming, aren't you?"

She straightened to look at him. "This is amazing. I can't imagine living here and being able to take a walk in these woods every day. And I can't wait to have that picnic you mentioned. I'd have a picnic every day if I lived here, and I'd take a walk every single day, rain or shine. Or even snow. I'm . . . I'm speechless." She took two hopping steps back toward the dry bank.

"That was quite a long speech for someone who's speechless," said Damion. "And I see you shall hold me to the promise of a picnic. Perhaps tomor—"

"Eek!" Alix slipped in the wet grasses and went down hard upon her posterior.

Damion ran across the bridge and down the bank, where Elizabeth was trying to lift Miss Adams, pulling on her hand. Damion took her other hand and easily pulled her to her feet. She winced and faltered as she tried to stand straight.

He was quick to grasp her by the waist before she fell again. "Are you all right?"

"It's my ankle. But I'm sure it's all right. If I may, I'll lean on you for just a moment." She tentatively shifted her weight, and grimaced.

"Miss Adams! I mean, Alix, are you all right?" Elizabeth looked anxiously up at Alix's face.

She made an effort to smile and calm her expression. "Of course, dear. I'm fine. My ankle felt a little sore, but it's fine now." She turned to Damion. "Shall we start back? Slowly?"

"Let's sit here a bit and rest. It will be dry up there by that tree."

"No, I'm fine, truly. What if your grandmother has arrived?"

"Then I think she'll wonder why you wear muddy dresses."

Alix's eyes widened in shock at the mess on her skirt. She brushed off the leaves, but their winter mold left dark spots. And marsh mud stained the hem where she'd stepped on it. "I can't believe this." Her eyes closed in mortification. "Now I truly must get back. Immediately. I have only one clean dress to change into."

She picked up her skirts, and took two quick steps toward the bridge before she stumbled again. Damion grabbed her elbow. "Miss Adams, stop. Can't you see your ankle is still weak?"

Alix tried to pull away, but his grip was firm. "Please," she said, "please let me go. I must go back to the hall."

"And I say we need to rest here a bit." He hadn't released her arm.

"I can't. I tell you, I must get back and change this muddy dress. And then I must see that it is washed, or I'll have no clothes to wear tomorrow."

Damion did not release her. "As interesting as that might be, I promise you the modiste will have something ready for you to wear tomorrow. I insist we rest here, Miss Adams."

80

Alix lowered her brows. "And I said I insist we return, my Lord."

"You insist? Are you sure?"

"Yes, I already said so."

"Well. Only because you insist." Damion swung Miss Adams up into his arms.

"Stop! Put me down. What are you doing?"

"If you insist on returning, then we shall return. But you are not going to walk back."

"Ugh! You are an odious man."

"And you are a stubborn woman." Damion carried the grumbling Miss Adams effortlessly. He glanced over his shoulder to see Elizabeth skipping along to keep up with his long strides. "I am suddenly worried about your meeting my grandmother, Miss Adams."

"Exactly my point. Whatever will she think?"

"Oh, not about your dress. I'm speaking of your stubbornness. I'm afraid you and Grandmother shall kill one another before the week is out. She can be a frighteningly stubborn woman, but I fear she's met her match."

"I have never been called stubborn, and I resent that. I am practical." Alix folded her arms, disgruntled, across her chest and refused to look up at Damion.

"Miss Elizabeth," Damion said without glancing back, "has your sister always been so stubborn?"

Elizabeth laughed. "Yes, my Lord. That is, as long as she's been my sister."

Alix looked around Damion, and her eyes went wide at the little girl, whose own eyes were laughing above the hand she clapped over her mouth.

Alix rolled her eyes. She fumed silently all the way back to the house.

Philbin was at the door. "Sir? Is Miss Adams injured? Shall I send for the doctor?"

"No, I don't think we shall need him, Philbin. But please ask the housekeeper to make up a compress for Miss Adams's ankle."

Philbin scurried down the hall, and Damion carried Alix through the hall and into the closest parlor.

Chloe rushed in. "What on earth? What is going on?"

"It's nothing," said Alix, at the same time Damion said, "Miss Adams twisted her ankle."

Chloe stared at the two of them: Miss Adams fitting into Damion's strong arms. "Do you plan to stand there holding her all night, Damion?"

He blushed as he realized he should have set Miss Adams down by now.

Alix looked embarrassed as well. Truth be told, she'd enjoyed being cuddled so close to his chest. Damion moved to the settee and deposited Miss Adams as if she were a precious vase.

Alix sat up and leaned forward, rubbing at her ankle. "I think it already feels better, my Lord."

"I accept your gracious apology. Oh, and your grateful thank you as well."

Alix grinned. "Thank you, my Lord. And . . . I apologize as well. Though I do believe you inherited your grandmother's traits, you know."

He smiled, and opened his mouth to respond, when they were interrupted.

"My Lord," Philbin hurried over to Damion. He leaned close, trying to speak for Damion's ears only. "I am sorry to interrupt, but there is a man here who's been waiting for your arrival. I put him in the side parlor. He insists on seeing you. Says it's of the utmost urgency."

Damion turned white. "Is it about my grandmother? Did he say who sent him?"

"No, my Lord. I asked him his business, but he said he must wait to give his message personally to you."

"Ladies, please excuse me." Damion executed a curt bow and strode out of the room, Philbin in his wake.

Alix looked down with distress at her gown. "Elizabeth, can you please ask one of the maids to prepare my other dress? I'll be up shortly to change."

Chloe waited until Elizabeth left the room. "How clever, Miss Adams. Well done."

Alix looked up in confusion. "Whatever do you mean?"

"You are here only a few hours, and you manage to establish yourself in the best guest room, take a private walk with Damion—"

"It was not private! Elizabeth was with us—"

"And have him carry you in his arms. How dramatic. And how contrivedly convenient."

Alix stared at Chloe, her mouth open. She didn't know how to respond to the preposterous accusations. Chloe spun on her heel and left the room.

A few minutes later, Damion entered the room, and she swiftly forgot her own feelings of frustration with Lady Chloe when she saw his face. "What is it? Bad news? Is it your grandmother?"

Damion came over to the couch where she sat, and took a seat next to her. Distractedly, he took her hand. "No, it's not about Grandmother, but it is news of the worst sort." He shook his head. "It's my friend, Greeley. He's one of my oldest school friends . . . he *was* one of my oldest friends." Tears filled Damion's eyes. "He's dead. His wife sent word with one of their servants. Sarah is devastated. Poor Sarah. And the children." Damion pulled his hands away and slid them over his face, pushing the hair off his forehead. "She asks for my help. She doesn't know where to turn, whom to appoint to oversee the land, what to do about the books, where to start. Miss Adams . . ." He looked up at her with wet eyelashes. ". . . I need to go to Sarah. It will only be for a few days. I'll help her interview a foreman, get her in touch with some others who can help her. And I'll be there for the funeral, of course. I'm so sorry to ask this of you, when you've only just arrived."

"Nonsense, Lord Woodhurst. Please, you don't need to worry about us, especially not at a time like this. You have enough on your mind. Go to your friend's wife, by all means. I'll be fine. Besides, I'll be here to greet your grandmother. We'll make your grandmother feel welcome, you've my word on that."

Again Damion took her hand. "Thank you. And I also give my word: I'll be back as quickly as I possibly can. Four days. Five at the most."

Neither said anything, just stared at one another.

"So much death surrounds me," Damion said quietly. "I can hardly stand it."

CHAPTER TEN

"Alix! Alix!" Elizabeth's clear voice sang across the gardens like the early morning's birdsong.

Alix turned toward the path, but couldn't see her charge due to the circular hedges. "Elizabeth. Over here, darling. By the statue of the deer."

Elizabeth came running, and Alix held her arms out to the rushing child. She caught Elizabeth against her dress, thinking how just one day away from the school had brightened the child's cheeks and her spirit as well.

Alix laughed. "Catch your breath," she said to the panting child.

"I ran as fast as I could." Elizabeth bent over, put her hands on her knees and theatrically caught her breath. When she straightened, she said, "My goodness! Your dress is so pretty!"

"Thank you, Elizabeth." Alix was pleased at the compliment; she felt different—pretty even—wearing the first of the morning gowns hastily delivered by the dressmaker, even if it was a bit too frilly and bright. She held Elizabeth an arm's length away. "And just look at *your* new dress, Elizabeth. That color is perfect for you."

The organza outfit provided for Elizabeth was a soft lilac, complementing the little girl's dark curls.

They'd spied the first of Alix's new dresses laid out this morning, and had been shocked to find a smaller dress for Elizabeth lying on the counterpane next to it. Elizabeth's included a doll-sized reticule as well, of matching fabric. Alix could still hear Lady Chloe's voice chastising the dressmaker:

"I did not authorize a dress for the youngster. I demand to know what you are thinking of, wasting our precious time on making children's clothes. I did not commission that, and I shall see you are not paid for it."

"But, my Lady, it was my Lord who insisted. He distinctly ordered me to make one dress for the child for every two dresses I make for Miss Adams." There had been a sly smugness in the woman's innocent reply to Lady Chloe.

Alix smiled now, as she had then, that Damion had done something so unexpected and considerate. It was wonderful to see the thrill in Elizabeth's eyes. "But surely, Elizabeth, you didn't run all the way here to the gardens to look at my new dress?"

Elizabeth shook her curls. "No. Lady Chloe said I should come find you." In a sing-song voice, Elizabeth quoted, "Lady Chloe says to tell you that Lord Woodhurst's grandmother has arrived, and that she's been here for a long time already, and that they want to know where you are."

"Oh, dear. So early?" The morning sun was still striping the dewy ground with long shadows of the yews.

Elizabeth pointed, her arm ramrod straight. "Alix, you got some dirt on your new dress."

Alix looked down and gasped. "Oh, dear." She pulled off her right gardening glove, clasping it in her other hand as she swiped at two powdery smudges on her skirt.

She should have known better than to pull weeds. She'd been told the dowager Lady Croxton might arrive any day, at any time. Why hadn't she resisted the urge to garden? She'd only meant to stroll, and then she'd seen a few weeds popping up in the raised beds—just a few. And she'd met the gardener, an older man with shaggy white hair and brows, patient and kind, who'd conjured a pair of leather gloves for Miss. It was such a quick task to bend and yank the stray greens from the dark fertile soil, and so fun that it made the gardener shake his head as he went on to his other tasks. Only, that had been some time ago. She hadn't meant to get so involved.

"Oh, dear," she repeated. "How thoughtless of me to soil this fine dress. I no longer see any spots on the skirt, do you?" As Elizabeth shook her head, Alix gave a final brushing to the candy-pink fabric. "Whatever was I thinking? It is imperative I be presentable to Lord Woodhurst's grandmother."

"She's not going to like us, is she?" Elizabeth made it sound more of a statement than a question.

"What?" Alix looked up from her skirt. "Why do you say that, dear? Of course she'll like us." But Lady Chloe didn't like them, Alix reflected.

"If she doesn't, do we have to go away? Does that mean I can't be your sister anymore? And I can't call you Alix? And I can't pretend to be a princess anymore in my new dress and my bedroom?"

Alix knelt down next to the small girl. "Elizabeth, listen to me. You are the nicest little girl I know. That's why I brought you here with me. I know you're nervous about meeting her. So am I. But Lord Woodhurst loves his grandmother, and he thinks she's really special. And you like Lord Woodhurst, right?" She waited until Elizabeth nodded. "Then I bet his grandmother will be exactly as nice as he is."

Elizabeth did not look convinced. She began twirling a curl around her finger, pulling it to her mouth, a habit she was often teased about at school.

"Do you want to know the trick for having someone like you?" Alix smiled mischievously.

Elizabeth nodded. "Is it a magic trick?"

"Sort of. And most people don't know this trick, but I'm going to tell you. Can you keep a secret?"

"I told you I'm the best secret keeper."

"Yes, and so you have been. All right. Listen carefully." Alix lowered her voice, and Elizabeth leaned in to hear her whisper. "All you have to do is be the nicest person *you* can be. Don't think about being nervous. Just think about being nice to *her*. Think about how maybe she wishes to have a friend as well."

"Maybe she can be our sister, too, if she can keep a secret."

"Well . . . let's not tell her about *that* secret. But we'll try to be as nice to her as we can be. That will make Lord Woodhurst happy, too, don't you think?" Alix straightened up and shook out her skirts one more time. She couldn't see any more of the fine dirt. "Do you see any other spots, Elizabeth?"

Elizabeth walked around Alix with her eyes scrunched up, carefully surveying. "You look beautiful to me, Alix."

"Thank you. And you look beautiful as well." Alix put her shoulders back with resolution and took Elizabeth by the hand. "Let's go and meet Lady Croxton now."

Alix wished she felt as confident as she sounded.

Lady Chloe regally entered the lavender parlor. "My Lady."

The Dowager Countess of Croxton, elegant in a dove-grey travelling dress of fine wool, dipped her head in acknowledgment.

Chloe glided across the room to where Damion's grandmother sat. "I am Lady Chloe Grisham. The Earl of Cantwell is my brother." She curtsied prettily. "May I offer refreshments?"

"That would be lovely, my dear. My throat is parched. I'd forgotten how dusty these local roads can be."

Chloe politely inquired further about Lady Croxton's trip until tea arrived. While serving her guest, she could not help eying the spectacular rings on the older dame's hands. She glanced up to find the dowager countess's eyes upon her. "I was admiring your garnet, my Lady."

"A gift from my husband when we visited Spain." Lady Croxton touched the stone and adjusted the heavy ring, which had slipped slightly off-center on her finger. "It was part of a set I admired, in southern Andalusia, where he insisted we go seabathing." She pulled the large garnet pendant from where it lay hidden by a pleated frill of lace at her neckline. Chloe's eyes widened at the perfect stone surrounded by a brilliant halo of diamonds. "He told me garnets were believed to protect their wearer against bad dreams." The countess smiled tenderly. "I told him I delighted in it because it reminded me of the ruby kernels of a pomegranate."

Chloe smiled indulgently. One knew by Chloe's expression that she did not plan to grow old or die, if senility were the price.

Alix entered in a swirl of skirts. "Lady Chloe, I'm so sorry. I wasn't aware Lord Woodhurst's grandmother had arrived." She rushed forward to Lady Croxton and curtsied deeply. "Please accept my apologies, my Lady. I do not wish to appear as if I ignored you."

"That is fine, dear. I am not easily offended. And your name?"

"Alix."

"Just . . . Alix?"

Alix blushed. "Miss Alix Adams. But I would be pleased—I mean honored—if you would call me Alix."

"All right. Alix. I am pleased to meet you, dear." Lady Croxton reached out as if to take her hand. Alix put her hand forward, but her eyes widened as Lady Croxton reached past and plucked a small twig from Alix's hair. "You've been in the garden?"

Alix blushed to her roots.

"Our Miss Adams is quite the outdoorsy young lady," Chloe said, a hint of aspersion in her voice.

"I must confess I do find myself enjoying the garden more than may be proper," Alix said. "You see, with your grandson away, I wish to spend as much time in these beautiful gardens as possible. The parterres of lavender would bring tears to your eyes, they are so beautiful."

"Miss Adams, please." Chloe raised her eyebrows as if being extremely nice to an errant child. "We wouldn't want to bore Lady Croxton." Chloe turned amused eyes to Damion's grandmother. "You must excuse Miss Adams. Having spent most of her life in the country, she is not aware that ladies do not preoccupy themselves with working in the soil. I am certain," she said, stressing the word, "that Lord Woodhurst would not approve of such . . . use of your time, Miss Adams. Nor his family—"

"Oh, no. Quite the contrary," said Lady Croxton with a husky chuckle. She gave an approving nod to Miss Adams. "I myself love strolling in gardens. You shall have to visit my home some day. I have a terrace of planters with tamarisk and myrtle. My late husband loved the flower of the myrtle. So fragrant."

"Even the berries seem aromatic," Alix said.

"Exactly," Lady Croxton said with approval. "I see you know your plants, dear. There is also an exquisite formal border of scented shrubs."

"It sounds delightful." Alix's voice was wistful. "I only know most plants from what I've learned in books. But the gardens here have everything I'd only seen pictures of! Perhaps you'd care to see—"

"Miss Adams," broke in Chloe.

Alix dipped her head in embarrassment. "Well. Perhaps not at this moment."

"I hope to be here for a few weeks, Alix. I hope we shall spend many pleasant hours strolling together." Lady Croxton turned to Chloe. "And exactly what is the relationship between you and Miss Adams, Lady Chloe?"

"I am Miss Adams's . . . chaperone." Chloe bit out the last word unpleasantly. "I have come from London at Lord Woodhurst's especial request. He and I belong to the same circles, you see. My brother, Lord Cantwell, is Lord Woodhurst's particularly good friend." Chloe leaned forward as if to share a bit of gossip. "You may not have guessed this, Lady Croxton, but it is Miss Adams who is Lord Woodhurst's fiancée. Not I." Chloe's eyes looked her apology.

"Oh! But . . ." Lady Croxton looked from Lady Chloe to Miss Adams.

Alix lowered her gaze, not wishing to witness the disappointment in his ailing grandmother's face.

Lady Croxton looked back to meet Chloe's triumphant eyes. ". . . But that is what I assumed all along, Lady Chloe."

Chloe's self-possessed feathers ruffled perceptibly.

"You are so very sweet and beautiful, my dear," said the dowager countess. "But you are, of course, not quite my Edmund's type."

Alix left the room to gather Elizabeth for introductions. By the time she returned, a delicate lemon and herb scent filled the parlor. Lady Croxton was alone and informed them Lady Chloe was suddenly indisposed.

Alix glanced back to find Elizabeth standing behind her skirts. She gently brought the young girl forth. "Lady Croxton, may I present my sister, Elizabeth." Alix was relieved to note that Elizabeth performed a perfect curtsy. She did not look to Alix for confirmation, but smiled tremulously at the countess.

"I am delighted to meet you, child. Come here so that I may see your beautiful dress."

Now Elizabeth did look up at Alix, who nodded with an encouraging smile. Elizabeth walked daintily and in a straight line over to where Lady Croxton sat.

"That smells good," Elizabeth said, peering into the empty tea cups.

"It is the tea brewing in the pot. Can you guess what is in it, Elizabeth?"

Elizabeth appeared to forget her nervousness in her effort to place the scent. "Mmm . . . lemon?"

"Well done! What a bright child you are. Would you care to sit here next to me, and we'll have some tea and biscuits and get to know one another better?"

Elizabeth remained standing. "I'm not allowed to have tea with the adults. But thank you, Lady Croxton. Oh! I almost forgot." Elizabeth buried her head, searching in her small reticule, until Alix asked what she was doing. "I'm looking for something I brought to show Lady Croxton."

Alix and Lady Croxton expressed their surprise as they made eye contact with one another. Elizabeth pulled out a rock and held it out toward the countess.

"What an amazing stone. Where did you find this?" asked the older woman.

"Outside," said Elizabeth. "Last night, when we were taking a walk with Lord Woodhurst. I love rocks, don't you?"

"Yes, I do." Lady Croxton turned it over, studying it. "And look at the little specks of white. I do declare, this reminds me of a bird's egg."

"That's what I thought, too!" said Elizabeth. When Damion's grandmother held the rock toward her, Elizabeth said, "It's yours, Lady Croxton. It's your welcome gift."

"Well, I thank you sincerely. Tell me, Elizabeth, why are you giving me such a precious gift?"

"Alix told me if you want someone to be your friend, you have to be nice to them and make them feel happy. And I have six rocks, so I decided to give you one. That one is my favorite."

"Your favorite? I am honored. Your sister is a wise woman." Lady Croxton smiled at Miss Adams. "Please come sit and have tea, Alix. And do allow your sister to join the ladies. She's so very grown up."

Alix noted the pleading in the child's eyes as she crossed the room. "Elizabeth, just this one time, since Lady Croxton requests it."

Elizabeth gingerly sat down, spreading the skirts of her lavender dress as she'd seen the ladies do.

Alix said, "The tea does smell delicious. Do I detect chamomile as well?"

"You do. My mother swore by a light infusion in her afternoon tea to protect against indigestion. Shall I pour?"

Alix sat in the nearest chair, accepting the saucer and steaming cup Lady Croxton offered. She had a pang of sympathy that this wise woman would soon depart the earth with its plants and herbs the lady reveled in. It would be sad to lose this kindred gardening spirit, not to mention Lord Woodhurst's more serious loss.

She inhaled the aroma appreciatively, and looked up to see the lady's eyes magnified comically through a lorgnette.

"My. What a bright color." Lady Croxton's pulled her face back from her spectacles several inches, as if the color of Miss Adams's gown would shift when exposed to the extra distance.

"Do you like it?" Alix bit the right side of her lip. "You don't think it's a little too . . . intense?"

Lady Croxton picked up her tea cup and took a sip. "What do you think, Alix?"

"I . . . please don't misunderstand . . . your grandson has been so very generous to me, but—"

"What? Never say Edmund chose that!"

"Edmund?" asked Alix.

"Edmund. My grandson. Lord Woodhurst."

Alix set down her tea cup. "Lady Croxton, Lord Woodhurst purchased all of my clothes. *All* of them," she said, a little forlornly.

"I don't understand."

Alix sighed. What to say? "Lady Croxton . . . I truly don't know where to start."

The older woman did not help her out. She placed an iced biscuit on Elizabeth's plate, then took a tiny bite of her own chewy biscuit, watching Miss Adams with total fascination. "Good heavens, Alix. I can't wait to hear this. Please, start at the beginning. No, wait. Start by calling me what my friends call me, please. I know we shall be good friends. I wish for you to call me Lady Charlotte." When Miss Adams nodded, she continued. "Now, start at the beginning of your tale."

"I . . . oh, dear. May I ask that you not repeat anything I'm about to tell you? To Lord Woodhurst's parents? I'm not sure he would be pleased that I'm even telling you."

Lady Charlotte held up two crossed fingers as she busily chewed.

"I had only two dresses to my name when I came here."

Lady Charlotte choked on her biscuit.

"My lady! Are you all right?" Alix moved to hurriedly set her cup down, but stopped as Lady Charlotte waved her off.

"Yes." The countess swallowed and hastily drank some tea. "Did you say two dresses?"

"Yes. Two. I am—I mean I was—a teacher."

Well, perhaps best not to reveal that she was still a teacher and would be returning to the school in a matter of weeks. She gave Elizabeth a warning glance. And she definitely could not reveal at this time that she was not a real fiancée.

"Elizabeth and I were both living at the school when we met your grandson. I had an extremely limited wardrobe, as you would expect of a teacher. Two serviceable dresses for teaching, so that I could wash one and have one dry," she added quietly, peeking up at Damion's grandmother. "I see," said Lady Charlotte, while her tone said she did not.

"Your grandson wanted me to dress well. Especially with family arriving." She shrugged. "I'm sure he was ashamed of my paltry wardrobe."

"I would hope *ashamed* is not the sentiment. I'd be most disappointed in my grandson if his male pride were that fragile."

Alix smiled. "Perhaps it was I who worried about shaming *him.*"

"Alix." Lady Charlotte set her teacup down with an authoritative clink to match her voice. "You are a wonderful addition to this family. If anything, I can see you shall give him reason for pride."

Alix faltered in the middle of sipping tea, unsure how she should respond. "I hope to do your hopes justice, my Lady."

"My dear, I know my grandson. And I can already see why he chose you for his future wife. His return letter to me sounded so. . . . well, content is the word that comes to my mind. And a grandmother can read between the lines."

Alix had to smile to herself, knowing she had nothing to do with Damion's happiness. "Oh, that. It is because he is treasuring his time with you."

"Yes, that must be it," Lady Charlotte said dryly. "You were saying? About your wardrobe?"

"When he discovered I had nothing presentable—Lady Chloe was right to point that out, to my embarrassment—he insisted on buying clothes for me." Alix blushed. "But I did protest." With a note of pique, she added, "And he not only ignored me, he bought too much. Much too much."

"Are they all . . . all similar to this one?" Lady Charlotte's words were delicately put.

"Well. I've only seen two so far. They *are* both quite bright.

And quite ruffly. I realize I should be grateful, but I feel a bit like a tea cake."

"Well, I'm relieved to hear you say so. Our sensibilities are similar. Perhaps you should have helped Edmund pick out your patterns?"

"Oh, no. Lord Woodhurst did not choose the dresses. His friend, Lady Chloe, insisted on directing the modiste."

Lady Charlotte's eyes narrowed. "Lady Chloe? But she does not dress in this fashion. Why should she choose it for you?"

"She told me . . ." Alix lowered her voice in mortification. "She said I had no sense of fashion, and I must leave the choice of a wardrobe in her hands. It's true. I've never employed a modiste."

"I think I begin to see. Do you care for it, Alix? Now, be honest, gel."

Alix shook her head. "No. I am much more comfortable in my plain dresses."

"I'm glad to hear you say something so prudent. I don't care for it either." At Miss Adams's surprised expression, she said, "And you say the other is similar to this?"

"Perhaps brighter." Alix shrugged. "This was the simplest, so I chose to wear it today."

Lady Charlotte rolled her eyes. "When is Edmund expected back?"

"He thought he could be back in four days' time."

"And when does he expect his parents—my daughter and her husband—to arrive?"

"He hopes to be back before their arrival. I believe he said they might be at Fern Crest Hall by the end of the week."

"All right. Perhaps we can do it." Lady Charlottes brushed the crumbs from her hands in a precisely military fashion.

"What shall we be doing?"

"Alix, yours is a classical grace. You should favor more of a slender Grecian look than . . . a tea cake, did you call it?"

Alix smiled.

"So, I shall send for my own modiste."

"Oh, no!"

"Don't worry. She doesn't only outfit matrons, as you shall see."

"That wasn't what I meant at all, Lady Charlotte. It's that—I can't possibly allow Lord Woodhurst to spend another farthing on clothes."

"Who said Edmund would spend it?"

Alix looked confused.

"I have my own money, Alix, and . . . well, as Edmund would be the first to admit, I shall have no need of it where I am going." Her eyes twinkled at Miss Adams's blush. "I choose—choose, mind you, so no arguing—to spend it on some appropriate dresses for you."

"But—"

"Tut-tut. I said no arguing, miss."

Alix shook her head in capitulation. "No wonder he loves you so."

"So just say 'thank you,' and we shall get on with it."

"Thank you." Alix crossed over to where the lady sat and kissed her cheek. As Alix returned to her seat, smiling, she did not see Lady Charlotte's stunned look.

The countess cleared her throat. "Elizabeth, while Miss Adams and I visit, would you care to gather a few toys and sit here with us? If your sister doesn't mind?" She raised her eyebrows to Miss Adams.

Elizabeth shook her curls. "No, but if I promise to be quiet and listen, Alix, can I sit here without toys? Please?"

"Elizabeth, did you forget to bring your toys with you when you left the school?" asked Lady Charlotte.

The little girl shook her head again. "I didn't have any."

"Then bring along one of your dolls, and she'll join in our tea party."

Elizabeth appeared embarrassed. "I don't have any dolls neither, my Lady."

"Why ever not?"

"Headmistress Staunton says that young ladies do not need friv—frivelly—"

"Frivolous?"

"Yes. Frivolous. Young ladies do not need frivolous things to keep their minds occupied."

"Oh, dear. I don't think I like this Headmistress Staunton."

This irreverence set Elizabeth off into giggles. Lady Charlotte's deep chuckles joined her.

CHAPTER ELEVEN

Damion returned three nights later, when the household was asleep. Philbin informed him that Lady Croxton had arrived, and asked did he need anything else.

"No. Thank you, Philbin. Please see yourself off to bed."

Finally home. His shoulders were tense with the stress of the last few days, the funeral, and Sarah's desperation. He'd done everything he could to get her household settled—at least the mundane matters. It would be a long time before Sarah and the boys would recover. Sarah, the raucous young girl he remembered, had been frighteningly quiet, even at the funeral. And seeing the two young boys grieving had torn at Damion's heart.

He got up to pour a drink.

"You've arrived." Alix stood at the door, a heavy robe wrapping her from her neck to the tips of her bare toes.

"Would you care to join me for a drink?"

He turned to face her, and she inhaled. "My Lord, you look awful."

"What a delightful welcome home from my fiancée."

"I'm sorry, Lord Wood—"

"I'm teasing. Don't apologize." He forced a smile. "You're right, if I look as I feel. Did you say you'd like a drink?"

"Yes." She crossed over. Yes, I'll join you. "She took one of the two deep armchairs in front of the fire. "It was bad?" It was more a statement than a question.

"It was hell." He handed Miss Adams a glass and took the

seat across from her. "But how self-centered of me to complain. I show up for the funeral, interview a foreman, and leave. They are left alone in their misery. I can escape, they cannot." He rubbed a hand through his hair.

"It's obvious you haven't fully escaped yet either. Have you lost someone close to you before this, Lord Woodhurst?"

He looked up at her with red eyes. "No. And you?"

She looked over at the fire and nodded. "My parents."

"Of course. You told me you were an orphan."

"And *you* told Lady Chloe." She didn't sound bitter; simply resigned.

Damion reacted as if slapped. "She said something to you? I told her of it when we were on our way to the school to gather you. Miss Adams, I only told her because I thought she'd be more sympathetic toward you."

"Humph. Sympathy is not a trait I'd ever attribute to Lady Chloe." She stared at the fire a moment, sipping her drink, and turned to Damion. "But I'm sorry. She's your friend and I shouldn't gossip. Tell me about your trip. Would it help to talk about it?"

"I don't know, truthfully. I've done nothing but replay the scenes at Greeley's home over and over in my mind as I rode here." He looked around the room. "You don't know how good it feels to be home." His gaze dropped to his glass. "And now I shall have to replay the scene soon with my own grandmother." He raised his eyes to Miss Adams. "How is she?"

"Wonderful. I mean, she *looks* wonderful. And she *is* wonderful. You are a lucky man to have such a grandmother, Lord Woodhurst. One would never suspect she is so seriously ill. I admire her attitude and strength. She arrived the morning after you left. Lady Charlotte—"

"Lady Charlotte, is it?"

Alix blushed. "She insisted. Do you mind?"

"Do I mind? Let me think about this. You've already made my grandmother enough at home that she asks you to call her by her favorite name, reserved only for her friends, and you ask if I mind?" He stared at her. "You are a marvel, Miss Adams."

"It's not me, I'm sure. She's such an amazing person, easy to get to know. And she loves plants. We've walked every day through the gardens, discussing the varieties. I could talk about gardening all day with your grandmother." Alix laughed. "Well, I suppose we already do. I've learned so much from her these past few days. And you should see her with Elizabeth. I've never seen Elizabeth happier. Oh, and thank you for the dresses you had made for Elizabeth. I wish you'd seen her eyes, my Lord. This adventure has been the best—" She shook her head. "Listen to me. Now *I'm* being self-centered, to find joy in this unhappy family situation." She set her glass on the side table, and stood to leave.

Damion rose and stepped into her path. "Why not find joy where we can? If my grandmother can be happy these last few weeks, you'll never know what it means to me."

He took Miss Adams's hand and moved closer. She had to look up to meet his eyes.

"You were the perfect choice for a fiancée, Miss Adams." He dropped her hand, but still he stood too close. "The perfect choice."

Aware of the impropriety, and much too aware of him, Alix stepped back and moved around him to the door. "I'll see you and your grandmother in the morning," she said from the threshold. "Welcome home, my Lord," she added lamely.

Damion entered the breakfast room to find his grandmother alone.

"Edmund, my favorite grandson!" Lady Charlotte had to reach up to hug him.

"Grandmother, am I not your only grandson?" He hugged her gingerly.

"Do you call that a hug? I'm not so fragile, young man."

"Yes, ma'am." He hugged a bit more tentatively. "Have you had your breakfast?"

"I was about to sit down. And you?"

Damion waved off the footman and seated his grandmother himself. "I was hoping to join you. Allow me to dish up your plate. You don't care for kidneys in the morning, as I recall."

"Sausages, please." Lady Charlotte glanced toward the double doors. "Edmund, I must tell you before the others arrive that I am delighted with your fiancée. I could not have chosen a more perfect young woman myself."

Damion beamed. "My thoughts exactly. I'm glad I went with my hunch." He froze as he realized what he'd said.

Lady Charlotte laughed gustily. "I should hope it was more than a hunch that made you propose. You are always such a teaser."

He sighed inwardly as his grandmother turned her attention to the coddled eggs, then jumped to his feet as Miss Adams and Elizabeth entered the room. He couldn't take his eyes from Miss Adams, dressed in a softly draped green morning dress that complimented her cloudy grey eyes and the lush twist of auburn hair knotted at the nape of her neck. As he seated her, he leaned close and said, "That dress is lovely. It makes your eyes the color of the lilies floating on the pond."

"The dirty water doilies?" asked Elizabeth loudly, who was close enough to overhear. She took the seat the footman offered.

"What was that?" Lady Charlotte had her lorgnette at the ready.

Damion straightened. "I was complimenting Miss Adams on her new dress, Grandmother. I said . . . it made her eyes look

102

the color of the lilies floating on the pond." He blushed at the poetic sentiment.

"That dress *is* beautiful on you, Alix," said Lady Charlotte. "It has . . . a classical grace, would you not agree?"

Alix smiled affectionately. "I would agree, my Lady. No tea cakes."

"Tea cakes?" asked Damion in confusion. "Were you wanting sweets with your breakfast?"

Alix shook her head, smiling. "No thank you, my Lord. I am very content."

Damion was content as well. He sat and beamed at his three favorite women. And remembered there was another lady in residence. "Will Lady Chloe be joining us for breakfast?"

Alix said, "She enjoys resting in the morn—"

"Insists on keeping town hours," interrupted Lady Charlotte with pursed lips. "Else, she does not care for our company at breakfast. Hasn't yet. Or at tea, come to think of it."

Alix's eyes were two round circles.

Damion cleared his throat; changed the subject. "So, Grandmother, I assume you've already met Miss Adams's charming sister, Miss Elizabeth?"

This worked to soften the woman. She looked fondly upon Elizabeth, who sat on her left. "Oh, dear, yes. Lizzie and I are already the best of friends."

Damion cringed. He saw Miss Adams holding her breath, waiting for the little girl to unforgivably give her elder a set down.

"You mustn't call her Lizzie, Grandmother," he said quickly. He watched Elizabeth, waiting for a scowl to mask her tiny angelic face. "She prefers to be called Elizabeth. Because Lizzie is rather common. Don't you agree?" he asked the little girl with a wink.

"Oh, no." Elizabeth calmly set down her fork and reached

out to put her small hand in Lady Charlotte's weathered one as she looked up at the older woman. "She may call me Lizzie if she wishes."

"I see," said Damion. But it was obvious he didn't.

"My Lord! You're finally home," cooed Chloe as she floated into the room and straight up to Damion's chair, ignoring the others.

He stood and bowed briefly over her hand. "Lady Chloe. We're honored you joined us for breakfast."

"But I wouldn't *dream* of your dining alone, Lord Woodhurst." Her pout looked sincere as she fluttered her eyelashes.

"Alone?" repeated Lady Charlotte, looking around the room at Miss Adams and Elizabeth.

CHAPTER TWELVE

"Edmund, where did your grandfather keep his hunting decoys?" Lady Charlotte looked around the library as if expecting to see them perched atop the highest satinwood shelves.

Damion tilted his head a bit to the side, as if to hear better. "Decoys? Did you say decoys?"

"Decoys, Edmund. Is there something wrong with your hearing, Grandson?"

He grinned. "No, Grandmother." He turned to his butler. "Philbin, would you please have the footman fetch a decoy from the cabinet in—"

"No!" Lady Charlotte held up her palm to detain the butler.

Philbin and Damion both turned as one to the older lady.

"I didn't ask you to have one *fetched* to me," she said. "I should prefer to pick one out for myself."

Philbin turned to Damion, his expression unreadable.

Damion studied his grandmother, seeing a spot of senility for the first time. "All right, Grandmother." His tone was soothing. "Of course you may choose your own . . . decoy."

"And don't humor me with that condescending tone, young man." She pinned Damion with her sharp gaze. "Philbin, please lead on." She marched to the door. Turning round, she skewered Philbin with that same gaze. "I said *lead*, Philbin, not follow."

"Yes, my Lady." Damion had never seen his butler show a

faster pace, but the man fairly scurried out the door.

Damion shook his head in amusement and returned to the books he'd neglected too long. Sooner than he wished, the door opened to another visitor. Chloe peeked around, and when she spied him she crossed the room to his desk.

"Damion, we need to talk." Her voice did not sound pleased.

"Yes?" He continued writing in the ledger. Perhaps if he looked studiously busy . . .

"I have to tell you there is something wrong with that woman."

He sighed and leaned back, steepling his fingers. "That leaves Elizabeth out. Which woman are we discussing? My grandmother or my—"

"Don't say it! Do not use that word to me. Not when speaking of her. We both know she's not truly your fiancée." She hissed the last word, but he'd already sensed displeasure by her body language. Her arms were crossed under her breasts, pushing them up amply; however, with Chloe, one never knew whether it was to express discontent or to enhance her assets.

"As it happens," she continued, "I'm speaking of your grandmother."

Damion glanced away disinterestedly from the enticingly low neckline. "Well, of course there's something wrong with her. She's dying, Chloe."

"Is it an illness accompanied by dementia?"

"What is that supposed to mean?" His voice echoed his annoyance.

"The woman is a bit senile, countess or no. Surely you've noticed?"

Damion replayed the decoy scene of the last few minutes. Regardless, his sense of loyalty to the grand dame would not allow him to admit anything. Not to Chloe. "I cannot say I have.

But what of it?"

"I think Miss Adams encourages her."

"Miss Adams? Encourages senility?" He laughed. "I suppose teachers are most effective when encouraging."

Lady Chloe did not laugh. "She caters to the dowager countess's silly fancies and stories."

"What would you have me do, Chloe? Lock her up in an attic room?"

"Miss Adams or your grandmother? Or both?" Chloe stared at the window as a gust blew spatters of large rain drops noisily against the glass. "I believe they are both making me crazy. I can't take being cooped up with them *and* with this rain. And then to have you gone so long, depriving me of any clever company. I find it tedious trapped here on my own."

"On your own? Chloe, I'm sorry this has been such a chore for you. I shall owe you a gratitude gift. When we're back in London, why don't you pick out a bauble or two, on my account?"

She perked up. "At Rundell and Bridge? On Ludgate Hill?"

"Anywhere that pleases you."

Chloe moved swiftly around the desk, and leaned toward Damion. "Why don't you pick out something for me, Damion? That would be so much more . . . personal. Meaningful." She moved slightly so that her body touched his writing arm.

Damion cleared his throat, but he did not move his arm. If he turned his head at all, he'd be staring down her dress. He looked down to contemplate the feather in his hand. "I have another thought. Now that my grandmother has arrived and the charade at the school is done, perhaps you'd prefer to return to the city. My carriage is at your disposal."

Chloe snapped upright as if his arm burnt her. "Are you implying you no longer desire my company?"

"No! That wasn't what I said. I'm only thinking of your

comfort. I don't wish to keep you here any longer than necessary if you are anxious for town entertainment. You'd be escorted, of course."

Her tone softened. "Would you be my escort, my Lord? And we'd do the jewelry shopping together that you promised?"

"That's not what I had in mind."

The pout was back. "Then you're not getting rid of me so easily. She'd enjoy that."

Damion had no idea what Chloe blathered about.

"Furthermore, I'm offended you should attempt it, Damion. Myles said this would be a daring adventure. But so far it's been boring. And annoying."

Damion sighed loudly. Leave it to Myles to con his sister with silly promises. Damion should have remembered how vain and demanding she'd been as a young girl before he agreed to have her here. He picked up the quill and dipped it. Scratching the parchment too vigorously left a tiny rip, and he cursed.

"Chloe, I am sorry this is the boring countryside. There is nothing I can do about that. There is nothing I can do about the weather. There is nothing I can do about changing fiancées. There is nothing I can do about my grandmother's health, or her frame of mind. There is nothing I can do about your room. Now, if you have no other complaints, I am rather busy."

He kept his head down, writing busily for a full minute before he hazarded a glance. Chloe was gone. He should have been relieved, but all he experienced was guilt. And a sense of frustration he couldn't explain, but it was not fair to take it out on Lady Chloe. She'd done him a huge favor. Well, he'd certainly make it worth her while when they returned, as he'd promised. He really should spend more time with her, but frankly, that didn't interest him.

A soft knock at the door came not five minutes later.

Who the devil is it now? he wondered. He might as well post an inn sign on the library door. "Come in," he ordered loudly.

Alix stepped in gingerly. "I'm interrupting."

For some inexplicable reason, Damion felt pleasure at seeing Miss Adams. This made him feel even guiltier about how he'd treated Chloe. "Not at all. Come in, Miss Adams."

"You look busy." She made it sound like a question.

"I need a break." He stood and stretched backward, his hands on his lower back. "I'm still tired from the ride. And a bit melancholy about Greeley. And Grandmother. And I feel terrible for snapping at Lady Chloe a few minutes ago." He looked ruefully at Miss Adams. "I might not be the best company, but do come in if you'd risk it."

"I may not be the best of company either. I'm wandering the house because I'm bored." Alix walked across the room and stood at the window, watching the millions of rain drops falling. They weren't large, just steady. "Ugh! I'm so tired of the rain. It seems it's been raining for three days straight."

"I was once in Scotland," said Damion, as he sat back down. His gaze remained on the young lady backlit by the tall window panes, "and they swore it was the one hundredth day of straight rain."

"Then why would someone want to live there?" She continued to stare at the flooding grounds. The water in the duck pond had already begun escaping over the surrounding grass.

He shrugged. "There are worse things than rain."

"Such as?"

"Scotland is a beautiful country, Miss Adams. Have you been there?"

"No," she said softly. She stared through the rain, as if she could see the faraway country. "I've never been anywhere, until here. Well, London as a child, but I hardly remember it. And Widpole Manor, of course. For most of my life."

"Hmm. Let me see if I understand: When you lived all those years at Widpole Manor—the school that is only a few miles from here—it never rained. Or, the rain never bothered you. Yet at *my* home you find the rain annoying."

Alix laughed. "Well, perhaps the company has something to do with one's perception of the weather."

"What a cruel guest you are, Miss Adams."

She turned from the gloomy day outside so he could see her smile as she said, "I thought a proper host is supposed to provide his guests with entertainment."

Damion surprised her by rising from his deep armchair and coming straight to her. "What type of entertainment would my fiancée desire? I can think of several things I'd wish to do to pass away a grey, rainy day."

Alix backed up until the curved window handle bumped her in the back. Watching his smiling lips, she had a mad desire to ask what he had in mind. Instead, she ducked her head and looked down shyly. "I . . . I don't know."

They remained almost toe-to-toe. She was sure he still watched her, and she flushed slightly. She'd felt the warm blush coming, but was helpless to stop it. "Cards?" she squeaked.

He laughed. She stared down until she saw his shoes step away from her field of vision.

"Of course." His voice came from farther away now, a safe distance. "That's exactly what I was hoping my fiancée would say."

Alix peeked up to see he stood at the bell pull.

When the footman appeared, Damion said, "We'd like a small tea, please, and a set of playing cards. For piquet."

Alix's insides were warm, but thankfully her face no longer felt hot. She left the window.

Damion fished in his desk for paper and laid it atop the small card table that stood on slender cabriole legs. "I was serious, you know."

Alix froze. Rather than meet his eyes, she ran her hand across the raised frieze on the table's smooth octagonal top. "Yes?" She gulped. "About . . . about passing the time on a grey day?"

His eyes sparkled. "No, Miss Adams. I apologize for frightening you. I don't know what got into me. I was feeling silly. And I'm sure Headmistress Staunton would never approve of my proposed curriculum." He fumbled about in a nearby escritoire for more writing utensils. His back to her, he continued. "But I still desire to know how you never had to deal with rain at the school, which resides in the very same county as this house?"

"All right, yes. We did have rain. There! I've confessed. It's just that . . ." her voice trailed off.

"Yes?" Still bent over the low drawer, he twisted to look at her.

"I have to think about it, so I can give you an honest answer." A few moments later, she said, "It's just that my time here is so limited. I must enjoy every single day, every chance to walk the grounds. And I was so looking forward to the picnics you suggested. I don't have time for it to rain!"

Damion straightened, additional pens in hand. "I like that about you, Miss Adams. Most ladies love to banter back and forth, and say the first silly thoughts to enter their heads, false or otherwise. Yet you—" He returned to the card table. "You consider every question I ask quite seriously. You weigh it and you deliberate on your answer, to ensure you are precisely honest."

"That makes it sound as if I cannot make up my own mind. I suppose you dread asking me a question, as you are ensured of a long wait for an answer."

"No. It only means I know you'll tell me the truth." He seated her, then took his seat at the small table. "You *have* always told me the truth, haven't you?"

Alix always knew when she was about to blush, yet the knowledge did not help her to keep it away. She knew from the heat in her cheeks that a light pink tinge would soon color her chin as well.

"Because," he pursued, "I wish to ask you more questions. May I."

She opened her mouth to speak, but closed it again without answering. His fingers drummed.

"Questions about what?"

"About Elizabeth's father," he said. "Your lover."

"No, you may not!" This was said more fiercely than Alix had intended.

Philbin entered with a tea tray, followed by the footman, and Alix jumped out of her chair. "Oh, Philbin. Here, let me help you."

The butler's eyes went a little round before they swiveled to Damion.

"By all means, Philbin. Miss Adams is trying to avoid my questions, so please do allow her to occupy herself—"

"That's not true," she snapped.

"Then sit." He pointed to the chair opposite. "Now, Miss Adams."

She folded her arms. "I don't care for your t—"

"Sit." He turned his commanding gaze to Philbin. "Serve."

All was silent as Philbin set the napkins and the tea service with amazingly quiet movements. The clocked ticked, and the logs on the fire popped just once, as if afraid to anger their master.

"Thank you, Philbin."

"Sir." Philbin scuttled out the door, closing it behind him.

"That was rather rude," she said.

"Then don't play games to avoid me. I told you: I value

honesty. I hate deceit."

"And if someone does not answer all of your bullying questions, you consider it deceit?"

The viscount chose not to answer, as he did not consider it to be a question.

CHAPTER THIRTEEN

Elizabeth stared at the large box with pink satin stripes as the footman carried it into the parlor. He set it gently upon a low table and exited the room, passing Lady Charlotte as she entered.

"Did you see what was found outside the parlor door?" asked Lady Charlotte, taking a seat close to the warmth of the fireplace.

Alix and Lady Chloe glanced up from their books.

"It's so prettily wrapped," said Alix. "Have you checked the label?"

"Label?" asked Elizabeth, moving closer to scrutinize the mysterious package.

"Yes, it appears to have a tag of some sort on it," said Alix. "Can you sound out the letters?"

Elizabeth dutifully began reading the letters aloud, slowly. "E-L-I-Z—" She looked at Alix with round eyes. "My name has a *Z*." She looked back at the label. "I think maybe it says my name?" she added hopefully.

"Why don't you read the rest of the letters," suggested Lady Charlotte, "and then we'll be sure."

"—A-B-E-T-H. I'm sure it's my name!"

"Why, I believe she's right. Alix," concurred Lady Charlotte. "Isn't that how *Elizabeth* is spelled?"

Alix smiled when she caught her wink. "I believe it is."

"Do you wish to open it, Elizabeth?" asked Lady Charlotte.

"May I?" The little girl looked to Alix for permission.

"Yes. You may." Alix's voice was gentle. "And thank you for asking first, Elizabeth."

Elizabeth didn't lift the lid; she touched the box with reverence. "It's so beautiful."

"Elizabeth," Lady Charlotte said her name softly. "Would you like to bring it over here and we shall open it together?"

Elizabeth lifted the box gently and walked it carefully across the room to the settee.

Lady Charlotte put an arm around the little girl's shoulders. "It's only a very small gift, darling. It's my welcome gift to you."

Elizabeth slowly lifted the lid. Inside was a piece of green velvet covering something lumpy. "I never had a gift. Except—" her small brow wrinkled. "Maybe I did, from my mama and papa. I can't remember no more," she whispered, running her fingers over the fuzzy nap of the emerald-green cloth. "It's so soft."

"Oh, heavens, that's just a piece of material I covered your gift with. It's nothing. Look underneath the cloth."

Elizabeth turned her face up to look at Lady Charlotte. "May I keep the cover? Please?"

The older woman squeezed the child a little closer. "Of course you may. Now, look and see what is beneath it."

Elizabeth lifted one corner and peeked. She peeled the layer away as if it were priceless gold-leaf. Peeling back a bit more of the cloth, she inhaled sharply. "Oh—my—goodness!"

Underneath the cloth a duck's head peered out. A worn wooden duck with smooth black head stared at the little girl with its round glass eye on the side facing her. Elizabeth scooped the animal out of the box and cradled it in her arms. "Ohhh," she cooed to it. She draped the green velvet cloth over his back. "It's his blanket," she explained to both women as she wrapped him in it. She pulled a bit on top of his head to shape a hood. "It's soft and warm. He likes it." Girl and toy duck both looked in Lady Charlotte's direction. "Thank you for my duck, my Lady."

"You are quite welcome, child."

"And he says to thank you for his blanket." She tucked him deeper into her arm. "May I be excused to show him our bedroom?"

"Yes," said Alix, at the same time Lady Charlotte said, "Of course you may."

Elizabeth stood, the duck cradled gently. She leaned over and kissed Lady Charlotte. "May I call you *Grandmamma?*"

"Elizabeth!" Alix was distressed at the familiarity.

"I'd be honored if you would." Lady Charlotte squeezed Elizabeth's hand.

Elizabeth carefully carried the little duck from the room.

After she was out of hearing range, Alix turned to Lady Charlotte. "I must apologize for her forwardness, my Lady."

"Please don't. I could not be happier." She shook her head, her eyes wet. "It's only a decoy, from my husband's old collection. I shall order a few dolls and children's toys from the village."

Alix opened her mouth, but the woman was faster. "And no arguments. I shall do as I please, and you know that by now, Alix. So just nod and say, 'Yes, ma'am.' "

Damion passed Elizabeth in the hallway, on his way to join the ladies.

"Why are you chuckling, Grandson?" Lady Charlotte spied her grandson as he entered the room.

"I just passed little Elizabeth in the hall, and now I know why you asked me about the decoy."

"Well, why else do you suppose I'd be wanting a decoy, at my age?" His grandmother raised her lorgnette in time to see his silly grin.

"To tell you the truth, I didn't bother to hazard a guess." When she looked away, he exchanged glances with Chloe, who had the grace to look embarrassed. "I came to announce that I saw a rainbow from my room, ladies. Could it be a sign we will finally get a break from the rain?"

Universal sighs of approval greeted this announcement.

"My arthritis will enjoy the break," said his grandmother, rising slowly from the settee. "I shall see you all later, at tea?" She touched Damion on the arm, and gave him a kiss on the cheek as she passed him near the door.

Chloe stood, closing her book, and moved close to Damion while he stood alone. "Lord Woodhurst, I've been waiting for a break in the rain to do a little shopping in the village. Perhaps in an hour." She gave a quick sigh of exasperation. "I don't recall an overabundance of shops, but one does what one must while in the country."

"And one must shop," he said, lips curving up.

Chloe smiled fetchingly. She faced him so that Miss Adams was blocked from their view by his broad back. Putting a hand on his forearm, her voice was low and husky as she said, "I'm glad you agree. Because I was especially hoping you might escort me."

He placed a hand over hers. "But of course. It's the least I can do after subjecting to you to so many days of rain here. Miss Adams?" He raised his voice without turning around. "Lady Chloe and I are planning a trip to the village in about an hour's time. Shall you join us?"

Chloe snatched her hand from his arm, narrowing her eyes.

"I'd love to. Thank you, Lady Chloe." Alix returned her attention to the book on her lap.

Chloe glared at Damion. In a lowered voice she snapped,

"Why don't you invite Elizabeth as well while you're at it?"

Damion appeared oblivious to the sarcasm. "That is quite generous of you. If you're sure she won't disturb you ladies, I think she'd be thrilled."

Chloe bit back a reply and marched out the door.

Damion strolled to a deep armchair near the fire. When Miss Adams looked up, he said, "Please, don't let me disturb you."

She closed the book firmly. "In truth, I'd prefer the company. This book is so sad, not the best choice to be reading on gloomy days."

"Is it a good book?"

She looked at it as she considered, then shook her head. "Not really."

He couldn't help laughing. "Then why are you still reading it? I have only twelve dozen more in the library for you to choose from. Ah, let me guess. Because your time here is so limited, you must read every single book in my library, as quickly as you can."

Alix held the book in front of her and studied its cover. "No. Though, I am only skimming through the pages of this one. While the story is melancholic, the scenery descriptions are fascinating. It's about Paris. In the winter. But I think Paris at any time of year would be fascinating."

"Is that where you'd go if you could travel anywhere? To Paris?"

"Oh, no. I'd travel to Bath."

He looked his surprise. "To Bath?" At her enthusiastic nod, he continued, "While I'd admit the natural scenery is intriguing, I think that in Bath—the town, that is—the natural scenery pales to the comic scenery. What *I* find most fascinating is the many exposed shapes of the Ton."

Her eyes lit. "You've been to Bath?"

"Many times. My parents enjoyed taking the waters there annually. But why does it interest you? Have you been there as well?"

"Oh, no. One of the teachers at the school has a brother who went to Bath. With his new wife. He sent my friend letters—the most comical letters—and we made her read them to us at night. More than once. But they were mostly about his heavy mother-in-law, whom he already disliked, and her airs and anecdotes. There was a little about the baths, and their walks, but I'd love to know more about the city itself."

"What do you wish to know?"

"Everything! I want to know what the Pump Room looked like, and the furnishings in the Assembly Rooms, and how they were different from one another, and where you strolled and what you did for leisure, and if you saw famous artists and actors, and—Could you see the river? From your room?"

"All of that? Is that all you wish to know?" His eyes laughed.

Alix dimpled. "Don't mock me, my Lord. I've never been anywhere."

"You said you'd been to London as a child."

Her laugh was short and scornful. "Not a part of London a tourist would want to visit, I assure you." She was quiet, her eyes focused far away, but returning to his quickly. "I've only known one tiny piece of London. And the school. Nowhere else."

"Sounds as if you dream of traveling?"

"Yes." Practicality ironed her smile to a straight line. "But I am wise enough to know that dreams are for sleeping. They do not hold true when one examines them closely by the light of day."

"You can't mean that, Miss Adams."

Her eyes held a gentle reproach. "Look at me. Look at my situation. Please do not think to humor me, my Lord. You know I shall never travel, other than here. But I shall remember this as the greatest adventure of my life."

"Ah. Then it is my duty to make sure it is a worthy adventure. Where to start?"

"Anywhere. Please. Tell me anything you remember about Bath. Or any other place you've visited."

"Let me think." He leaned back into the deep cushions of his chair, as Miss Adams leaned forward in hers.

She gripped the arms of her chair in anticipation. "Your favorite sight at Bath. Or your favorite memory."

"You'll laugh, because it's not the Pump Room, nor the Assembly Rooms. It's a bridge."

"A bridge, yes?" Her words rushed, pulling her imagination along. "Tell me why. I want to hear all about it."

Damion watched her eyes as he talked. "It is located a little outside the city itself. I've always had an appreciation for architecture. And landscaping. But even landscaping strikes me from an architectural or structural point of view. So, through a friend, I was able to visit Prior Park one day. It's an estate in the Bath vicinity. It happened to be the middle of summer, late afternoon. I was walking the grounds, admiring the gardens. Of a sudden, I crested a rise, and saw a lake. A small lake, not remarkable for a manor. Its surface was the color of wet stone: dark grey, with patches of green moss floating near its edges."

He looked away, to a spot at the center of the hearthrug, seeing another place, on another day. "In its reflection I could see the trees behind me, and the bright grassy bank I stood upon. But spanning it was a bridge such as I'd never before seen. I thought at first it was a Roman temple floating on the pond, for this bridge had a structure above it." He returned an intense gaze to her. "First, picture a railing along the entire bridge, with supporting balusters. Delicate, as if a master carpenter had turned the spindles of each. Then, in the center of the bridge, a roofed structure supported by columns. Flanking the row of columns at each end was an open portico of arches."

He looked into the fire now, seeing more memories. "I spied a pathway below me that strolled along the bank toward the bridge. I shall never forget that walk, with large honeysuckles on my right, and the green lawn sloping down to my left, to the opaque waters. I half expected to see a rock rise from the murkiness, and King Arthur's sword float up upon a hand, and . . ." Damion blinked and looked up from the fireplace. "I'm sorry. I am carrying on—"

"No. No, don't apologize, please. It . . . it was magical. I can see it all."

He noticed she wiped a hand across her eyes. "Are you all right, Miss Adams?"

Alix smiled and nodded. "You are a wonderful story teller, my Lord."

"I'm sure I'm not. I'm just a traveler with silly imaginings."

The footman entered to announce that Lady Chloe wished to depart for the village.

Alix rose, taking Damion's extended hand. "Will you tell me other stories? About Bath?"

"I fear my travel stories, combined with the rain, may soon have you ready for Bedlam."

"Not at all. I think that even if it were a perfect day, I should prefer to sit inside by the fire and hear of your travels. Will you promise to tell me another? Soon?"

He shook his head in disbelief. "If you wish, but I do believe you are merely being a polite guest." He crooked his arm for Miss Adams to accompany him.

She looked up at Damion with obvious admiration. "The woman you marry will be fortunate, my Lord." When he arched his brows, she added wistfully, "Your stories will entertain her nightly."

Damion paused out of earshot of his footman, and muttered, "I hope, Miss Adams, that I should have other entertainment to offer a wife at night besides story-telling."

Alix and Elizabeth laughed as they exited the confectionery shop. Elizabeth had a smudge of cinnamon on the side of her mouth, and Alix stopped the little girl. Stooping down, she gently dabbed the flecks away with the edge of her handkerchief.

"There. Now you look like a young lady again, Elizabeth."

"Elizabeth, is it?" came the gruff voice of a man.

Alix spun around at the voice, and immediately straightened. She grabbed Elizabeth's hand tightly and began walking quickly down the street.

"Wait! Miss Adams, I need to talk to yer." The slurring stranger was dressed shabbily. Small greedy eyes peered out of his round, unevenly shaven face.

"Miss Adams," Elizabeth said. "He knows your name. Shouldn't we stop and talk to him?"

"No! Elizabeth, don't stop. Hurry." Their carriage waited about a dozen doors away. "No! Don't turn around. We must get back to our carriage."

As they neared it, she saw Lady Chloe had already completed her errands, and stared at them impatiently, while Damion waited at Chloe's side. Alix glanced over her shoulder. They'd lost him. He most likely had been too full of drink to be able to follow their hasty path.

"Elizabeth," Alix whispered hastily. "Do not talk about this in front of Lady Chloe. Or Lord Woodhurst. You and I shall discuss it later."

Elizabeth started to turn so she could look for the man, but Alix pulled on her hand. "Don't look back, Elizabeth! Did you hear what I said?" They were almost to the carriage.

"Is this another secret?"

"Yes, dear. Yes, it is." Alix handed the little girl up the steps and shuddered as the carriage pulled forward.

CHAPTER FOURTEEN

In two days' time, the dark rain clouds had been banished to memory. The sun had done its job and dried the grounds, putting a crisp spring back into the grasses.

"Tell me about your childhood." Damion sat on a green knoll next to Miss Adams, a picnic lunch between them, the warm meadows releasing their wildflower perfume to mid-day heat.

His grandmother had commandeered Elizabeth for a tea party, and Damion took advantage of the chance to have some private time with Miss Adams while Chloe napped.

She picked a dandelion and twirled it as she considered what to say. "There's so little to tell." He waited, so she sighed. "All right. But remember, you asked." It took her another moment to begin. "I never knew my father." Her chin came up with determination. "I am a bastard, my Lord."

He didn't blink. "That does not signify with me, Miss Adams."

"Oh, of course. I am only a pretend fiancée. Still, I am pleased to see you did not rescind our agreement."

"Do you think persons should be punished for their parents' foibles and actions?" he asked in a serious tone.

"I . . . I don't know. I've never really given it thought."

"Well, if so, let me know soon, please, before you meet my parents." His seriousness melted with a twinkling in his eyes. "Else, I am sure to be condemned in your eyes."

She laughed sweetly, like a wind chime. "Why is that? Can

they be so horrible?"

"I suppose everyone thinks of their parents as odd."

"And will your children think the same? Of you?"

"Of course not. I will be the perfect father. And you?"

She looked over at the pond. "If I can be half the woman my mother was, I shall be grateful."

"You remember her. Then, you were older when—when you were orphaned?"

She nodded, not trusting her voice to speak for a moment. "I was eight. I still remember her so clearly." Alix stared at the still water. "It's hard to believe she's gone. She's frozen in my memory at that age."

"Do you prefer not to talk about it?"

She shrugged. "You would not want your relatives to know any of this, I am sure."

"That's not true." He sounded a shade angry. "Don't judge me too harshly. I've never cared much for the approval of others."

Alix glanced at him. "And your parents? What shall I say if they ask of my birth?"

"I've always found it easier to tell the truth than to lie. But tell them whatever you like, Miss Adams. They know me well enough to realize it would not matter one whit to me whether you were an orphan or the daughter of a duke."

"Easy to say for a pretend bride," she said dryly.

"What? You doubt my sincerity?" He clapped a hand over his breast.

She raised one skeptical brow as she smiled. Focusing on the dandelion instead of Damion, she said, "My mother never told me much about my father. She said he was exceedingly handsome, and she said he was kind. But I don't believe it. For he very unkindly left her when she became with child. I always believed he would return, of course. I was sure my dashing father had joined the military, so that he could return as an officer and afford a family. He would show us the riches he'd found in his travels. His eyes would light up when he discovered me, his daughter. And then, he would marry her." She twined the stem in between her fingers. "But when he didn't appear, I worried he'd been killed in battle."

"What battle was that?"

She turned to him, but her cool glance looked through him. "Does it matter? I don't even know if there was a war going on at the time. It was what I believed as a child, what I wanted to believe, as an excuse for him. I clung to it, but said nothing to my mother. She refused to talk about him, except once, to say I should tell others she was a widow. That was fine, as it would be even more exciting to see her surprise when he arrived at our door. I convinced myself he was still alive, else he could never show up."

Damion watched her. Self-consciously, Alix brushed away a leaf that had floated down to land on her skirt. "Then she died. After I got past the shock of her death, I experienced a second shock: how would my father find me? Without my mother for him to recognize, I was truly lost . . . twice."

Damion plucked a dandelion within reach and handed it to her. "Then it is possible you are not truly orphaned. Do you wish help in finding him?"

She shook her head. "No, but I thank you. No, I don't even know his name. He is dead to me, one way or the other. I don't know his first name, let alone his surname. I have no picture of him, other than that I made up in my head, where he is standing so forthright and handsome in his military uniform." Her smile was grim. "No. I hear it's a typical orphan's dream. I let it go the day I knew my mother could not return from the dead."

"How did you end up at the school?"

"I was amazingly lucky, my Lord. But enough about me.

That's a tale for another day, assuming you are interested. Tell me about yourself."

"I'd rather hear more about you. And what of Elizabeth's father? I wish to know of your relationship with him."

"No." She shook her head quickly. "No. I already told you there is nothing more I shall say on that subject. Not today nor any other day."

"Not even to your betrothed?" he teased.

"No. Please don't ask." She concentrated on adding to her dandelion bouquet.

She should tell him the truth. That Elizabeth was only a student of hers, and no relationship at all. Would he send the little girl away? Alix didn't think so. He seemed to have a genuine affection for Elizabeth; who wouldn't?

But he said he hated deceit. And she'd deceived him. Though hadn't he deceived his family? He could defend his actions because of love, but couldn't she claim the same, for love of Elizabeth?

On the other hand, why bother telling him, when she and Elizabeth would only be here a matter of weeks? An inner voice answered: because she longed for something more. She wished she could have begun on an honest note with this man. She wanted to be a true friend to him. He was so easy to converse with, so comforting to be with. She had a desire to tell him all her secrets. Alix was sure that sharing would help her burdens; she was tired of bearing them alone.

She wished she could tell him about the man who'd accosted her and Elizabeth in the village. Lord Woodhurst made her feel safe. Protected.

But even he could not stop the nightmares that had begun again.

Four small guests sat at the miniature table having tea. Tiny lavender and blue flowers twined with green vines decorated the whitewashed table and chairs. Delicate painted cups and saucers mimicked the floral patterns.

Elizabeth presided. "Would you care for more tea, Mrs. B?" This was directed to the pearl-white porcelain doll sitting to her left. "I have some very fine . . . oh-long tea. Oh-long," she repeated, sounding unsure.

"Oolong," Lady Charlotte said, as she peeked around the door.

"Grandmamma! Please come in and join us. We are having our tea."

Lady Charlotte entered the playroom and glanced around. "I am afraid I would not fit in one of your delicate chairs. Let me pull up another, from over there, and join you." She scooted a paneled oak chair from a corner arrangement. "What are we having for tea? It smells delicious."

"Oo-Long tea," enunciated Elizabeth carefully. "That is what Mrs. B is having." She pointed at the first doll, dressed in a white frock with frilly blue apron and matching bonnet. "But Lady Apricot . . ." Her finger swung to the other side of the table. ". . . prefers blackberry tea."

Lady Apricot was a long, thin wooden doll with jointed arms and legs. She was covered in peach muslin from head to toe, a jaunty smile painted on her oval face.

"And who is this charming gentleman sitting across from you?"

Elizabeth beamed. "You remember Mr. Fizziwig."

"Mr. Fizziwig! I beg your pardon, sir. No wonder you looked familiar."

The smooth wooden duck just stared across the table with his glassy eyes.

"And what is Mr. Fizziwig drinking?" asked Lady Charlotte.

Elizabeth leaned toward her, a hand shading her mouth so

the duck couldn't hear. "Don't tell Lord Woodhurst, but Mr. Fizziwig enjoys the sherry that Lord Woodhurst drinks in the evening."

Lady Charlotte laughed. "Oh, my. No, I won't tell my grandson. But I did notice the decanter seemed emptier than normal. Do you think Mr. Fizziwig is drinking too much sherry?"

Elizabeth wagged a small finger at the duck. "Mr. Fizziwig."

"I came to see if you would care to join me in the Lemon Parlor for tea, just we two ladies, but I'm thinking I should ask Philbin to serve us here. Which would you prefer?"

"Tea in the adult room!" Elizabeth jumped up from the table. She took Lady Charlotte's hand and they moved toward the door. "Oh, excuse me, Grandmamma, I forgot." Elizabeth ran back to the table and pulled Mr. Fizziwig from his seat. She wrapped him in his blanket, the square of green velvet he'd sat upon.

"What about Mrs. B and Lady Apricot?"

"They live here."

"Mr. Fizziwig does not?"

"No. He lives in my bedroom, with me."

"Oh. I see." Lady Charlotte smiled her amusement that in spite of the new dolls and other toys that had been delivered for Elizabeth, the child still insisted on toting the worn wooden duck everywhere she went. "I think we need to find a button and some thread, and make that blanket into a gentleman's cloak for Mr. Fizziwig. Do you think he would like that?"

Elizabeth's eyes lit up. She lifted Mr. Fizziwig up so that he stared at her, eye-to-eye. "He said he would appreciate that so very much, Grandmamma."

"Excellent. Then we'll start on it after tea, shall we?"

About an hour later, Alix and Damion returned to find Lady Charlotte and Elizabeth huddled together over a small gilded table, shears and pins and needles covering its glassy scagliola surface.

"Did you have an enjoyable tea, ladies?" asked Damion.

"Yes, and now we're making a cape for Mister Fizziwig!" said Elizabeth.

"And I believe we're finished, Elizabeth," said Lady Charlotte. "What do you think? Shall we see if it fits him?"

Elizabeth held up their creation for Alix and Damion to see. Two corners of the green velvet came together, clasped with a loop over a large bone button fastener. She picked up her duck, and gently pulled the open end of the material over his wooden head. The woven square rested comfortably on his back, staying attached thanks to the button closure at his neck. Elizabeth found she could pull up an extra triangle of material for a hood. She turned the hooded duck for everyone to see.

"This is for when it rains," she said. Then she pulled the hood down so it gathered on his back. "And this is for when the sun is out. But he still prefers to wear his cape, because some mornings it's chilly even when the sun is out. And . . ." She touched his cape. ". . . he likes it because it also makes him look so handsome. Just like Lord Woodhurst."

Damion laughed. "I only wish my tailor could make me look half as handsome!"

"I agree," said his grandmother with a twinkle in her eye. "You could never hope to be as proper and formal as that duck, Edmund."

Elizabeth got up from her seat and came around the table to Lady Charlotte. She leaned in to her and gave her a hug. "Thank you, Grandmamma. I love it, and so does Mr. Fizziwig."

"You are both certainly welcome, child." Lady Charlotte touched her napkin to her eye. "But perhaps we should ask Mrs. B and Lady Apricot for their opinions."

"Shall I retrieve my cloak as well?" asked Damion. "Then we can see if they can tell the two of us apart."

Elizabeth giggled and set Mr. Fizziwig in the center of the table so everyone could admire his new clothes.

CHAPTER FIFTEEN

"Do you know, you look quite domestic. One would never suspect you were a bluestocking teacher." Damion leaned against the doorjamb.

Alix set aside her embroidery. "The only needle I've held in the past ten years has been a darning needle, and this is much more fun than mending moth-eaten socks. I've never held a paintbrush, but see how similar this is, as I have a rainbow of silk threads to choose from." She picked it up again, briefly, to frown at the messy knots on the back of the fabric. "Besides, I must find something to occupy me when your parents arrive other than sticking my nose in a book." She gave him an arch look. "I rather thought they'd enjoy the engaging sight of their son's fiancée as she sits charmingly at his feet with her embroidery hoop."

"At his feet? With an embroidery hoop? And will she have a worshipful look on her face?"

"Please, my Lord, I thought the intent was to be believable, if I'm to earn that money."

He strolled into the room and stood above her. She stilled as he leaned over. "You, Miss Adams," he said, touching the end of her nose twice, "have a cynical little bite to you. Perhaps I should have heeded Headmistress Staunton."

Alix sputtered and shoved his hand away. "Exactly what do you mean by that?"

Damion straightened and with a crooked grin he said, "She

warned me about you. Said I would be better off with another teacher."

Alix made a rude noise. "I don't believe this! What exactly did she say?"

"Oh, let's see . . . I believe the word 'unmanageable' was used once or twice."

"That is quite untrue. I was the most manageable teacher in the—What other teacher? Did she name another teacher?"

Damion's eyes glittered with amusement. "She was quite adamant that I should be much happier with Miss Eccleston. Is this true?"

Alix dropped her embroidery on her lap at the same time her mouth dropped open. "Miss Eccleston! I don't believe it. She is a termagant!" Alix narrowed her eyes. "Did she give you any specifics?"

He studied his knuckles. "Overly independent? Not biddable? Did she say *headstrong?* Perhaps not. I believe that was my impression, not hers." He ignored Miss Adams's glare. "I'm sure climbing trees would not be counted as an asset."

"Well, it would have served you right if you'd brought Miss Eccleston here. She'd have made your life miserable, my Lord."

"Would she have allowed me to beat her at piquet?"

Alix stared at his innocent look, and could no longer contain her laugh. "You are too egotistical for your own good, Lord Woodhurst."

"Then would you care for another match of cards? Or perhaps dice?"

"Dice? My, if Headmistress Staunton heard you even say the word in polite company, she would have refused to allow me to come here. She loves giving advice from an old proverb: "The best throw of the dice is to throw them away.""

Damion laughed. "Well, since you trounced me thoroughly in piquet, my male pride demands we try another game. Do you think cribbage would be acceptable to Headmistress Staunton?"

"I don't know. However, since she's not here, we shall play. You'll have to teach me. But I'm a fast learner when I set my mind to it."

He studied her with a warm gaze. "I am sure you are. And I am a very patient teacher."

Alix blushed, but wasn't sure why. "If we play, I want to learn more of your visits to Bath."

Damion crossed the room and opened the door to ask a footman for a cribbage set. As he returned, he said, "I'll tell you a little more about Bath, but there will be a price to pay."

Alix dimpled. "No, I shan't allow you to win at this game either."

He seated her at the small table, before he settled across from her.

"No, that is not the price I had in mind, Miss Adams. I will tell you of my travels, but you must tell me a little more about yourself. All I know so far is that you were orphaned, and your mother was deserted by the man who fathered you."

She hunched her shoulders slightly in a feminine shrug. "Why do you wish to know more about me? Elizabeth and I shall be leaving shortly."

Damion's brow furrowed. "I don't know why," he said softly. "I tell myself it's to be prepared for any questions my grandmother or my parents may ask. Except . . . that's not the truth. The truth is, I desire to know more about you." He shrugged without embarrassment.

"Why *didn't* you bring Miss Eccleston to your home? Why me?" She held her breath.

"Because I saw you that day on the wall. And I thought—" He paused at the knock on the door and waited as the footman set down board and cards.

Damion pushed whittled pegs into the wooden board, until

he heard the door click shut. "I thought you were a caring person, Miss Adams, to rescue the little lad as you did. And . . ." He held her eyes. "I thought perhaps you wished to escape."

More than you could know, thought Alix. Briskly she said, "Now, teach me the rules so that I may hear more of Bath."

Philbin knocked at the door to see if Lord Woodhurst required anything. Hearing no reply, he silently entered. Damion and Alix were studying their cards, frozen as he'd seen them the last two times he'd popped by.

"Sherry," said Damion.

"Two," said Alix.

Philbin left.

Damion discarded two cards to the crib. "I'm surprised."

"That I'm winning? Don't you dare say it's beginner's luck."

"No, I meant that you requested a sherry."

Alix dropped her cards in startlement. "Is that what we were ordering?" She laughed. "Then I am also surprised at myself. I was too busy concentrating to listen."

They continued their play in silence until Philbin returned.

"Enough cribbage." Damion pulled out the pegs as they finished the round. "That's two games each." He puffed air through his cheeks. "Do you wish to concede?"

"Do *I* wish to concede? You arrogant man!" Alix thanked Philbin for the small liqueur glass and said to Damion, "However, I am also ready to stop, as you promised more tales of your travels in Bath." She took a gulp with smiling lips as she watched him over the rim of her delicate diamond-cut glass. "Mmm, this—" Alix coughed, inhaled loudly, then coughed again.

"Are you all right?" Damion jumped up, but she waved him back to his seat.

"I'm fine," she rasped. She coughed, cleared her throat, and in a more normal voice, said, "I swallowed the fumes is all. My, that is potent."

"Next time, Miss Adams, try *breathing* the fumes and taking a tiny sip."

She took his advice. "It feels so warm in my throat." Her eyes opened wide. "It's delightful. I do believe you've spoiled me. Sherry, picnics by the river, the view from my bedroom, piquet and cribbage . . . I've never had a more wonderful time in my life, Lord Woodhurst." She took another sip. "Goodness. I see why men love sherry after a fine meal."

Damion watched her as she closed her eyes and took another sip. "Sherry is meant to be coddled, Miss Adams, and appreciated, and lingered over . . . like a fine fiancée."

Her face went as warm as the sherry trickling down her throat. She couldn't look away from his intense gaze.

"There is more I could teach you besides cribbage and drinking sherry." His eyes held hers in a hooded vise.

The huskiness of his voice sent a shiver through Alix. She made herself break eye contact, and chose a safe spot to stare at on the table between them. "Would it be on the headmistress's curriculum?"

"Absolutely not." Damion grinned, deepening the crevice in his cheek, and topped off both their glasses. "You know, I still chuckle, picturing you the day we met, when you were assisting—Tommy, was it?—the lad who was stranded on the wall."

She laughed. "Yes. It seems my life before I came on this adventure was quite monotonous. Teaching children and rescuing Tommy from himself."

"Why *did* you save him that day?"

She pondered. "I'd climbed that same tree myself. Many times."

He pulled his head back, tucking in his chin. "What? Why would a teacher go tree climbing?"

Alix chuckled. "Not as a teacher. I think you are teasing me." With a wistful smile, she added, "As a student."

"Were you young when you were first enrolled at the school?"

"Yes. After . . . she died," Alix said softly.

"It is a charity school, then?"

"No, it is a boarding school, though they arrange to take in a few of the parish's poor." Alix stared at the amber liquid in the glass and shook her head. "After my mother died, I was quite fortunate to be given a spot at the school." She looked at him and explained, "One of the women my mother worked with—a wonderful woman—had an aunt who taught at the school. She was kind enough to mention me to her aunt.

"The aunt came to meet me, to look me over, actually, and I went back with her to the school to meet the headmistress. It was possible, I was told, that I might be given a position at the school if I agreed to stay on and become a teacher. It was more than I could hope for. Apparently, they believed my speech and sensibilities would be an asset in preparing young women." She glanced at Damion to judge whether her long story was tiring him, but he leaned forward and nodded for her to go on. "In addition to the regular subjects, Headmistress Staunton finds it convenient I should instruct the young ladies in deportment and social conventions as well."

"You instruct them in those additional classes at no extra wages, I am sure."

Alix paused with her glass halfway to her lips. "I suppose so. I've never given it thought. After all, I am given one annual sum, to teach. To teach whatever is asked of me. And if it helps the young girls, then I am only happy to do it. For the less fortunate girls, it means a better opportunity to find jobs as servants to good houses."

"And how did you learn such speech and manners yourself?

Most certainly not from Headmistress Staunton, the guardian gargoyle."

She laughed. "No." Her smile turned to a grim line. "From my mother."

"Tell me more about her."

Alix sighed. "All right. But I will expect to learn more about your parents as well, before they arrive." She twisted her ring around her finger, wondering where to start; what to confide. "She'd been raised a gentlewoman." At his look of surprise, Alix continued. "Her father and mother had raised her to become the wife of a genteel landowner, similar to themselves. Or perhaps a merchant. Their neighbors and acquaintances often had relatives to their home who dabbled in the higher trades. Bankers, merchants. It was expected she would marry within their circles. There were many opportunities, I am sure; my mother was a beautiful woman." Her mouth twisted. "I should be grateful I did not inherit that."

"You surely don't believe that. I don't mean whether you should be grateful. I mean . . . Miss Adams, surely you know you are a beautiful woman as well?"

Alix blushed and shook her head. "Please. Don't say so. I was not fishing for flattery. You had never seen my mother, or you would not say such a polite thing. No. My mother was beautiful. Too beautiful. Her beauty was the undoing of her life."

"What happened to her?"

"She 'rose above her station,' as they say. Her head was turned by a nobleman. From the little she has said, I know he was a second son."

"And you mentioned the other day that you never knew his name."

She shook her head.

"Any idea where his family seat was located?"

Shaking her head again, she said, "I know it's amazing to

imagine, but I have told you in its entirety everything I knew about my father. He was a second son of a nobleman, and he had income to his name. That is truly all I know. Except that he was dishonorable. My mother foolishly believed he would marry her. He said he would. But, as often happens, when she found herself with child, she found herself just as suddenly without a prospective husband. He disappeared, abandoning her.

"What did her parents do? Could they not have forced him to the altar?"

"If she'd told them his identity, I don't doubt that would have been their course. She had been visiting her cousins, and there'd been too many unsupervised parties. Evidently her parents never forgave her aunt for the neglectful chaperonage. Even her cousins could not name the beau whom she met in secret."

"Then, what did her parents do?"

"They did what any loving parents would do." Alix sounded bitter. "They disowned her. Forced her to leave."

"I cannot believe it."

Alix gave a disgusted snort. "Her father was stubborn, an extremely proud man. My mother tells me he was also strict. Her mother was a weak woman who did whatever her husband told her to do. 'Love' is the one word I never heard my mother use to describe my grandparents. She begged their forgiveness, and they turned her out. My mother only faulted herself, though. She never implied she held them at blame for their part."

"Are they still alive?"

With a shrug, she said, "I don't know. Nor does it matter. I would not turn to them if they were."

"Parents sometimes mellow as they grow older, Miss Adams. Regret their mistakes and—"

"No. It is too late. In memory of my mother, I would *not*

turn to them. And I do adequately on my own.”

“Hmm . . . I don’t suppose you inherited any of your grandfather’s stubbornness?”

This made her smile.

“So your mother was forced to leave her home.” He shook his head. “A young, pregnant gentlewoman. It is a sad story.”

“And a common story, I hear. One that often ends in tragedy. Well, this one did not have a tragic ending. My mother found a job in London. And she was allowed to keep me with her. She told me she was lucky, as many women gave up their babies, but she . . . was stubborn.” Alix smiled up at him.

“A gentlewoman who took a job in a strange city in order to keep her young daughter. I am impressed,” he said with a sad smile.

“No one else was impressed, I can tell you.”

“Why do you say so?”

Alix made a face. “They thought my mother and I both talked above our stations.”

“What did your mother do? What was her station?”

“She was a laundress.” Alix said it firmly, unequivocally, as if challenging him to contradict her. “They didn’t think a laundress, or the daughter of a laundress, should speak with such diction. Said we had airs . . . They told me I must imagine myself better than them because I was not allowed to say ‘yer’ or ‘guv’neh’.” She smiled, a guilty smile. “When my mother was not in hearing, I spoke a below-stairs accent with the best of them. I lived two lives. As I am doing now?” she mused.

“So you grew up in a laundry,” said Damion.

Alix blushed. “Not exactly.”

“But you said your mother was a laundress? Was she a laundress in a grand house then?”

Alix considered. “Yes. It was certainly a grand house.”

“And?”

"And what?"

"Tell me about the house your mother worked in. Where you grew up."

"It's nothing to mention. I can't imagine you want to hear about a house in the middle of London."

"But I do."

"There's nothing to tell." Alix sounded slightly exasperated. "We had a hard life, but I know it was harder for her than for me. I helped her as soon as I was old enough to fold and to iron. She had problems with her hands cramping as she got older, so I did what I could. And I remember being happy," Alix said with wistfulness. "Very happy. My mother and I were happy together . . . until her death.

She looked up at him. "She died suddenly. It was unexpected." Alix touched her locket and looked down at the table, seeing private memories in its crystal ball surface.

Damion cleared his throat. "I am sorry. I didn't mean to distress you."

She drained her glass. "May we speak of happier things now, my Lord? Tell me more of Bath, as you promised you would."

He reached for the decanter. "Well, I can tell you an amusing story I learned. But I don't know if it is true. You really can't believe half of what you overhear in the Pump Room."

"Do tell me." She held out her glass for a refill. As she took a sip, Alix wondered if she should be drinking a second glass. Or, was this her third?

"I was told that Bath was discovered accidentally by a swineherd."

Alix laughed. It was a little loud, she realized too late. She took another sip of sherry to hide her embarrassment.

"Supposedly, a lad—who later became the father of King Lear—had a skin disease. So he was sent to take care of a herd of pigs which also had a skin disease. One day, the pigs went wallowing in the hot mud of a steaming swamp by the river's bank, and they came out healed. So our royal lad plunged in and found it cured his leprosy as well."

"So, you are saying that when you bathe in the public pools of Bath, you are bathing in waters where diseased pigs once wallowed?"

"I'm afraid I am. Do you still want to go to Bath?"

"Ever so much!" She watched him, thinking how companionable this was. It seemed so natural to sit in the parlor with Damion, chatting about travels and playing cards. She wondered how it would be if one were truly married to this man. She was sure he would enter the breakfast room each day and capture his bride in his arms with a morning kiss.

"Why do you blush?"

Her mouth opened in surprise. What had gotten into her? "It must be the fire. I'm simply a bit flushed. It's rather warm." She lamely pointed at the fireplace and almost tipped over her glass, but caught it clumsily. "Tell me how you spent your mornings—Days. I meant days." She blushed further as images of his freshly-kissed wife interrupted her muddled thoughts. "I meant, how did you spend the rest of your day in Bath?"

Damion narrowed his eyes. He looked at her empty glass and studied her before continuing. "In the morning, the baths are visited unbelievably early. We would be up at dawn, and in the waters. We were always skinned by eight o'clock in the morning."

"Skinned?"

"Relieved of our coin. For, after bathing, one must tip everyone who stands between himself and the hotel. There is the Sergeant of the Baths, and of course, there are guides. Then there is the woman who hands out the drying cloths."

"And then what did you do?"

"We would return to our hotel and cool off and get dressed

for breakfast. You would love it. Some mornings we'd take the ferry across the river to the Spring Gardens. We'd listen to music as we breakfasted. It's a delightful, romantic place. One would be tempted to sit there all day."

"But one didn't?"

"Of course not! If one is in Bath for the waters, one must partake of *all* of the water. Bathing in it is not enough. We would then make our pilgrimage to the Pump Room, where we would dutifully drink our three glasses of the healthful waters as prescribed."

"Was it silent? Folks quietly lining up to drink? Just the clink of drinking glasses?"

"Oh, no. I think visiting the Pump Room was only an excuse to do more socializing with friends. To learn the latest local gossip."

"What a lazy morning." Alix leaned a chin upon her fist, eyes bright.

"It gets lazier. We'd stroll to the library or the reading rooms. It was imperative also to catch up with the gossip from London. I don't remember doing much during the mid-day. If my parents insisted, I would attend church with them. But I don't remember doing much else until it was time for dinner, about three in the afternoon. It was in the evening that the real festivities began. Card playing, dancing, plays, music. It's a bright fairy land nearly every night."

"And then?"

"And then, my dear Miss Adams, we would stumble to our beds, and wait for the rooster to order us to begin the whole cycle again."

She shook her head. "I envy you. I know it's a sin to envy."

"It's a sin to covet. I believe envy is normal."

"And I don't believe there is a difference. I think you make up these moral terms as you go." She lifted her glass to her lips;

143

was surprised to find it empty. "Is there more sherry?"

"I think that is all we shall have tonight, Miss Adams." Damion reached for her glass, but she misunderstood, putting her hand in his.

"Tell me . . ." He kept her hand, studying it, and then met her eyes. "If you were truly engaged, where would you wish to go for a honeymoon?"

Without hesitation, Alix blurted, "I would go to Bath."

"Bath!" He barked a laugh. "What of Italy, or France?"

She shook her head. "I know nothing of Italy or of France."

They turned to the door as his grandmother entered the room. Damion dropped Miss Adams's hand and stood.

"Sit, sit," said Lady Charlotte. "What did I hear? Are you discussing your marriage trip?"

"Just imagine, Grandmother." Without thinking, Damion covered Miss Adams's hand with his larger one. "We are thinking of a grand tour."

"A grand tour? Capital! What part of the continent?"

His eyes twinkled as he winked at Miss Adams. "We have decided we wish to visit Bath."

"Bath?" The older woman's brow wrinkled. "Did I hear you right? Bath is not a grand excursion."

"He is teasing me, my Lady." Alix primly removed her hand from his. "Did you know your grandson has a mean streak?" She scooted her chair over. "Come and join us in a game of cards. And perhaps *you* can make him behave."

CHAPTER SIXTEEN

Alix stretched as she yawned, placing her hands at the small of her back. She should go down to breakfast now that she'd dressed, but found it difficult to leave her bedroom. A light breeze stirred the duck pond, and the early sunlight glittered on its waving surface.

Unlatching the white mullioned window, she pushed one of the large frames outward. The breeze was cool, but not uncomfortably so. It promised a warm day to come. A picnic day, Alix thought with a smile. She leaned her elbows on the sill and surveyed her world. The river at the bottom of the hill snaked along, but was a dark green ribbon today. How could water look so different every day, even within one day? She still couldn't believe she was here, looking out this window, at this scene. For the rest of her life these memories would hold a special magic: Lady Charlotte, picnics and strolls, Lord Woodhurst—she shut that thought cupboard. She wasn't ready to examine her feelings for him too closely; perhaps when she returned to the school and could put some distance between her heart and this adventure.

She heard the ducks complaining as they bobbed on the choppy pond. She'd learned already to distinguish the drakes from the hens. She was counting the ducks when she gasped. Something was wrong with one of the ducks: it was drowning. She couldn't see its small head; it was tipped, its head under the water, with only its triangular tail pointing to the sky. Its webbed feet were tucked against its body lifelessly.

Alix flew out her bedroom door and rushed to the stairs. Perhaps she would be in time to rescue it.

"Whoa!" Damion avoided a collision as he exited his room. "What is your hurry, Miss Adams?"

She stopped, blocked by his body, but her voice raced. "My Lord, it's the duck! I'm sure it's my favorite duck. It's drowning. I must hurry."

He put his hands on her upper arms. "Miss Adams, ducks don't drown, they're water creatures." He quirked his brow, and one corner of his mouth nearly smiled.

"No, you don't understand. It's upside down. It can't breathe. I saw it from my window, and its tail is sticking straight up in the air, and its little webbed feet are just dangling uselessly. It can't even tip itself back up and it will drown if I don't help it. Excuse me." She escaped from his grasp as she talked, squeezed by him, and headed to the stairs.

"It's feeding," said Damion.

She stopped on the top step and turned back to him in confusion. "What?"

"It's feeding." He strolled toward her. "Eating its breakfast. That's how ducks feed, from the bottom of the pond. They are like young boys showing off, standing upside down upon their hands." He stood above her at the landing. "You're a teacher. Surely you've seen young lads and their antics?"

Alix groaned. "Oh, I'm so embarrassed. And here I was about to run into the pond, into the water, and rescue a duck." She had to grin at herself, looking at her shoes, and a laugh escaped as she shook her head.

Damion's eyes shone. "It's enchanting to see the world through your eyes, Miss Adams. And I'm utterly charmed to think of you wading into the pond to rescue a duck." The crevice in his cheek deepened with his smile. "I can't remember the last time I've enjoyed being home so much. You and Miss Elizabeth have a way of brightening each day." He put a hand on the staircase balustrade. "In fact . . ."

"Yes?" Alix looked up at Damion as he towered above her. She was too aware of him as he stepped down onto the same step as she.

"I'd have hired a fiancée long ago, Miss Adams, if I'd only known."

The step was not as wide as she'd first thought. She swallowed as Damion moved lazily to the next step below. They now stood eye-to-eye.

"Known?" She swallowed.

Damion moved closer, crowding her back against the banister.

"And I think . . ." He fingered the seam at the shoulder of her dress, tracing it from her neck to the top of her arm. "If we want my family to believe in this ruse . . . that is, for you to keep your part of the bargain . . ." his hand cupped her shoulder, gently moved her toward him. "I think I'd like it if you should call me by my first name."

She looked to the side; he was too close.

He asked, "May I call you Alix?"

She thrilled at the way he said it so softly . . . a sibilation. "Alix." She closed her eyes. *Oh, dear.* She had to put a stop to this. It would end in a few weeks. She could not—must not—let herself be carried away by this man.

"Say it," he whispered in her ear.

Chills went down her shoulder, starting with the hairs on her neck.

"Say my name," he repeated. His lips moved from her ear and brushed a soft path across her cheek, toward her mouth.

She swallowed. With eyes closed, she knew at any moment she would feel the caress of his lips on hers. She knew they would be warm and soft; she'd memorized their fullness.

147

"Say my name." His lips touched the dimple in her cheek.

She had to break the spell. Now. Or never.

"Yes," she whispered, "my dearest Edmund."

He jumped back as if burnt. "What did you say?"

Her eyes twinkled.

"My name is Damion. Nobody calls me Edmund except my grandmother." He ran his hand through his hair, and shook his head slightly. "You certainly know how to splash ice water upon a fellow's mood, Miss Adams."

She stepped past him, continuing down the stairway, and looked over her shoulder. "Please," she said in a purr, "call me Alix."

In the breakfast room, she was pleased to find Lady Charlotte, a safe haven from the thoughts and feelings that faltered her steps as she'd descended the stairs.

"Are you ill, child? You look terribly flushed," said the countess.

"Ill? I—No. I mean, I am feeling fine. Thank you for asking." Alix moved to take a seat, nodding to the footman to pour coffee.

Damion strolled in behind her and planted a kiss on his grandmother's cheek. Lady Charlotte looked from her grandson to Miss Adams, who blushed again, and she picked up her lorgnette. "I see."

Alix looked at her plate and gave great concentration to stirring the cream in her cup.

"I thought I'd stroll the gardens after breakfast," Lady Charlotte said to Miss Adams. "And I would love the company. But perhaps you've grown tired of an old woman's constitutional?"

Alix shook her head. "A stroll? I'd never tire of that, my Lady. It's what I look forward to most each day."

"But surely you have other interests, other hobbies. What hobbies do you enjoy, Alix?"

"Hobbies?" asked Alix. "I'm sorry," she said with a sheepish grin. "I must stop repeating your questions. I've . . . never been asked about . . . hobbies." She glanced at Damion guiltily, but he only watched her with a polite interest. Should she have made up hobbies in anticipation of the question? She chose honesty as the safest harbor. "I'm afraid I haven't any."

Two narrow eyebrows raised over the lady's periwinkle blue eyes. "Surely you have things you enjoy doing in your free time, child."

Alix smiled as she shrugged. "I haven't had much free time these last years. I stayed pretty busy helping at the school. In between classes there are meals to assist with and assignments to plan. And the girls' dormitory needs supervision after dinner. The mornings begin at sunrise, as we have prayers. And I escort the girls in my hall to breakfast. And Cook usually needs an extra hand once the girls have finished and left to clean their rooms. Then it's time to escort the youngsters in the next—"

"Alix. I thought you were a teacher," said Lady Charlotte with a teasing frown. "You've just described a slave, a governess, a cook, and a maid. Is there anything you don't do at that school you came from?"

Alix looked sideways at Damion and chuckled. "Apparently I don't obey. Nor do I conform to expected behavior."

"Good for you. I like a gel with spirit. Well, you're mistress of this manor now. You'll never need to return to that life."

Alix worked hard to school her features to a calmness; not to look over at Damion. She thought every single day about how hard it would be to return to the school after this precious adventure. Once more she felt the urgency that drove her to absorb every memory, treasure every moment with Damion and with his grandmother. Those memories would have to last her a lifetime.

His grandmother, lifting a spoonful of curried eggs, asked,

"Was it difficult for Elizabeth, living there?" She studied Miss Adams as she took a bite.

"It was the only life she knew," Alix said softly. "Elizabeth and I had each other, so it made each day easier."

"Yes. Tell me about Elizabeth. How difficult was it to manage a group of girls when one is your sister? Sometimes it's more natural to be stricter with your own than with others' children."

"Oh, no. Elizabeth—" Alix stopped in the middle of cutting a sausage. This time she did glance Damion's way. Dear God, she'd been about to declare that Elizabeth was not related to her! How would she ever work her way through all of the deceit and webs of untruth? "Elizabeth is the most obedient of children."

"Speaking of hobbies, do you ride?" interjected Damion, rescuing her.

Alix set down her knife and fork, hoping he could read gratitude in her eyes for the change of topic. "Do you mean horses, my Lord?"

One eyebrow dipped down, and a corner of Damion's mouth on the same side quirked up. "What else would one ride?"

"I don't know. I've led a sheltered life, haven't I?" Alix laughed at herself. "A camel?" She picked up a toast point.

"You have me there, Miss Adams. I admit I have heard of folks riding camels, though I don't think they were in England."

"No, my Lord, I've never ridden a horse."

"Are you afraid of them?" he asked.

She'd already taken a bite of toast, so she chewed slowly as she considered his question. "I don't know. I don't think I've ever been close enough to a horse to decide. I don't believe I would be, though, because they look so beautiful and appealing from afar."

"How does a young lady grow up in the country without ever having been near horses?" asked his grandmother.

"Wait. Let me guess. If it's not on the curriculum . . ." said Damion.

Alix laughed. "Will your parents be scandalized that I cannot ride?"

"Pish-posh!" said Lady Charlotte. "They shan't dare criticize you, or they shall have to answer to me."

Damion laughed. "And a dowager countess is a fearsome force, as you can see, Miss Adams."

All three chuckled.

"The reason I asked," Damion said around a bite, then swallowed, "is that I was thinking about what you said the other day, when it was raining."

"That I wished it would stop?" Alix grinned.

"No. About a person making the most of every day. And that made me think of Elizabeth. She's such a sweet child. I find her amazingly appealing, and I didn't think I cared for children."

Alix's teacup was almost to her lips. "Similar to how I feel about horses? Afraid of them, were you, my Lord?"

"You're brutal, do you know that?" He held her smiling eyes with his until she blushed. "I admit I haven't been around too many children. And I've no nieces or nephews. I'll be honest. Your sibling charms me. As does her elder sister."

She choked on her tea, and then quickly looked at Damion's grandmother to discern the lady's reaction. His grandmother smiled indulgently. The grand dame appeared to enjoy, perhaps to condone, their improper banter.

"Are you all right?" he asked.

She continued coughing, but nodded "Yes." And she held up a hand to stop him as he rose in place. As soon as she had voice, she said, "I'm fine. Truly."

He leaned forward. "Miss Adams, I was thinking it might be fun for Elizabeth to have her own pony to ride. What do you think?"

Lady Charlotte clapped her hands. "What a capital idea, Edmund."

Alix looked straight down at her napkin, then whisked it up to dab at her eyes.

"Miss Adams?" Damion asked.

Alix lowered the square of ivory linen, and looked at him with moist eyes. "Elizabeth would love it. You are the kindest man I've ever met, Lord Woodhurst."

"Well, if you've never been close to a horse, I daresay you've never been close to a gentleman, Miss Adams, so you don't have many to compare me to, do you?" Seeing his grandmother lay her napkin beside her plate, he pushed back his chair and moved behind to assist her.

"I so enjoy being with the two of you," Lady Charlotte said. "However, I wish to check on Lizzie before we take our stroll. Alix, shall we meet in a quarter hour?" As she reached the door she added, "But please, do not hurry on my account."

"Yes, my Lady." Alix put her own napkin down as she rose, and jumped, startled to find Damion so close to her chair.

"Miss Adams, I didn't mean to frighten you, but if I know my grandmother, she is conniving to give us some time alone. In private." He moved a step closer, if that were possible. "With my fiancée."

"And you know I am not your fiancée." She practically hissed the sentence, in her effort to keep her voice to a fierce whisper.

"We have some unfinished business. While we are private, I must tell you something I wanted to tell you on the stairs: I desire to get to know you better while you're here."

Alix surprised herself by meeting his eyes boldly. "I'm sorry, my Lord, but I don't believe that's on the curriculum for the governess of Fern Crest Hall." She took a step back and turned to the doorway, but stopped at the hand on her arm.

"I shall speak to the headmistress," he said, "and we'll rectify that."

She searched his face, knowing she'd be making a mistake if she got too close to this man. With careful formality, she said, "Thank you for your kind offer of riding lessons for Elizabeth, my Lord. She'll be so excited. We are both grateful."

She'd been walking with an older woman, the sun filtering everything an unnatural yellow, but within one minute she stood alone on the path and it was so dark she could barely see. Who was the woman? Alix twisted in the bedcovers. The woman—she couldn't focus on a face. Alix's feet were locked on the path, wending toward a darkened mansion straight ahead; not one light lit its staring windows.

She didn't want to walk toward the weathered building, but her feet wouldn't obey her wishes. They kept moving her steadily closer. The woman was back again, standing stiffly on the side of the path. Lady Charlotte? The name came to Alix in her dream. But the woman's oval face was blank; no features marked the flat, smooth flesh framed by curly grey hair. The blank mirror of a face stared toward Alix, but there was no mouth with which to speak, or to warn, and the woman would not accompany her on the path. Alix kept walking toward the house, which was breathing now, and the woman on the path shimmered to nothingness. In her place was a silent Lord Woodhurst, watching her—judging her?—but not moving. Only his eyes moved, following her progress along the path, toward the threatening house.

Inhaling, exhaling, the door was a devouring mouth, and Alix couldn't make her body stop its floating journey forward. She tried to turn away, to move toward Lord Woodhurst, but the path wouldn't allow her feet to veer. It did not matter. The faceless Lady Charlotte and the silent, watchful Lord Woodhurst had both disappeared.

Alix's body continued to drift toward the waiting lintel framed in black wood. No, not wood. Those were pointed, rotten teeth bordering the heavy door. And someone watched her approach from the window. It was *him*.

She began moaning, "No. No, I don't want to." She was at the door, waiting for the teeth to snap her in half. But it was the school's door. She was at Widpole Manor. Where were the other teachers? They'd form a sisterly circle around her so he couldn't touch her.

But he would. And he did. He always did, in her dreams.

She was in his grasp. When had she moved through the door? They were in a parlor. No, they weren't in a parlor. They were outside now, in the dark fruit arbor. The black, rotten plums assailed her nostrils. She might vomit.

He had a face, but it only had two features: great ogling eyes and leering lips—greasy lips that slithered toward her face like twin snakes. Rough hands grabbed her shoulders, hurting as deeply as knives.

She dropped her lantern—where had the lantern come from?—and it illuminated Simon Blackthorn's ghoulish features on a bloated face just before it blinked out in a crash of glass. She screamed at his next cruel squeeze, but no sound came out.

Alix screamed again, and woke.

Her pulse raced. Had she screamed aloud? She held her breath, but didn't hear any doors in the hallway, or see candlelight approaching her bedroom. She was alone.

She wiped a hand across her sweating brow. She was safe. She forced herself to take deep breaths. She was at Fern Crest Hall. She was not at Widpole Manor. He could not touch her here. As if in denial, her eyes snapped in fear to the tall windows. No dark faces leered through the clear panes.

Her racing heart settled, and she closed her eyes. When would the nightmares stop?

Alix attempted to go back to sleep, but Simon Blackthorn haunted her still. He'd seen her in the village. Had he recognized Lord Woodhurst? Lady Chloe should not be recognizable to him, since she lived in London. But did it matter? He would go to the school and ask his cousin. The woman would tell him where Alix could be found. Or would she? Alix didn't know what confidences they shared.

Her mind took her back to the first time she'd seen Simon Blackthorn. He was visiting his cousin, Headmistress Staunton, at the school. Alix was a girl, not yet a woman, though her body surprised her as it metamorphosed to her dismay, pushing her closer to adulthood.

He came to visit his cousin, but it was the young women he watched. He had an eye for adolescent girls. They talked about it at night, when the lights were out, when they were not supposed to be talking. They whispered their disgust of the man who came regularly to call on his cousin—perhaps a pretense.

Alix couldn't remember how old she was when she'd caught him targeting her with his piggish eyes. She shuddered, remembering how his gaze frightened her. She was with friends and there he would be, standing at the corner of the wall. At first she thought he watched all of them. Unnatural shivers told her he singled her out, perhaps because she was an orphan with no one to protect her.

It was inevitable he would approach her.

She was able to avoid him until the following spring. That was the year she became a teacher. It was not so easy for a staff member to hide as it had been for a silly schoolgirl.

He surprised her when he intercepted her alone, trapped her in one of the classrooms. Other teachers strolled across the grounds. She wanted to call to them but could not find her voice. If he touched her, she'd find it. She would scream. But, to her surprise, he did not. Simon Blackthorn was amazingly polite.

He held out his hand, asking her to take a walk with him. Her hands sneaked behind her skirt, and she looked down at the worn splintered floor instead.

He made a sound of impatience, then spoke quickly, earnestly. Said he could give her a home, if she'd marry him. Told her she should gratefully accept his proposal, as she had no other options than to remain a slave to his cousin's school until she shriveled and died, alone.

Blushing, she stammered her refusal. She said it as politely as she knew how, glancing nervously toward the door. When she forced herself to meet his gaze, she flinched at his angry flush. He gained control of his jaw muscles and expression and blandly bade her good day, asking her to reconsider, promising they would speak again when she'd had time to dwell on the merits of his offer.

Headmistress Staunton called Alix to her office later that day and asked her what had transpired. The headmistress claimed to be curious about the exchange. Alix wondered if the headmistress thought it improper, whether she would be punished for being alone with a man, for speaking of such things with a man. But the woman, a strict moralist, who inculcated virtue and censored with a firm hand, didn't appear to be angry.

No, Headmistress seemed in an odd mood. Alix next feared the woman would dismiss her for turning down her relative, but Alix was to suffer no repercussions. She was surprised.

Surprised, that is, until she confided to another teacher, her friend Lucy Greene. Lucy told her the headmistress needed Alix as cheap labor, and must have been relieved to see Alix turn down his offer. Beware, Lucy added, as it was also possible the headmistress was jealous. The woman had never married; perhaps she expected an offer should come from her cousin, who visited with such attentive regularity. Perhaps she would be vindictive, as he'd turned to a younger woman.

Alix was fearful. She wanted to keep this job. She was afraid of the world, afraid it was filled with men like Simon Blackthorn. She knew she would never leave on her own or seek other employment.

Exactly three days later, Alix had ushered the children to her hall as evening fell. They were preparing for bed when Alix was told the headmistress wished to see her in her office. Lucy's warnings bubbled like yeast in Alix's stomach. It was a most unusual request at this late hour.

Alix grabbed a lantern and hurried across the wide lawn separating the dormitories from the administrative wing.

She was about a third of the way when she was grabbed by the shoulder. Gasping, she dropped the lantern. As it crashed to the ground, it had illuminated Simon Blackthorn.

Alix stood in the dark struggling against his grip. Blazed into her memory was the ugly look on his face when she'd faced him in the last moment of light before it blinked out in a cacophony of glass.

"So, you think you're too good for me? You? An orphaned slut?"

She smelled sour liquor on his breath. "Let me go. Please. I'll scream."

"Bloody good it will do you out here." He held her tightly against his chest. "My cousin's told me all about you, Miss Adams. How she rescued you from that brothel. You've probably already given yourself to dozens of men, but you think you're too good for me? No other gentleman will ever have you. You're soiled goods. As soiled as the laundry you scrubbed in them tubs."

"That's not true. I was only a laundress. I stayed below stairs in that house. I've never . . . been with a man."

She saw the faint gleam of his yellowed teeth in the evening. "Well, now. That's even better. I do enjoy a virgin. If you won't take my offer of marriage, I'll have you anyway. You know you're always teasin' me when I come to visit my cousin."

"That's not true!" Alix almost pulled free, but he jerked her back.

"I watch your saucy ways. You know exactly what you're doin', miss." He put his pudgy lips on hers, bumping foreheads in his haste to find her mouth in the dark.

Alix pulled back, turning her face as far to the side as she could.

Just as he grabbed her roughly by the chin and snapped her face to the front, someone called her name.

"Miss Adams! Miss Adams, is that you?" Lucy's skirt billowed with her long strides as she hurried along the path, a circle of light forming a hoop skirt around her.

Mister Blackthorn dropped his hold and took a step back. But not before he whispered harshly, "Don't say anything, or I'll tell everyone your secret."

"Are you all right, Alix? What are you doing in the dark? Who's that with you?"

Alix looked from his warning face to her kind friend, biting back tears. "I . . . I dropped the lantern on the path. Foolish of me. Mister Blackthorn offered to escort me back to the hall. But since you're here . . ." She turned to Simon. "I'll go back with Miss Greene. Good night."

Alix moved quickly to hug Lucy's arm as if it were a spar floating by in a perilous sea.

Her friend must have noted that Alix did not say "Thank you" to the man. Nor did she curtsy. But they never talked about it, even though Alix believed her friend would not betray her. Lucy must have known something was terribly wrong. But she was enough of a friend to avoid further pain for Alix.

Thinking of it now, as Alix lay awake in the dark room, she wondered if she should have confided to Lucy. Perhaps, if they'd talked about it that same night, the nightmares would not have started.

She never confided in the headmistress; instead, she never went out alone when the school grounds were dark. She looked over her shoulder often. She was careful, very careful. She'd not been confronted by the man since.

Not until the other day while she and Elizabeth were shopping in the village. And now the nightmares had begun again. And she couldn't confide in Lord Woodhurst, though her heart wished her to. It was not his problem. He did not need the scandal of her upbringing. She would never admit to him that she and her mother had lived in a brothel. Her mother was as innocent and virtuous as her daughter. Alix firmly believed it.

The moon pushed aside the clouds and threw a circle of light on the bed covers. Alix welcomed it, though it had no warmth to dry her tears. She missed Lucy and the students. But there was nothing else she missed at the school.

She thought while she was here, she would be safe from him. She must be careful. Very careful.

CHAPTER SEVENTEEN

Dear Ardis,

I need your help. I know you dislike social upstarts as much as I, but this one is threatening a bit too close to home. I have the unfortunate duty to tell you she is attempting to seduce our dearest Lord Woodhurst.

His grandmamma is dying—not too nice a woman, let me tell you, as I've had to spend a number of days in her company—and Lord Woodhurst hired this young woman to pose as his fiancée. Yes, I said pose. She is a penniless opportunist.

You'd think he would have at least chosen a woman who was presentable. She's quite the unmannered country mouse. Yet now she attempts, in her greed, to seduce him. He is in such grief that even he is not aware of what he is succumbing to.

Forgive me, if I ramble, but I am most upset. Besides, you will see all of this for yourself when you arrive. Yes, dearest Ardis, I am imploring you to come to Fern Crest Manor in the greatest haste, before it is too late.

If you still have feelings for Lord Woodhurst, as I know you do, dearest Ardis, then we must unite to see her gone. You would not believe it, but it is taking all my sweet nature not to screech at her.

I remain Yr. dearest friend,
Lady Chloe

CHAPTER EIGHTEEN

"I'm afraid I'm going to fall off." Elizabeth's voice was a bit higher than normal, and tremulous.

"It's a normal fear, Miss Elizabeth." Damion placed a steadying hand on her knee. "Everyone worries about falling off a horse the first time they mount."

"Did you?"

"Absolutely. I was terrified. That's when they made up the phrase, 'shaking in his boots.' It was about me." He smiled when she giggled. "Do you know what we're going to do about your fear?"

"Learn to balance better?"

"How about learning to relax first? Did you know that when you are nervous, it makes NellyBelly nervous? You don't want her to be frightened, do you?"

"Oh, no." Elizabeth patted the pony gently, and smoothed her hand over the pony's coarse brown coat.

"Do you know why I love riding horses?" he asked.

The young girl stopped patting NellyBelly and shook her head at him.

While talking, with Elizabeth distracted, Damion began walking the pony on its lead. "I love horses because I learn something every day from my horse. He teaches me."

"Like one of the teachers at the school? Like Miss Adams?"

"Exactly like Miss Adams. But let's not tell her we compared her to a horse, shall we?" He glanced over at Miss Adams, who watched their lesson from the other side of the ring's fence. This earned another bubbling laugh from his young student. "Sometimes," he said, "my horse is in a bad mood, and other times he wants to play around. We have a good relationship because we respect each other's feelings. And every horse is different."

Alix crossed her arms atop the railing, and dropped her chin onto her arms as she studied Lord Woodhurst. The man was fascinating.

He appeared humble, admitting his fears as a youngster to Elizabeth. And his concern for the animal's peace of mind was an enigma. Everything she'd ever heard about men predicted they were self-centered. He didn't seem to be.

Did he know she eavesdropped? Their voices carried across the empty ring. Did he speak thus because he knew she listened? But why should he care to impress her? She'd be gone soon.

Though his grandmother did not seem any more ill this morning at breakfast than she had any other day of Alix's visit. Perhaps hers was a malady that would strike with no forewarning.

Alix was surprised to find a wet spot on her sleeve, when there was not a cloud in the sky. She wiped her cheek; she must not think about losing Lady Charlotte. The woman was as dear to Alix as Elizabeth was. As dear to Alix as Lord Woodhurst.

Alix didn't shy away from the thought as she watched Lord Woodhurst patiently walking in circles, the little girl on the pony, and the peaty loam climbing the fine leather of his boots. Her eyes moved from his boots up his strong legs, and to his muscled arms casually controlling pony and rider.

When he spoke of his relationship with his horse, Alix had to smile at the pinprick of envy she felt. Jealous of a horse?

Was it possible a man—one of those necessarily vile creatures the other women constantly complained about—was it possible a man could feel the same kinship to a woman? Could a man be attuned to the shifts of mood in a woman he cared for? Could there be mutual respect? She'd come in contact with so few men during her life. She'd based all her opinions of men on the dark shadows of various sizes who slipped up and down the stairs of the London house, never speaking. And based her opinions on the repulsive Simon Blackthorn. Finally, based her opinion on what the other teachers had told her in disgust as they berated their brothers, their brother-in-laws, their fathers. But none of the teachers had been married; none had ever lived with a man as husband.

Alix had lived in this manor for a number of days now, and nothing they'd told her seemed to apply to Lord Woodhurst. Of course, they'd told her, men change after they marry. Sweetness and gentility dissolve as quickly as the bridal cake icing after the vows. That's what they said.

Her only other experience with men had been of paper gentlemen in the books she read. But they were always heroes. And it was only fiction. She knew, though, she'd not be able to pick up a book for the rest of her life without the hero taking on Lord Woodhurst's features. The hero would have his ash-grey eyes that creased at the corner when he smiled, his build, his slightly long hair.

She wondered if Lord Woodhurst had any idea how she felt about him. How her body betrayed her when he was near. Probably not, if she were to believe the older, wiser teachers who said men were more in tune with their horse's feelings than with women's. That made her snort.

NellyBelly, a female, snorted her agreement.

Alix shaded her eyes against the strong sun, watching and listening to man and girl, wondering whether Damion brought back memories to Elizabeth of her own father. Elizabeth's father had never meant to leave his daughter. Death had yanked him forever away, whereas Alix's father hadn't cared enough about Alix to be in her life for even one day. How different life was with a family. *Don't be maudlin,* she chastised herself. You had a loving family of two, and very lucky you and your mother were for eight years. Eight special years that many children never have.

The first riding lesson finished, Damion and his charge disappeared into the cool darkness of the stable. Alix heard him telling Elizabeth a good rider also knew how to care for a horse, and brushing was one way to thank their friend. Alix was surprised. She'd assumed a viscount would carelessly toss the reins to one of the stablemen, and would not bother himself with such menial work. Perhaps he did this only for Elizabeth's education. She certainly wouldn't have a stableman standing by for flicked reins when they left Fern Crest Hall . . . Of course, neither would she have a horse to ride.

It was too hot standing here by the dusty track, thought Alix, slapping away a large fly. The flies buzzing the stable yard seemed so much larger than the flies she was used to living with at the school. *Noble flies.* She smiled to herself. Puffed up with pride because they live at a nobleman's mansion.

She pushed away from the fence rail and strolled the sloping grounds to seek the shady cavern of the willow trees by the pond. Her imagination fancied the leaves also drooped from the heat. Under the arching branches a single bench was placed, its mottled verdigris imitating the mossy undertones of the water's surface.

This area of the grounds could be seen clearly from Alix's bedroom window. If someone were to stand at the bedroom window, the eye would be drawn to the circle of water. Otherwise, it was not easily visible from the major rooms of the ground floor. The woodland border along the terraces effectively isolated the pond from the manor.

Dragonflies of metallic hues darted to the water plants. Alix watched hypnotically as they hovered, flew backwards, and performed loop-the-loops. She rested against the arm of the bench, closing her eyes as the heat and insects hummed around her.

In the solitude, a skylark sang its plaintive song of flutelike whistles. She did not hear the footsteps cushioned by soft grasses, did not know the man approached.

"Miss Adams."

A half-scream escaped, and Alix spun around in fear. A man was outlined in the harsh sunlight, his face hidden by the rays blinding her as she stared.

"I didn't mean to startle you." It was Damion's deep voice.

Her heart was pounding. She'd been half asleep, and thought she woke to a living nightmare of Simon Blackthorn.

"Miss Adams, you're shaking. What's wrong?" He slid to her side. "Your hand is trembling." He cupped it protectively.

Alix bit back tears of relief. "I . . . I'm fine. It's nothing. A bad dream. I must have dozed. Please . . . forgive me." She pulled her hand away. "I'm quite embarrassed," she said, looking down at her hand on her lap, willing it to stop shaking, willing her heart to calmness.

"I shouldn't have frightened you. I am the one to apologize."

She forced her lips to a smile and shook her head. "Nonsense. I am fine now." She was able to meet his eyes, her lungs no longer heaving.

She must be more careful. What if it had been Mr. Blackthorn? She shuddered.

"I don't think you are fine at all. It's hot, yet you shake as if with fever." He placed his palm above her brow.

Alix let her eyelids close in relief at the security of his broad, cool hand upon her forehead. And her eyes flew open in mortification. She pushed against the bench to rise. "I think I should check on Elizabeth."

Damion dropped his hand, looked up at her. "No need," he said calmly, watching her with an expression she could not decipher. "She should be along shortly. She said she was going by the garden to pick a few flowers for tonight's dinner table."

Alix's irritation at herself irrationally jumped to his lordship. "You realize, my Lord, allowing Elizabeth to dine with the adults is not doing her a favor for the life she must return to." She sounded like a shrew, even to her own ears.

"But riding a pony is deemed acceptable? Oh, of course, surely every child there rides ponies back and forth between classes. You are in an odd mood, Miss Adams." He sighed and leaned back, angling an arm along the back of the bench. "However, whether Elizabeth dines with us or alone won't change her world when you return to Widpole Manor." He insolently remained seated while she stood. "If children of gentility do not eat with their elders, it is not a lesson she must learn. While she is with us, if I choose to avail her of a pony, I shall. And if I choose to have the company of my fiancée's 'sister' . . ." His look was sardonic. ". . . then I shall. Besides, *she* does not avoid answering my questions."

"Whatever does that mean?" she snapped, in a mood to argue.

"I am curious. I've been patient, but I think it is time I should know a little more about Elizabeth's birth."

His assumption annoyed her. "And why should you?"

"An interesting choice of words, that. Not 'what would you wish to know?' That would be too polite. An invitation to share confidences. Yours is more of a demand. A defensive move. 'Why should I ask?' "

She knew she was being ungracious, and strove to regain her composure. "All right," she said a bit too sharply, crossing her arms. "What do you wish to know?" She eyed him warily.

"Though I may choose not to answer. I retain that right."

His dark frown finally cleared, and he nodded. "Fair enough. So . . . what do I wish to know?" He looked dangerous. "There are so many things I would like to know, it is more a question of which to start with, rather than a single question."

They stared at one another. The drone of dragonflies was the only interruption to the stifling air surrounding them.

"You've never referred to her with a surname. Is her name Elizabeth Adams?"

Alix needed her wits about her if she were not to be caught in her web of deceit. "That's because she's only a child. And I don't believe you've ever asked me what her surname—"

"Why would you go by 'Miss Adams'? Why not 'Mrs. Adams'? Was that the surname of Elizabeth's father?" He leaned toward her, watching her expression.

She was careful to show none. Finally, she said, "I have never been married." Though she told the true statement with confidence, its implication made her blush.

"You two don't actually look alike, though you both have striking looks. She must look like her father, then. Is he a handsome man?"

"Do you hold that against me?" She grew weary of this dangerous cat-and-mousing.

"Tell me." He unfolded himself from the bench and moved closer. So close, she saw the tightness in his jaw muscle. "Do you still hold a tendré for him?"

She froze, and the ice brought an edge to her whisper: "How dare you ask something so personal."

"Do you know what I suspect?" His large hand circled Miss Adams's wrist tightly. "I think you still love him." He sounded angry. "Are you in love, Miss Adams?"

I thought I was . . . with you. "No," she whispered, alarmed by the sensations of his warm hand wrapped firmly around her wrist. Alix jerked her hand away. Rubbing her wrist, she added, "I am done answering questions."

He moved around her, blocking her escape to the path. "I have a right to know."

"What gives you the right?" Her voice was husky with disgust. "Because you are a viscount, you believe you can bully innocent young women on your estate? But you will not bully me, though you may fancy yourself a feudal lord. Now, move."

He did not move. "Innocent young women? You are hardly innocent, Miss Adams. The blackguard never married you. That is why you are so secretive about it, and Elizabeth knows so little. But we both know you were intimate with him."

Alix slapped Damion, hard. His head snapped to the side and he did not meet her eyes. She pushed past him and started up the trail toward the stables.

Damion called out, "Miss Adams! I have a right to know more about my fiancée, if only to ensure you will not embarrass me in front of my family."

"Do you know what I think?" She turned halfway 'round. "I think you use that as an excuse for your meddling rudeness. I have already told your grandmother and Lady Chloe that Elizabeth is my sister. They happen to believe it, as I told you they would. And I shall tell your parents the same. And I tell you, Lord Woodhurst, that this is the *last* time we shall have this discussion. If your family is as nosey as you are, they shall be told it is none of their business as well."

Alix was still shaking as she closed her bedroom door.

Out of breath after running up the sloping path and up the stairs, she crossed her arms beneath her breasts and stood at the window, taking deep breaths. When her breathing returned to normal, it hadn't lessened the distaste that filled her mouth. She was disgusted, but more with herself than with Lord

Woodhurst.

She should have shrugged off his words and accusations. But she couldn't, and with a dread realization, she knew why. How had this happened? She'd allowed herself to fall in love with him. Foolish, foolish girl.

She'd been attracted to him from the moment they met. She should have known their increasing familiarity would only make it more difficult for her to part from him. The idea of leaving Lord Woodhurst filled her with a hollow melancholy.

Of course, she knew she'd miss Fern Crest Hall. Looking out the window, she spied a blue heron on the sparkling pond's border, spearing its dinner. And the late afternoon sun was brushing the rose gardens in golden shadows as it put its paints away for the night.

No, it wasn't the room, or the house, or the view she would miss. It was its master.

And she'd miss his grandmother, more than she'd expected. Sadly, Lady Charlotte's time must be almost up. Alix tasted salty moisture on her lip and realized a tear had slid swiftly down her face. She wiped a hand across both eyes.

She'd grown to love his grandmother. As had Elizabeth. The thought of Elizabeth losing the woman who had become so dear to her sent fresh tears escaping. Alix pulled a delicate square of linen from her pocket and wiped one cheek and then the other. She swiped it across her eyes as she turned from the window.

And saw the note on her dressing table by the door, lying atop an ornately carved salver.

Putting her handkerchief away, she crossed the room and picked up the ivory envelope. It was quite light, with an unadorned wax seal; she flipped it over. On the front was scrawled "Miss Alix Adams" in a childish hand.

Alix smiled. She pictured Elizabeth following Lady Charlotte's advice on how to properly address a card to an unmarried lady. Her dimple deepened, anticipating an invitation. To a tea party? A picnic?

She opened the topmost narrow drawer and withdrew a silver-handled letter opener. With great care she slit the envelope, wanting to store both the letter and the envelope with the few treasures she had to her name. Reaching in, Alix extracted the folded note with the tips of her fingers. Still smiling, she unfolded it. And dropped it in shock.

She backed up as if the note lying on the floor were a snake, waiting to strike.

The short missive was explicit:

Meet me at six o'clock tonight at the inn in the village.

He knew where she was.

CHAPTER NINETEEN

"Well, well, well. Aren't you the grand lady. I heard you were gettin' comfy in the gentleman's home." Simon Blackthorn sneered. "Though I bet he ain't actin' like no gentleman with you." He didn't bother to lower his voice in the noisy tavern.

Alix sat straight, afraid to lean back against the dirty wood. It was dark in the low-ceilinged room, and she couldn't discern whether those were grease spots or blood stains. "He is a perfect gentleman," she said, tilting her chin up. "I am merely—" She stopped. She'd been about to blurt she was acting a part, but this was more information than a man such as Simon Blackthorn needed to know. "We are engaged to be married."

Simon reacted as if he'd been punched, but recovered with a whispered, "Are you now? My cousin said nothin' of that."

"She doesn't yet know." Alix realized she might have unintentionally closed the door on the only livelihood she knew, and she wondered if the headmistress would allow her to return to the school. Surely, when she told her the engagement was off, when she groveled . . . It was nothing more than the headmistress expected from all the teachers, wasn't it?

She could see the wheels turning behind Mister Blackthorn's squinty eyes. "Does the gentleman know you've been compromised?"

"I have not! By whom? What are you talking about?" Alix

shuddered. She might have been, by this man, if her friend hadn't appeared that night. What if she'd been forced to marry this brute?

"By them men in the brothel." His lip curled into a leer on the word. "Does he know about that? That you grew up servin' men in a brothel?" He watched her with narrowed eyes.

"I did not serve any men. You know I was a laundress. I worked in the basement. I never went upstairs. You know that."

"Do I?" He sat back and picked his teeth. "I guess I forgot. My memory's bad as I get older. But I tell you what. You give me a little blunt, and I'll forget to tell your fi-an-cé." He sneered as he dragged out the last word.

Alix was speechless. Her mind worked furiously. It wouldn't matter if Damion found out, because she'd be gone in a matter of weeks. But meanwhile, how to keep this man away from Damion's home? The appearance of Simon Blackthorn would cause Damion the deepest embarrassment in front of his family, whether they believed this man or not.

No. The real truth bubbled up, bursting into her noble thoughts. It was important to her that Damion not believe this man because she'd had dreams . . . dreams in which Damion respected her; dreams of his falling in love with her. Silly dreams. This man had the anvil to smash those delicate dreams all around her. Damion would never want her for a true bride after Simon revealed her past.

"I will make you a deal." She bit one side of her lower lip, thinking a plan out loud even as she spoke. "You must let me think about this . . . this offer." *Extortion* was what it was, but she would not risk further antagonizing the man. "Let us meet in one week, here, and I will give you my answer." She stood. It was best if she seemed confident; decisive.

"One week? Why not? And you'd better be here, Miss Adams. And perhaps you should bring some money with you. Else I'll have to go up to that fancy house and explain why I'm lookin' for you."

CHAPTER TWENTY

Early the following day, Damion strode into the parlor and stopped halfway between Elizabeth, who played on the plush rug by the settee, and Miss Adams, who sat on the settee reading.

He bowed stiffly. "I am thinking of escorting Lady Chloe to the village this morning. I am assuming you and Elizabeth will accompany us?" Damion's voice was as cold as his neck was stiff.

Elizabeth snapped her head toward Alix, her face lit hopefully. "May we, Alix?" She paused while tying a bonnet on her porcelain doll.

Alix turned white, as a stone dropped heavily into her stomach. "I—no, Elizabeth, we cannot." She turned to Damion. "Thank you, my Lord, but I would prefer not to go into town today." When he waited for an explanation, she lamely added, "I have plans . . ."

"That's fine. Lady Chloe mentioned she desires another excursion, but we haven't decided whether we'll go today or tomorrow. We'll go tomorrow, then."

"No. I . . . I don't think I'll be able to join you tomorrow, either." Alix could not reveal her fear to him. She must find some way to avoid going back into the village. Thinking of running into Simon Blackthorn made her nauseated and lightheaded; she feared she might faint. "Please, why don't you go today? There's no reason to wait on my convenience."

Elizabeth returned to dressing her doll, as it appeared no trip was in store. Alix was sure Elizabeth knew why, and was grateful she did not ask about the man who had confronted them last week.

"So this is how you plan to proceed, Miss Adams? Will we be playing these games for the remainder of your stay? I don't believe that was part of the bargain."

"Elizabeth." Alix looked warningly at Damion, and then over to the child. "Could you please gather your dolls and their clothes and take them to your room to play? Lord Woodhurst and I need to talk in private."

"Yes, Alix." Elizabeth was up in a trice.

Alix waited until the door closed behind her. "Please, Lord Woodhurst, I must insist you not air our disagreements in front of the child. Conflict upsets her, and—"

"I know what this is all about, and I told you I detest dishonesty. It is childishly obvious why you pout and refuse to accompany us. It's because of our argument at the pond, isn't it? You're teaching me a lesson, and that's why you refuse to go to the village. If you choose to be petty, it is a shame to punish Elizabeth when what you want to do is strike back at me." He rubbed a hand on his cheek. "Again."

Alix opened her mouth to protest.

"Well, Lady Chloe and I shall take Elizabeth with us, and she shall enjoy herself in spite of your small-mindedness, Miss Adams. Though I must say, I'm disappointed." He spun to leave, and as he opened the door he almost bumped into Chloe, who must have been listening to every word.

Chloe waited until he was out of earshot. "Tsk-tsk. The happy couple is fighting? We mustn't let Grandmother know. Not good for the heart," Chloe confided to Miss Adams, a small feral smile upon her lips, then turned to follow Damion down the hall.

Alix shook with anger, with humiliation, with dread of Simon Blackthorn. She picked up her book, but it was no use trying to concentrate, especially with tears blurring her vision, making the words swim. She refused to allow the tears to fall. *You are not allowed to feel sorry for yourself!* She took a calming breath, more of a shudder, actually. It seemed everything was going wrong. How had this happened? She'd been so happy these past weeks; she'd even fancied herself in love. Silly, romantic dreams. Was she finally seeing through the haze of her fairy tales, to the man's true soul?

The door opened, and Alix hastened to wipe her eyes. It might be Lady Charlotte, and Lady Chloe's words reverberated in Alix's head. She would not upset his grandmother. "Good afternoon," Alix called with false cheerfulness.

Elizabeth peered around the corner. "Alix, Lord Woodhurst has invited me to go to the village this afternoon. He's taking Lady Chloe. May I?"

"Yes, dear, you may." Alix opened her arms, and Elizabeth skipped across the room and returned the hug, then plopped beside Alix.

"Will that man try to talk to me again? The man we're not supposed to talk about?"

Elizabeth glanced to the door to be certain they were not overheard. Quietly, she said, "I don't think he'll recognize you if I'm not there. You do understand that's the only reason I'm not going? I did not mean to keep you from an enjoyable outing, Elizabeth."

Elizabeth nodded, playing with her hair, winding and unwinding a curl. She stuck the end of a glossy dark curl into her mouth.

Alix knew it to be a sign of worry. "Is there something you wish to talk about?" she asked, putting an arm around the child.

Elizabeth nodded, pulling the hair out and pushing it behind her ear. "Are we done with our secrets yet?"

"Why do you ask?"

Elizabeth studied her shoes, scuffing the toe of her boot in the carpet. "I don't want to keep secrets from Grandmamma anymore."

"I know how you feel. I love Lady Charlotte, too."

"Then why don't you call her Grandmamma, as I do?"

"That's something special between the two of you."

"But you shouldn't keep secrets from people you love, should you?"

Did she love Damion? "I don't know, Elizabeth. When we started on this adventure, I thought I knew. It seemed so easy. I'm not sure I know the answer anymore."

They sat companionably, listening to the crackle of the wood in the fireplace. A cloud passed its hand across the sun, the sudden gloom reflecting the veil settled over Alix's heart.

"Perhaps we should not say anything yet to Lady Charlotte. She doesn't know we're going back to the school after this visit."

"But, won't it make her sad? To be left alone?" Elizabeth's eyes turned forlornly down at the corners.

Alix couldn't tell Elizabeth that Lady Charlotte would have left *them* before that time. Alix bit her lower lip to keep it from trembling and nodded. "Yes, I'm afraid it will. That's why it's a secret still."

She paced, perspiring, listening and watching for their approach on the drive. Alix made herself sick, imagining Simon confronting Elizabeth in the village. Damion would know her darkest secret. When he learned she'd grown up in a brothel, he would demand she leave his home immediately. He had not pushed her out when he'd learned she was born out of wedlock, but that paled in comparison to the scandal she'd bring upon this house.

This was not a minor deceit, like pretending Elizabeth was her daughter or her sister.

Arms crossed under her breasts, she replayed the last few days. All of the arguments with Damion had concerned Elizabeth's father. Alix didn't even know Elizabeth's father! This was ludicrous.

The more she analyzed it, the sillier the arguments appeared. Arguments were always thus. Held under a magnifying glass in the sunlight, they lost their brittle shell and collapsed into an invisible wisp of smoke.

Perhaps it was her fault she and Damion were at odds. She'd been snapping at him like a fishmonger's wife, and all he'd done was inquire about another man in Alix's past life. Was he jealous? She blinked at the idea. No, of course he was not jealous. He could not possibly feel for Alix the same as she felt for him. He flirted with her, yes. But she'd been told it's what men do; it meant nothing, according to all of her female mentors.

Why, oh why, did she make up the tale about Elizabeth? Thinking back to that day in the headmistress's salon, though, she remembered his unyielding stance when she'd asked to bring along a child. He didn't know her then. He'd have refused her, certainly. And she and Elizabeth would never have had this grand adventure. No, she'd have said and done exactly the same again. That wasn't *quite* true. She'd have taken back the word "mine," and said "sister," as she'd meant to do. Oh, to be able to swallow words before their sound reached another's ears. That had been the worst slip. If he'd thought Elizabeth were her sister from the start, she would not be evading his questions of late.

That was it. She would confess to Damion the truth about Elizabeth. The truth was overdue. Well, perhaps not *all* the truths. But she could begin with this one. She would admit that Elizabeth was neither daughter nor sister. She'd explain about the child's history. Lord Woodhurst had shown he was a compassionate man. He'd take her hand, his eyes shining, telling her he admired her for her generosity of spirit. He'd understand. In fact, he would think it quite humorous; they'd share an intimate laugh . . .

Of course they wouldn't. The understanding, fictional hero faded away. In his place stood the true Lord Woodhurst, his mouth pursing, his jaw clenching. He'd know she had lied to him, and she'd be as untouchable as the fallen woman he had earlier imagined her to be.

She wasn't wanton! She must stop thinking thus. She could not help where she'd been raised as a child, and her mother had done the best she could. Alix's only accountable misstep was telling a tiny fib. A *very* tiny fib, when she thought about it. Nothing compared to the whopper *he'd* told his family: that he was engaged. She frowned in annoyance. He'd done nothing but lie from day one. How dare he condemn her for a fib?

She sighed. She was no closer to a solution. Continue fighting, and feel the pain of her broken heart. Or admit the truth, and feel the pain of his despising her.

A clattering of gravel and a jangling of harness broke the morning's quiet. She hurried over to pull aside the lace curtain and saw the horses smartly trotting home. The occupants of the carriage were laughing. They didn't look like a shocked, angry mob about to drive a silver stake through her heart.

No matter; her heart was already split.

Early the next morning, the sun rose at exactly the same time as Miss Alix Adams, and with it rose her spirits.

She would tell Damion the truth today about Elizabeth. Today, she'd tell him Elizabeth was her student. Not her sister; not her daughter.

She'd tossed and turned and thought about it all last night, until she made the decision. With it came peaceful sleep. No nightmares robbed her few remaining hours of rest.

She realized their relationship needed some darning in order to mend. As it could not get any worse, she had nothing to lose by confessing. If he chose to condemn her for fabricating in order to bring the child to Fern Crest Hall, so be it. Even if he was still cold and wouldn't talk to her, she was sure he would not send her packing. Not this close to her final days here.

She could no longer stand the frosty politeness buffering them. She missed the teasing Lord Woodhurst with the sparkle in his eyes and the sensual, inappropriate whispers in her ear. She couldn't wait to see him, to put her plan into action. He'd mentioned he'd be busy with errands this morning, so it would have to wait. Still, contentment filled her. With the resolution behind her, she practically bounced as she descended the stairs to the breakfast room.

Yes, the moment she saw him, she'd speak honestly—about Elizabeth, that is. She sipped her tea, refusing to think about the other things she hid from him: Simon Blackthorn and her upbringing in London. Well, they weren't fibs, though, just omissions. This soothed her conscience, which she swallowed with a bite of toast.

Alix finished breakfast quickly and rehearsed her speech all the way to the stables. Elizabeth would be continuing her riding lessons today with Sam, Damion's trusted stable manager.

Alix would begin by telling Lord Woodhurst she had a confession to make. That smacked of honesty, now, didn't it? Then, she'd tell him about Elizabeth's first few days at Widpole, and how the child had latched on to her heart. Finally, she'd conclude with the night she'd decided she could not leave her special little charge alone at the school. Surely he'd admit Elizabeth had been a wonderful present to his grandmother's final days. The two were practically inseparable.

Alix would apologize very prettily. Yes, she thought as she walked briskly toward the heavy stable doors, this would work. It was a sound plan, and he was a reasonable man.

She felt so much better.

She found herself smiling as she watched Elizabeth go through her routine with the pony. Alix actually looked forward to her coming meeting with Damion.

"No, Elizabeth. Remember? You need to cinch the girth first." Alix reached out a hand to slow the little girl's actions.

"I can do that for her." The stableman hurried over.

Alix held a hand toward him. "Wait. I think Elizabeth needs to learn to do this herself, as Lord Woodhurst has pointed out."

Alix knew Elizabeth would never be a gentlewoman with stablemen to wait on her. And being able to saddle a horse might be a skill that would come in handy in Elizabeth's future employ.

"Do you ride, my Lady?" Sam turned to his mistress.

"Oh, no. I know nothing about horses. Except what I've learned watching you and Lord Woodhurst with Elizabeth."

"Well, you're an apt student. Would you like us to saddle up a small horse for you as well?"

Alix's mouth dropped open in surprise. Her heart raced, but she was feeling brave and determined this morning. If she could face Lord Woodhurst, she could certainly face a dragon . . . or even a lady's horse. "May I saddle up my own? As you've taught Elizabeth to do?"

Sam looked at Garrett, his young stable hand. "I . . . I don't think we should allow that, my Lady. It's our job, and you're the lady of the manor, and—"

"And his lordship would be quite unhappy should he find out," added Garrett.

"Oh. I see." Alix tried to hide her disappointment. "Is there anything a lady is allowed to do with her horse—besides sit upon it?"

Sam tilted his hat and rubbed a grizzled jaw. "There's curryin'."

"Yup," chimed in Garrett. "I've worked for noblemen's ladies who were quite affectionate with their horses. Like best friends, they were. And they would insist on currying 'em."

"What is currying?" Alix asked.

"That's brushin'," said Sam. "You know, how little Elizabeth brushes down her pony after they've had their ride? It soothes 'em. And especially if they've been sweatin', it helps the horse to cool down."

"And these—these genteel ladies—they are allowed to do this?" Alix asked hopefully.

"Yup." Sam gave a single nod.

"What about treats?" Garrett asked the older man.

"What about 'em?" Sam sounded gruff as he looked over his shoulder at his apprentice.

"I've also known ladies who bring treats to their mares." Garrett added, subdued.

"Oh. Of course." Sam nodded, turning back to Miss Adams. Very officially, he decreed, "Ladies are allowed to bring treats to the stables."

"So. I can curry the horse. And I am allowed to bring treats. May I feed the treats directly to the horse? Or am I only to bring them to a certain line that's been marked in the hay?"

The two men looked confused, but when she laughed, they realized she was making a jest.

"Aye, you may feed them to the horse yourself, my Lady," said Sam, with a twinkle in his eye.

Alix pursued. She wanted to experience as much as possible. "Is there anything else a lady is allowed to do around horses, then? Other than ride them, brush—I mean curry—them, and give them treats?"

Both men looked to the rafters thinking, and then shook their heads at about the same time.

"I don't think so," said Sam.

"Not as I can recall," Garrett added.

Alix sighed. "All right. How annoying to be a real lady." Realizing what she'd said, she looked her mortification, but they didn't seem to have noticed.

"So. Shall I saddle up one of the mares for you?"

"Would it be a gentle mare, Sam?" she asked.

"Of course, my Lady."

"Could we start with a pony? Like Elizabeth's?"

"Hmmm. Best not to. Ponies are for children. But we've got several ladies' mares here."

"Do you have any that are smaller than the others?"

"We do, and I have one in mind." Sam's eyes lit up. "Why, there *is* something else that I recall ladies can do. They can tour the stables!" He grinned widely, quite pleased with his joke. "Let's meet the other horses, and see if you get attached to one."

"Attached? Why would people get attached to a horse?"

Both men smiled at one another, thinking this was the silliest question they'd ever heard.

"If you love horses, you'll soon understand, my Lady. Let's start over here. Garrett, you see to young Miss Elizabeth." Sam led the way to the furthest set of stalls.

Alix was amazed that it took a full minute to traverse the length of the stable house. She'd never been past the entry. Partially open wooden shutters gave enough light to see by, once her eyes adjusted to the tunneled dark. Close to the end, their steps stopped crunching in the straw.

"This is Celery." Sam stopped in front of one of many identical stalls.

A chocolate-brown mare turned and looked at the visitors with one eye. Alix watched her warily, and Celery returned her evaluation.

"Ye've got to talk to her. See if she likes your voice."

Alix took one hesitant step closer to the stall. "Hello, Celery. My, you're a pretty girl."

Celery shook her mane as if in agreement. She took steps closer to the stall's gate, her hooves crunching through the straw and clicking on the boards beneath.

Alix laughed. "She likes my voice!"

"Yup," Sam said, "I think she does."

"Why is she named Celery? Rather than Chocolate, or . . ." Alix could not think of another food to match the horse's beautiful brown coat.

Sam leaned his arms on the gate, studying the mare as he spoke. "We had a stableman who worked here named Rufus. Didn't last long." Sam cleared his throat. "We suspected he was a little too fond of drink, even during the day. He'd sneak celery leaves from the larder into his pockets, thinking if he chewed 'em, their smell would cover the ale odors of his breath." He looked over at Miss Adams with a lopsided grin. "Well, we come to find out this little mare—can't recall what her name used to be—developed a fondness for celery leaves. She'd always smell Rufus when he was near, and she'd poke her nose against his pocket. Gave him away every time. She came to expect a little snack of celery. We all started calling her Celery. Can't remember a time now that we didn't. Even after Rufus was let go, the name stuck."

"May I bring some celery out for her?"

"Why, it would be just the way for her to get to know you." He lifted the latch and led the small horse out. "Though I'd be careful not to give her too much, my Lady. We wouldn't want to get her ill."

"I promise. Just a taste. I'll go see if Cook has any." Alix began to hurry ahead, and then spun around. "And thank you, Sam. I . . . I think I do wish to try riding Celery. It would be a wonderful surprise if I could ride when Lord Woodhurst's parents arrive. Could I learn to ride within the week?" Her eyes, wide with hope, belied the casual words.

"Well," drawled Sam with not a little skepticism, "we'd best start today, and let's just see how you do. Can't make any promises, though."

"I'll look for a bit of celery, and I'll be right back." Alix picked up her skirts and hastened from the barn.

She laughed as she ran. Damion would be so surprised!

CHAPTER TWENTY-ONE

Alix swung the celery stalk, its flat leaves fluttering, as she walked briskly through the house, peeking in one room after another. She discovered Lady Chloe sitting in the crimson parlor.

"Have you seen Lord Woodhurst?" Alix asked, short of breath. "I've been looking everywhere for him."

Chloe studied her before answering. "You obviously didn't want his company yesterday afternoon, so why seek him now?"

Alix's back stiffened. "That's not true. I simply wasn't in the mood for a trip to the village. That was all. And I don't believe my actions are for you to judge, Lady Chloe."

"Well, it was your loss, as Damion—" Chloe emphasized his Christian name while flashing her hand to catch the light slanting in the window. "—insisted on buying me this small token while we were out shopping."

Alix moved farther into the room on wooden legs. The amber ring winked, a golden rainbow of soft shades. "It's beautiful," she said. A slight pang twinged in the pit of her stomach, like indigestion. It couldn't be jealousy, as she had no hold over Lord Woodhurst.

"But this is nothing." Chloe admired it in denial of her own words. "Wait until we get back to London. He's promised me something . . . special." Chloe's voice was breathy, and she watched Miss Adams from the corner of her tilted eyes, waiting for more questions. None came. "He's promised something more intimate. We shall pick out a piece of jewelry from Rundell and Bridge. I'm sure you've heard of them."

Alix had not. "Of course," she said.

"Of course," agreed Chloe, with a knowing smirk. "He said it would be to show his especial . . . gratitude." Chloe reclined against the arm of the Chinese-red settee, propping her chin on a graceful forearm. "He's promised *me* jewelry. And, what has he promised you, Miss Adams?"

"Picnics," Alix whispered, her spirits as limp as the celery stalk.

"How charming. A picnic." Chloe smiled a bored smile, and then turned back to her book.

"Ah, there you are, Alix." Lady Charlotte entered the room, regal in a teal-blue skirt and matching watered-silk blouse. "Did I hear someone mention jewelry?"

Chloe chose not to answer, forcing Alix to say, "Yes. Yes, you did, my Lady. Lady Chloe was showing me a lovely ring, a gift to her from Lord Woodhurst." The words almost stuck in her dry throat.

"How coincidental! And I had only recently mentioned to Edmund that I'd decided to give his bride-to-be a gift. Perhaps this triggered his thoughtfulness. Anyway, I've been looking everywhere for you, Alix."

"I was outside," she said, holding up the celery stalk. "Feeding the horses."

Chloe snickered, but stopped in surprise as Lady Charlotte glided across the room to Miss Adams, and made a fuss of clasping a pendant round her neck.

"This is what I wanted you to have, dear." Damion's grandmother stepped back, and a brilliant teardrop garnet surrounded by diamonds caught the light, as scintillating as a chandelier.

Chloe gasped. "It's the garnet—from Spain!"

Lady Charlotte stood close to Miss Adams, turning just her head toward Chloe. "Why, yes, it is the very necklace I believe you were admiring on my arrival. What a good memory you have, Lady Chloe."

"But . . . but it is part of a set. A most expensive set. You can't give it to—" Chloe caught herself.

"To my future granddaughter? Of course I can. And I may. And I did." Lady Charlotte's smile was frosty, and she sailed back out of the room as quickly as she'd swept in; before Alix could properly thank her, or properly refuse the gift.

Alix, in shock, looked down at the radiant pendant, which hung above the valley of her breasts.

"What are you doing?" said Chloe with a whispered hiss, appearing at her side. "You cannot accept something so valuable."

Afraid Lady Chloe was about to shake her, Alix stepped back and said, "I know." She shook her head, confused. "I . . . I didn't mean to."

"You must return it. You know you're not a real fiancée." Chloe bit out the angry accusation. "It's a priceless family heirloom. Damion will want to see it passed to his true wife."

"Of course I'll return it . . . When—" Alix swallowed, unable to complete the morbid thought. "I'll be certain to return it," she said, feeling helplessly guilty.

"Damion and I shall see that you do," said Chloe, shaking her head in disgust as she left the room.

Did Lady Chloe fly out to hunt down Lord Woodhurst? Alix wondered, feeling worse than ever. But it wasn't her fault; she hadn't had time to refuse. When she saw Lord Woodhurst, Alix would explain and confirm her intent to return the gift. But *after* she told him about Elizabeth. First they'd clear the air on that account. She had so many things to talk to his lordship about.

She touched the red stone, already warm against her skin.

Then she noticed the celery and inhaled a sharp breath. "Oh! Elizabeth and Sam are waiting."

Damion came around the corner and heard laughter. He slowed to listen.

"I know, I know! It's just that there is so much to remember." It was Miss Adams's voice.

"If you remember nothing else, my Lady, remember that you don't walk behind a horse. You always pass in front, so he can see you. They don't like sudden noises behind them. If you must go around back," said Sam, walking toward the horse, "then let him know you're there. Touch him briefly." He demonstrated. "Talk to him, and be quick about crossing behind him." He looked at her from the other side, over the top of the saddle. "But you'd better trust him. Because he can still kick out at someone he knows is there."

"All right. May I brush her now?" Her voice was young with anticipation.

Sam nodded. "I think we're done for today. I'm sure she'd appreciate it."

"Miss Adams. What are you doing?" Damion's loud voice echoed in the quiet stables.

Alix almost dropped the currying brush. "Oh, Lord Woodhurst! I'm so glad to see you. I've been watching for you all morning, as I wish to have a talk about—"

"I asked, what are you doing?" Damion's eyes were as cold as his voice.

Alix swallowed. "But . . ." Perhaps this was not the right time for a companionable confession. Their discussion would have to wait. "I'm . . . I'm brushing down Celery."

"I can see that. I mean, what are you doing brushing down a horse? And visiting in the stables?" He turned his angry gaze upon his stablemen.

Sam avoided Damion's eye. "My Lord. My Lady." He tipped his cap and left. Garrett, looking down at the straw-laden boards, bobbed his head and swiftly followed Sam to the tack room.

Alix stared after the stablemen. "That was extremely rude, my Lord. Sam and Garrett have been most kind."

"And I'm still waiting for an explanation."

Alix debated telling him about her lessons, but didn't want to spoil the surprise. Besides, she didn't care for his bossiness. "I'm not a prisoner, am I? I mean, I *am* allowed to go wherever I wish? To talk to whomever I wish?"

"Madam, we made a deal. While you act the role of my fiancée, you shall conduct yourself exactly as I would expect my future wife to conduct herself."

"And how is that, my Lord?" she asked with cool disinterest.

"The same as I do. *Not* hobnobbing and laughing with the stablemen like some common—"

"I see. So, you are hoping for a wife who behaves exactly as you do?"

"That is correct. One who carries herself with decorum—where are you going? I'm still talking to you."

Alix, her back to him, did not turn around. Loudly, over her shoulder, she said, "I am merely imitating my future lord. I am endeavoring to be your twin: cold. And rude. And snobby. I believe I shall start practicing this instant."

He lunged after her and grabbed her by the arm. "Wait. We are not finished. We shall finish this discussion during our picnic."

Alix looked at him in disbelief, shaking off his hand. "I hardly think—"

"I came to find you because on our way home from the village yesterday, I promised Elizabeth a picnic today. She thought you would be pleased. I'd hate to disappoint her. She's had Cook pack a basket. She's bouncing with excitement, and we're ready to leave."

Alix wanted to go; she wanted to mend everything with this man, but her stubborn lips said, "Perhaps I don't wish to go." She had to admit, though, she was touched by his thoughtfulness toward the little girl.

"So, you would deny a picnic for Elizabeth?"

"Elizabeth has plenty of distractions to occupy her. You needn't worry she will suffer if she misses one excursion."

"What about your philosophy to make the most of each day? Wouldn't you enjoy an opportunity to accompany Elizabeth on a picnic?"

"Perhaps I don't wish to accompany *you.*"

His look said he wanted to shake the haughtiness from her. But Elizabeth came skipping up, calling out.

"Alix! Lord Woodhurst is taking us on a picnic." She grabbed Alix's hand and began pulling her toward the doors. "Aren't you excited?"

"Quite," muttered Alix, gritting her teeth.

Elizabeth didn't seem to notice what a somber picnic it was.

She burbled happily through their cold collation of leftover partridge pie, a selection of cheeses, pickled beans, and hard-boiled eggs. Alix had to remind the child to chew the thick bread before swallowing, rather than washing it down with lemonade.

Between sips of cider, Alix stole surreptitious glances at Damion over her glass, but no words passed between them during awkwardly long silences. They directed any discourse via the young child, who was thrilled to be the center of conversational attention.

"May I go and pick dandelions?" Elizabeth asked much later, a bit of bread pudding on the side of her mouth.

Alix reached over and wiped the child's cheek with a starched napkin. "Yes, you may. Thank you for asking, and see that you don't wander too far."

Both adults watched Elizabeth amble across the meadow in a zigzag path, bending over to scoop up a daisy or a weed as each caught her eye. For five minutes, complete and total silence prevailed, punctured only by a whirring dragonfly skimming by.

Damion cleared his throat. "Shall we talk?"

"About what?" sniped Alix, though she hadn't meant it to come out so sharply. In a milder tone, she said, "Oh, yes. You haven't asked me about Elizabeth's father in at least twelve hours, I believe."

He laughed, a short laugh. "All right, I agree, I deserve that. It seems every time we are together lately, we waste our time bickering. And it is a shame, don't you think?"

"Actually," Alix said, mollified, "I myself wanted to bring up that very topic once more. *Just* once more," she added, noting his brows raised in surprise. "For I have a confession to make."

He paled; but at least he didn't look angry, as she'd feared he might.

"You see," continued Alix, "I have not been entirely honest about Elizabeth."

It was so quiet. She turned her face away from his stare and busied herself packing up picnic cutlery, quietly, one at a time, into the wicker hamper. Still not looking at him, she said, "Elizabeth is not my daughter, my Lord." Silence. "Nor is she my sister."

"Then what . . . who . . ."

She focused on the picnic items. "There is little to tell you about her parentage, though there is much to explain. Her father—whom I vow I never met—died of typhoid, as did her mother, within a week of one another." Alix gently wrapped the crock of pickled beans in a large napkin and nestled the jar in the basket, as if she were cradling young Elizabeth. "She is an orphan, like me. I first met her when she was delivered to the school. I was already a teacher at the time, and I took her under my wing."

Alix looked up at Damion, but could not read his expression. He appeared to be waiting patiently for further explanation. "You must understand how it was," she pleaded. "The child was incapable of speech. She didn't talk. Not one word, to anyone. I'm sure it was the shock of losing both parents at once. I cannot begin to imagine." Alix stopped packing, studying his face, speaking earnestly. "She clung to me. I felt . . . I felt as if I had a chance to go back in time and to console myself—the lonely, frightened little girl I'd been the day I arrived at the school. I knew it was what she needed."

She returned to the hamper. "When you made me the offer of employment . . . When I thought of leaving Elizabeth there . . . I couldn't." Alix shook her head, and whispered, "I couldn't." Her chin in the air, she said, "I had decided I would decline the offer that day you came to retrieve me, if you would not allow Elizabeth to accompany me. But—" Alix shuddered, remembering. "—you looked so forbidding when I attempted to ask I decided to tell you she was my sister, then I slipped and said she was my daughter, and then . . . and then it was too late to correct myself." Alix looked up at him with wet eyes. "Please believe me, I wanted to tell you the truth, but I didn't know you well enough then. I had no idea how wonderful a person you were, and how thoughtful and kind you'd be to Elizabeth."

He reached over and touched his warm fingers to her hand. "I understand, Miss Adams. I can appreciate your predicament."

She ducked her head shyly. "Thank you, Lord Woodhurst, for understanding." *Yes, that was nicely done,* she complimented herself. It was exactly as she'd pictured it would be. Alix was sure she looked quite fetching in the viscount's eyes: the contrite, feminine penitent. She kept her gaze averted modestly, studying the blanket.

His next lecturing words, however, undid any self-satisfaction.

"Mind you, I do not say I condone the fib. And doesn't it feel better to tell the truth? Honesty is always the wisest path."

She bristled at his self-righteous, stentorian tone, and raised innocent eyes to his. "Then may I assume, Lord Woodhurst, that you'll be telling your grandmother I'm not truly your fiancée? The moment we return to the manor? You may feel better telling the truth," she added, too sweetly.

Damion narrowed his eyes. "I believe we were speaking of *your* transgressions."

Alix fought the effervescence of stubborn spirit beginning to bubble up from her toes. "There is a saying, my Lord. Something about what is fit for the goose and the gander both, I believe."

"Miss Adams, in addition to being a viscount, which entails responsibility, I am a man of some experience. I do things for a reason, not on a silly whim. I don't believe you appreciate the difference between a lie about one of your students, and my altruistic endeavor to lessen the pain of a dying woman."

Alix's mouth dropped open. "How dare you imply that if a man lies, it is a sign of responsibility, but if a woman fibs, it is a silly whim?"

"Please." He held up both hands. "Let's not argue again. At least not on this point. I've said I understand, and I've given you my forgiveness." His voice rose in volume slightly as he affirmed his graciousness impatiently.

She squinted, turning her head to the side, recollecting. "I don't recall asking for forgiveness." She didn't sound confused; miffed would be a more precise barometer.

"Miss Adams, I wanted nothing more than to point out that being honest makes one feel better."

Her lips thinned. If she truly intended to mend their relationship, she must respond graciously. She'd told herself she wanted the old Lord Woodhurst back. And he'd made the first move, after all. She swallowed her pride, and said, "I do agree."

"I'm so glad to hear that. So . . ." He raised his eyebrows.

He seemed to be waiting for a response. "Yes?" she asked.

"So . . . is there something else you'd care to tell me?"

Alix froze. *He knows about Simon Blackthorn.* Elizabeth said they hadn't been approached, but perhaps while Elizabeth was shopping with Lady Chloe . . . Her palms were sweaty of a sudden. "What . . . what do you mean?" She wiped them surreptitiously on a napkin, pretending to pack it around a plate.

"I think you know what I mean. Is there anything else you wish to ease from your conscience? As you've already agreed, it will make you feel better," he reminded her.

She shook her head. "No," she said in a small voice. "I can think of nothing else."

"May I give you a clue?" he asked gently.

She nodded her head like an errant child, afraid to speak.

"Necklace?" he prompted.

Alix frowned. "Necklace?"

"Necklace," he repeated. "A certain, very valuable necklace?"

"Lord Woodhurst," she said with a mix of relief and impatience, "the only confession I can make is that I don't know what you are talking about."

Damion watched Miss Adams closely. He was frustrated and a little sad. Frustrated in his own judgment, for he'd grown to care for her, and once more she'd disappointed him.

In a sterner voice, he said, "All right. I was hoping you would have the honesty to tell me yourself, but I see you do not. Miss Adams, as your employer, I believe we need to talk about the necklace you convinced my grandmother to give you this morning."

She didn't respond for a full quarter minute. *"What?"* she exploded.

"I happen to know you have a necklace that belonged to my grandmother. A rather sentimental heirloom, as it was given her by my grandfather, who is no longer alive." Noting her silence, he continued. "I want you to know I understand your predicament. I'm sure anyone without money, in your position, would be tempted to do the same."

"To do what the same?" Her face was cold, but her eyes were alight with hot grey sparks.

"Lady Chloe already explained to me—"

"My, wasn't that kind of her! And exactly what did she explain to you, my Lord?" Alix bit out the last two words.

Damion tried to be as gentle as he could. "She explained how you were desperate for extra income, and so you dropped broad hints about the jewelry—"

Alix screeched.

Damion saw Elizabeth's head snap up from across the meadow. When the adults didn't move, she calmly went back to her task of collecting wildflowers.

"And you believed her?" Alix's chin thrust out at him, her jaw tight, and her neck strained. "Oh!" she said in a disgusted tone, "Why am I not surprised? I'll bet she couldn't run from the room fast enough in her haste to tattle." Alix snorted.

"Surely you can't blame her. Lady Chloe knows you're only . . . That is, you're not truly my future viscountess. And that is a valuable family heirloom, according to—"

"You couldn't possibly believe I planned on keeping it!" Alix's face turned red with anger, or embarrassment; he wasn't sure which.

"I hate to be blunt, but according to Lady Chloe, you cajoled it out of my grandmother. She said—"

"Stop!"

He had to press on. He didn't want to confront this issue any more than Miss Adams did. "You and I both know my grand-mother has grown quite fond of you. And we both know there are other women in dire straights who could not help but—"

"Lord Woodhurst." Alix picked up a heavy piece of crockery. "If you say one more word suggesting I intentionally maneu-vered Lady Charlotte into giving me the necklace, I'll—I'll dump this partridge pie upon your head. So help me, I will."

Damion wasn't sure how to proceed. So he said nothing as Miss Adams banged the dish into the wicker basket.

When the missile was safely wedged in and the hamper hadn't splintered, he said, gently, "Miss Adams, I didn't mean to slur women of poverty. I can tell you I know any number of women in my *own* circle who wouldn't hesitate to accept a similar gift."

Alix slammed the cover on the bread pudding. "Then that is something positive I shall be thankful for when this charade is over. Living sheltered, away from your 'polite society'. Because I can promise you: not one of the teachers whom *I* know—women of poverty, I believe you called us—would be despicable enough to finagle jewelry they didn't feel was theirs." With a violent move, the bread pudding joined the crock.

Damion's eyes widened, watching her pack hastily, tossing fine china plates helter-skelter into the basket, as if they were unbreakable iron.

"Furthermore, whether you believe it or not, I did *not* ask for this necklace. And I fully intended to give it to you as soon as . . . as soon as . . ." Alix bit back a sob. "As soon as she leaves us," she cried. Clutching the gem that hung around her neck, she appeared ready to yank it off. "In fact, you can have it now!"

Damion stretched out a hand. "No. No, I believe you. That is not necessary." He was relieved to see her return to her packing. "Besides," he added with a raised eyebrow, proud of his logic, "my grandmother will wonder why you are not wearing it."

Alix pointed the cheese wheel at him, as if it were a rapier. "Lord Woodhurst, this picnic is over. As is this conversation. Our business arrangement did not specify that you may badger me with Lady Chloe's spiteful, untruthful accusations."

She threw the cheese toward the basket's mouth. It hit the rim and rolled away, picking up speed as it escaped downhill toward a patch of prickly brambles.

Alix came to her knees and rose from the blanket. "I can't believe I let myself care for you. You're a . . . a snobbish cad, exactly like your friend, that evil Lady Chloe. Elizabeth!" she hollered to the child, who squatted in a patch of wildflowers across the meadow.

Elizabeth looked up, rose, and began walking toward them, her eyes on the field blooms in her path. She continued to pick, adding stalks to her bouquet.

Damion stood, and Miss Adams turned her back on him, arms folded. They stood without speaking until Elizabeth arrived with her nosegay of wildflowers and weeds.

Alix bent over and gently told the child they would return to the manor now, and leave Lord Woodhurst to collect the blanket and the basket. And his conscience, she said over her shoulder as she took Elizabeth's hand and left with hasty strides.

Damion stood, stunned. Chloe had lied. And he'd believed Chloe, not Miss Adams. He deserved the lady's ire; he should have known better. He'd witnessed Chloe's petty spitefulness all his life. Why hadn't he questioned it this time?

Because, he said, *you were ready to believe the worst.* Why? *Because every time you are near Miss Adams, you feel an inexplicable anger.*

He didn't realize why until just this moment. Now he recognized it: jealousy.

He broke into a foolish grin. Jealous of a lover who didn't exist! She was not Elizabeth's mother. She'd never slept with Elizabeth's father. She was still an innocent.

He'd wasted precious time being angry at a ghost of a man he thought had captured her heart and made love to her. A man he wanted to pummel, a man he wanted to fight for her love. A man who did not exist.

And—she said she cared for him, didn't she? Well, perhaps not at this instant, but she'd get over their minor tiff. And he'd make it up to her, just as soon as he returned from checking on Sarah Greeley and the boys. He'd promised to return for a brief visit; it couldn't wait.

Besides, it would give Miss Adams time to cool. The women he knew could never hold moods for long.

Damion congratulated himself. He might very well be an ass, as she suspected, but he'd never been happier.

CHAPTER TWENTY-TWO

Alix was furious. As she stomped into the parlor, shoulders down and fists clenched at her side, the last person she wished to see was Lady Chloe. Opening her mouth to let out a typhoon-worthy torrent, the emotional wind was deflated with Chloe's next words.

"Has Damion already left, then?"

"What? Left? Left for where?" asked Alix.

Chloe looked at her speculatively for a few moments without speaking. "Oh, he didn't tell you? How interesting."

Alix was speechless and churning with mixed feelings. She was sure she hated Lady Chloe. Perhaps Lord Woodhurst as well. And she hurt inside. But she wished she hadn't asked about his whereabouts.

With everything that boiled inside her, she needed the sanctuary of her bedroom. She refused to spend one more tick of the clock with this woman. She turned to leave.

"Damion's real fiancée is returning."

Those words stopped her for several ticks of the clock, and more. She didn't say anything, but when she turned to face Lady Chloe, the other woman must have read it in her expression, in her eyes. She looked triumphant, Goliath slaying the annoying David.

"You did know, of course, that he's been engaged before? A *true* engagement?" asked Chloe. When Miss Adams didn't respond, she tilted her head to the side. "I'm sorry to be the one to have to tell you," she simpered in a falsely sympathetic voice. "Damion should have told you about it. But then . . ." Chloe shrugged. "He didn't tell you he was leaving this morning, either, did he?" She sighed and straightened her shoulders, as if she were put upon to explain.

Alix knew the other woman relished the telling. She moved farther into the room, only as far as the first armchair. She felt faint. It might be wise to take a seat. The chair faced a roaring fire, but her insides were cold.

"It was a sad story." Chloe spread her skirt and clasped her hands upon her lap, as if she were a teacher telling a fairy tale to a group of young girls. "A little over a year ago, Damion had a fiancée. A real fiancée," she added, with a meaningful look. "A lovely lady. Of course, you would never have met her, as she is a member of *our* circle—Damion's and mine. Her father died, and she was distraught. So distraught that she and her mother immediately left the country for her grandfather's estate in Scotland.

"You can understand, I'm sure. In our society," she said, emphasizing the two words so precisely it stung, "there must be a proper mourning period. There would be no wedding in the immediate future, and she and her mother needed to recoup their spirits. Lord Woodhurst and his fiancée should have remained engaged until she returned, but . . ." Chloe looked toward the far wall, with her eyes scrunched slightly, as if straining her memory. "We were never sure who broke the engagement. Rather, *she* cried off, but we suspected it was Lord Woodhurst who wished it ended."

"Why didn't he wait for her to return?"

"I think he began regretting the engagement, as many of the town's bachelors have been known to do. At least, he certainly did not waste any time pursuing other ladies of my acquaintance."

Alix detected a note of . . . what?—Annoyance? Bitterness? . . . in Lady Chloe's voice.

Chloe continued. "Well, if it was his choice and he allowed her to cry off first, at least he gave her that small gentlemanly courtesy. Not that he acted in a gentlemanly fashion, for they'd been pledged, but evidently . . . Well, out of sight, out of mind as they say.

"None of us—their closest friends—could understand why it happened, but we knew with certainty that time would heal her spirits, and that they would both regret their hastiness. They were so perfectly matched." Chloe looked her defiance at Miss Adams. "They *are* so perfectly matched."

Alix sat transfixed. She had no idea he'd ever been engaged. He'd never mentioned it. But then, why should he? She was nothing more than hired help, wasn't she? She'd been foolish to imagine there could ever be more. Foolish.

She realized Lady Chloe was talking again.

". . . such wonderful news! We learned she is not only recently returned to England, but she has also written of her interest in renewing her relationship with Damion. Such perfect timing."

Alix's heart began a slow spiral. He loved another woman; he'd asked this woman to be his wife. Alix couldn't bear the image of another woman in his arms. She couldn't stand the picture of him leaning close to another woman to drop a teasing whisper in her ear.

Though she knew her playacting as his fiancée was now dead and purposeless, she couldn't resist asking, "Won't Lady Charlotte be upset? If we switch fiancées in the middle of . . . before she . . ."

"I think she will be so happy to see him wed, it will not matter. She'll understand that he wanted her to be happy before she dies." Chloe seemed to have no problem referring to Lady Croxton's demise. "Substituting you was such a thoughtful thing to do, when one considers. Just think, now Damion can go through with the ceremony immediately, as soon as his parents arrive."

Alix's heart stopped. In a short time, Lord Woodhurst would belong to someone else. Forever. "Will . . ." Alix forced herself to continue the question, though it cut little ribbons into her heart. "Will his fiancée be arriving soon as well?"

"She's on her way," Chloe bubbled with enthusiasm. "Her name is Lady Ardis." Chloe's eyes gleamed with an idea. "Ardis. And Alix. How coincidental. Damion's grandmother is so dotty, I'm sure she will barely notice the switch, your names are so alike." At Miss Adams's frown of censure, she hastily added, "The important thing is, Damion will be able to confess to his grandmother that you were merely standing in for his real fiancée while he waited for her return. Which is the truth, is it not?"

"I wouldn't know. He never confided in me," said Alix, not making eye contact. She twisted the ribbons at her waistline. "But I know he would agree the truth would be preferable. And Lady Charlotte is a very straightforward woman." Alix was so fond of the woman she'd never see again. She bit back tears. They'd have to wait, but she felt them overflowing within.

Chloe stood. "I am so excited. I'll be here at Fern Crest Hall to see the lovers' reunion. It will be the talk of the *ton* when we return. Damion will be so thrilled, as will his parents. They both *adored* Lady Ardis. What a wonderful, wonderful surprise for them. I cannot wait to see the look on their faces!" Chloe clapped her hands together, the clap of a conjurer.

For when Alix looked up from the rose-patterned hearth rug, Lady Chloe had disappeared.

She should have escaped to her room to cry, instead of sitting in shock, staring at the flames through teary eyes, crying silently. Too late, she heard the door open.

Alix hastily wiped her eyes with the edge of her hand, and pulled out a handkerchief, swiping at her nose. She patted her hair, and concentrated on looking down, fluffing out the skirts of her dress.

"Alix?" said Lady Charlotte. She moved closer and said gently, "Look at me, dear."

It was the "dear" that was Alix's undoing. Tears spilled again, though she rubbed at them ineffectively, first the left cheek, then the right. "I'm sorry," she managed to whisper, before burying her face in her hands.

"Alix, don't apologize for being upset, just tell me why you are!"

She shook her head, but wouldn't make eye contact with Lady Charlotte.

"Child, what is wrong?" The countess sat on the arm of the chair and put an arm around the young woman's shoulders.

"Everything." Alix caught her breath, taking hiccupping gulps of air, wiping her eyes with the fine linen handkerchief. It wasn't her handkerchief, she thought dully, as these weren't her clothes. By right, they belonged to his new bride.

Lady Charlotte waited patiently, a hand still resting on the younger woman.

Alix drew in a deep breath. Should she be the one to tell his grandmother about the arrival of his true fiancée? No, her grandson should do it. Instead, she'd tell another half truth, which was all she seemed to do lately. "It's just . . . All we do is fight, lately, when we are together."

"Is this what your tears are about? A little lovers' argument? Alix, this happens to everyone. Why, if I had a shilling for every argument I'd had with my Alfred . . ." She chuckled. ". . . I'd be a wealthy woman today."

Alix shook her head contritely, missing the irony that the Dowager Countess of Croxton was, in fact, an extremely wealthy woman. "I know this is not appropriate behavior, when all you want to do is see your grandson happy while you can." Her lips trembled as she looked at the woman through wet eyelashes. "I'm sorry. I'm sure it's all my fault."

Lady Charlotte sputtered. "What on earth? Why would you say that, child? I can see my grandson is as stubborn as a mule. Don't think I take your side solely because we are female. I can see he is pouting like a young boy. I've half a mind to tell him so."

"Oh, no!" Alix pulled the handkerchief away from her eyes. "Please. Do not say anything. He would be so distressed should we cause you any discomfort."

"Discomfort? Fiddle-faddle! It's nothing to concern yourself about."

Alix stared at the flames, downcast.

"I don't wish to pry," Lady Charlotte said, "but would it help to talk about your disagreements? It usually helps me, woman-to-woman. We all know men can make life so impossible."

Alix heaved a long sigh. "There is so much I wish I could share with you, my Lady."

"Well, you know I'm quite a hopeless busybody."

Alix smiled at the countess, then looked toward the door, listening.

"What is it? Is someone there?"

"I . . . I don't think so. But I don't wish to be overheard. By Lady Chloe or by Elizabeth."

"Then I suggest we take a stroll so we can talk in private. Besides, a walk in the fresh air and through the gardens will do your spirit good. Oh! Have you been inside that charming little gazebo?" Lady Charlotte jumped from the arm of the chair so quickly, Alix thought she might fall and injure herself. "I've decided I'm in the mood for some lemonade."

Alix stood. "I'll ask for refreshments to be sent . . ." She moved to the door. ". . . to the gazebo?"

"That would be delightful." Before Miss Adams reached the threshold, Lady Charlotte added, "Oh, and I believe a few of those iced tea cakes would go nicely with lemonade, don't you agree?"

"Absolutely," Alix agreed with a broken smile.

Chapter Twenty-Three

The stone path, its edges softened by mosses, curved around the old rhododendron beds. It meandered right up to the square reflection pool, and then parted at the last moment to outline the water folly. Joining again, it pulled the wanderers toward the white gazebo. Past the structure, the path veered sharply to the left and rambled on, a river of rock, ending at a waterfall of steps leading to the upper gardens.

The gazebo was encircled by a white rail running waist-high around its circumference. Spindle posts gave it an open, airy feel, as did the open wrought-iron dome wrapped with clematis and capped by an ornate white cupola.

The ladies took a seat inside the circle, fanning themselves. The air was hot, and so still it seemed one would be able to feel the beat from the bees' wings, if one sat motionless. Neither said much of consequence until the footman and under butler delivered refreshments and departed.

When Alix could no longer see their bright livery along the curved path, she said, "It seems it all started over Elizabeth's father."

"*Your* father, do you mean? I assume you shared the same father if you're sisters. Or . . . are you stepsisters or such?"

"Lady Charlotte, I have not been honest with you. Elizabeth is not my sister." Alix could see wheels spinning in the older woman's intelligent eyes. "Nor is she my daughter, as your grandson believed."

Alix watched the countess sip her lemonade, letting this new information sink in. She continued, "Elizabeth is, however, very, very special to me. You see, ever since she first appeared at the school, she followed me like a tiny duckling. She might as *well* have been my younger sister; we had so much in common. We both lost our parents at an early age. We both were sent to Widpole Manor—to the school—as young girls. While *my* father may still be alive, I wouldn't know as he abandoned me. Elizabeth lost her father to typhoid. The same time as her mother."

"Oh, dear. Poor little Lizzie."

"I have keen memories of arriving at the school and being taunted as an orphan. I didn't want her to bear those same feelings alone. I wanted to help her through it." Alix was thoughtful. "Do you know, I prefer to think there was a reason—a grander scheme—why I suffered through those years. I think it was so I could help Elizabeth. At least, that makes me feel something positive came out of it, and it was not all for naught."

"What a wonderful outlook, Alix." Lady Charlotte clucked her tongue. "So, do you plan to tell him about Elizabeth? That she is not your sister, I mean? And, of course, that she is not your daughter?" Before Miss Adams could answer, she said, "My dear, if I may make an observation—and please forgive me for prying—having secrets is not the best way to begin a marriage."

Alix nodded with furrowed brow. "I could not agree with you more. This keeping of secrets has been most troublesome! But it's been a good lesson for me. Next time I agree to become engaged to someone, I shall certainly take care to walk an honest path." Alix froze, realizing what she'd revealed.

Lady Charlotte laughed loudly. "Next time! La, you are so enjoyable, Alix." Her belly laugh shook the ruffles on her dress.

"Well," Alix said quickly, "he does know now. I told him, just this morning."

"Then, why do I find you crying? What else did you two love doves argue about?"

Alix fingered the fine chain encircling her neck. "This necklace. Damion accused me of finagling it out of you."

"What? Where is that boy? I shall box his ears myself. Oh, I forgot, he has gone to check on the widow Greeley. Well, I'll box his ears when he returns."

Ah, thought Alix. So that is where he went. Though it stung that he hadn't told her, she defended him with a loyalty that surprised herself. "To be fair, it was what Lady Chloe told him."

"Ooh, I'd like to box her cat ears as well. I don't care for that woman, or her airs. Alix, listen to me." Lady Charlotte pinned her with a steely look. "I gave you that necklace because I heard that annoying woman bragging to you about the ring my grandson bought her. Not that I approve! *Most* improper. Him engaged to you, and buying her jewelry. Whatever is wrong with that young man? Regardless, she's been eyeing my garnets and diamonds since the morning I arrived. I gave it to you, in front of her, precisely to set her in her place. And I'd do it again, if only to see the smugness wiped off her face. It was worth every carat, let me tell you." She gave a hearty "Harrumph!"

Alix made a decision. She must tell Lady Charlotte the truth. She reached for the clasp. "Actually, I am returning this to you."

"Stop! Don't remove it, dear. What are you doing?"

Alix paused. "I cannot keep it, for I'm not to become his wife."

The gazebo echoed with silence.

"But . . . The engagement has been broken? Over a trivial argument? You can't! Misunderstandings can—"

"No. I . . . You see . . ." Alix returned her hands to her lap, and looked down contritely. "There was no engagement to break. The truth, my Lady, is that I am not a true fiancée." She looked up. "Damion asked me to . . . to stand in as his fiancée, while you . . . until you . . . Lady Charlotte, I am an imposter."

The countess looked stunned and disoriented. "This cannot be."

Alix sighed. "I wanted to tell you the truth, but I felt it was Damion's secret to tell. Please believe me." She leaned forward in earnest. "I've grown so close to you. You're the grandmother I never had."

"Words of flattery will get you nowhere, Alix." But Lady Charlotte smiled weakly to belie her words. "I know how you feel, dear. I feel the same way about you. Now, continue. Out with it. I demand to know the whole story."

"And please don't hold it against Damion. He only wanted your happiness."

Lady Charlotte pursed her lips grimly. "It's because of my failing health, isn't it? Is this why he proposed to you?"

"Well . . . he didn't exactly propose in the normal sense. It was more of a *business* proposition. You see, when he received your letter, telling him—telling him you would not be . . . *here* . . . for long, he wanted to do something special for you."

"Drat," said Lady Charlotte. "Makes me wish I really were dying."

Alix's eyes flew wide.

"I'm not, Alix. Not dying, that is."

One hand flew to Alix's mouth, and she inhaled on a sob.

"Don't be so disappointed, gel." Lady Charlotte reached over and touched her. When Miss Adams looked at her in mortification, she quickly said, "I'm teasing, of course."

"Oh, Lady Charlotte!" Alix laughed, a half-sob of glee. "I'm so happy you're not going to die!"

"Well, of course I'm going to die—"

Alix stopped and stared.

"I mean, aren't we all? I'm simply not ready to go *yet*." Lady Charlotte leaned back and folded her hands on her lap. She sighed, then continued. "My dearest friend, the Dowager Duchess of Elderberry, did die, though. I wrote Edmund of her death, in a letter. I realized later that he misunderstood. You see," Lady Charlotte said, looking up from her gnarled hands, "her sudden death upset me terribly. I was a bit dazed for days. Then I decided I would travel. I'd take that trip she and I had always promised ourselves. We met as young girls, while traveling with our parents in Wales." She spoke softly, her eyes far away, in another country.

"Well, as I explained, I was quite distraught after Ellen's death. I'd been dwelling on how short our lives are and brooding about death, and it seemed the time to seize the moment. I wrote and told Damion I wanted to see him, before I was gone."

"Before . . . you were gone." The corners of Alix's lips turned up. She chuckled. And then she laughed out loud. "Oh, he will be so happy." She looked toward the manor, as if she could spy him from here. "I cannot wait for him to hear the—"

"No!"

Alix snapped her eyes back to Lady Charlotte. "No?"

"No," repeated the grand dame. "And ruin this farce? Absolutely not. I shall not tell him, and neither shall you, my girl."

"But . . ." Alix was confused. *Oh my word!* she thought, Damion did not need a fiancée after all. He would be so relieved. Or would he? She recalled Lady Chloe saying he'd be thrilled at the return of his former fiancée. "But why would you not tell him?"

"Let me ask you a question first: When did Edmund propose to you?"

Alix turned red.

"Aha! I thought so. He would not have been prodded to

finally ask the question if he did not think I was dying, would he?" She smiled a Cheshire cat smile. "I knew it! I told his parents so."

"His parents know?"

"Oh, yes. We had quite a good laugh over it. Well, *I* had quite a good laugh. Edmund's father does not have much of a sense of humor. Hmm, neither does his mother, for that matter, and she's my daughter. I've always suspected someone switched babies on me whilst I was giving birth. I was not all that cognizant, you know."

Alix giggled, in high spirits again. "You are incorrigible, my Lady." She thought about the intricate webs Damion and his grandmother had spun around each other. "Well, Damion truly is your grandson. You are both too alike to deny it."

Lady Charlotte appeared pleased with this observation, just as she appeared to assume it was a compliment.

Alix asked, "Aren't you worried his parents will tell him the truth?"

"I forbade it. They also realize your fiancé finally set a date because of the misunderstanding. They are as content as I to let him follow through. Why, if I'd known all along this was all it would take, I'd have staged my own death long ago."

"When your grandson finds out . . ." Alix shook her head slowly. "I don't plan to be in the vicinity. He'll be furious with anyone who took part in this secret."

"That is fine, as I don't plan for him to discover this secret," said Lady Charlotte firmly, her lips pressed together.

Alix sipped her lemonade, thinking. "But he'll eventually realize it, when . . . when . . ."

"When I don't curl up my toes?"

"Please don't say that!" Alix shuddered.

"Anyway, I do plan to tell him something. I plan to tell him the doctor gave me wonderful news! A miracle!"

"Oh, I suppose that's all right then." Alix was relieved. "And when do you plan to tell him, my Lady?"

"After the wedding, dear." The dowager countess sat back in her chair. "So, I believe you owe me a story, miss?"

Alix sighed softly. "Where to start?"

"I'd suggest when you met Edmund. How do you two know one another?"

"We don't, not really." Alix wrinkled her brow, and then a smile cleared it. "I mean, I think I do know him now. As well as I could after such a short time. But I didn't know him a mere month ago."

"That's absurd!"

"Yes. It is." She smiled mischievously at Lady Charlotte. "I fell at his feet. Literally. He was a gentleman knight, and he assisted me."

"How charming. I love romantic meetings. You tripped?"

"I wish it were something so delicately feminine as that. No. I fell off a wall."

"At your age?"

"Yes." Alix laughed. "There was this small student, Tommy, climbing a wall. He's one of my wards, always into mischief. He found himself up on the wall and was afraid to climb down. In essence, it's simple. I climbed the wall, I helped him down to safety, but then *I* fell."

Lady Charlotte raised her eyebrows.

"And Lord Woodhurst was riding by on his horse. And . . . that was that. As you can see, it was a chance meeting."

Lady Charlotte clapped her hands, once. "But, Alix, I believe there is no such thing as a chance meeting."

Alix looked surprised. And skeptical.

"Believe me, dear. I've lived a long and full life. And I've observed—no. I firmly believe. I *believe*, Alix. There is only fate. This was meant to be. You and Edmund are meant for one another. You are perfect together. Tell me. Don't you feel it?"

Alix blushed. "I . . . I did imagine, I mean I thought . . . But how silly of me."

"No, Alix. It's not silly. Trust me. It's meant to be."

Alix shook her head. "No, it is not. I mean, if he *is* meant to marry, it will not be to me. There is more. This morning I learned his true fiancée is returning to London." His grandmother gasped, and Alix rushed on. "Lady Chloe says his parents adore her, and he is still very much in love . . ." Alix's voice faltered. ". . . in love with her. They broke their engagement, but they will soon be reconciling."

"Oh, my! No, he cannot be." His grandmother appeared distressed, disoriented. "You don't understand." Leaning on the arm of her chair, she rose slowly, then paced to the other side of the gazebo. Turning in agitation, she said, "Alix, I never met the girl myself, it was such a short engagement. My daughter was ecstatic when they announced the engagement, of course, but it is what I would expect of her, the silly thing. However, my closest friends, a most astute pair of ladies, one of them being Lady Elderberry . . ." Lady Charlotte frowned. "What was it they told me about her?" She looked at Miss Adams. "I cannot remember, but it wasn't good. I do remember that much. They told me in no uncertain terms that he was well rid of her. And I trust their judgment, Alix. He cannot think to be marrying her. He cannot. I will tell him I won't allow it!"

The idea of Lady Charlotte telling her grandson he could not marry almost made Alix smile. She stood.

"Alix, let us return. I must think on this. Surely, something can be done to prevent it." The countess shook her head and moved to the gazebo entry. "Oh, by the way," she added, as she paused on the gazebo steps, "I must insist you continue to wear the pendant, as a favor to me. I wish to annoy Lady Chloe."

Alix grinned and moved to the entry, hoping she'd been right to reveal Damion's secret. But time was running out.

Lady Charlotte cleared her throat and said, without turning, "There is one more secret you haven't told me, Alix."

Alix stiffened, her hand on the gazebo rail. Lady Charlotte stood about five feet away, but hadn't turned around. "There is?"

Now the countess turned. "Yes, dear. I see it in your eyes every day."

Alix froze, holding her breath.

"And, often I hear it in your voice. I think you love my grandson."

Chapter Twenty-Four

The heavy tavern door swung open, allowing the bright afternoon light to pierce the smoky darkness inside. Just as quickly the vertical bar of light narrowed and disappeared as the door was closed behind the tavern's newest guest.

She squinted as her eyes adjusted to the cave-like gloom. A serving girl stopped in front of her, balancing a round platter of mugs. "Who be ye lookin' for?" She looked the young woman up and down.

"I'm meeting Mr. Blackthorn."

The worker jerked her head to the right. "Ye'll find him in that corner table."

She moved hesitantly further into the dark. "Mr. Blackthorn?"

"Aye. Have a seat."

"Don't you even want to know who I am?" Chloe's petulant displeasure was mirrored in her voice as she eyed the dark stains on the tavern bench with disdain.

"I've seen you with her. That's all I need to know. Best not to know names sometimes, girlie." He grinned at his own cleverness, showing wide gaps between the two remaining upper teeth.

Chloe swiped the wood ineffectually with a gloved hand before sitting on the edge of the seat. "You said you had some information for me."

"Aye. And you said you had some coin for me."

She looked around. No one was in hearing distance, and the

tavern was loud. "First, your information."

"How about first you show me the blunt?"

"Blunt?"

"The money, dearest."

Chloe reached into her reticule and produced several coins. She pushed them toward the center of the table. When he reached out to grab them, she yanked her hand back as if burned. He slid the money quickly across the table and off the edge into his palm, then into his pocket in one motion.

"That'll do for starts."

"There isn't going to be anymore, Mr. Blackthorn. You promised to give me information about . . ." She lowered her voice. "About Miss Adams."

"What is she to you?"

"I am her companion. But I was hired by her fiancé, Lord Woodhurst. It is important he know the truth if there is scandal in her past. You can understand, can't you, how damaging it would be if he discovered any secrets in Miss Adams's past?"

"Well, now. I wonder what you mean by secrets? Her companion, eh? Did she tell you she was born in London?"

Chloe nodded impatiently. "That much I already knew. What else?"

"And where in London did she tell you she grew up?"

"She said she lived with her mother. Her mother was a laundress."

He barked a loud laugh. "Ah, that's a rich tale."

"She was not a laundress?"

"Oh, she may have done some work with the sheets. But between the sheets would be more likely."

Chloe's eyes widened, and she leaned slightly forward. "What do you mean?"

"I'm thinkin' you know exactly what I'm sayin'. Our little

Miss Adams didn't grow up in no grand house. She lived in a brothel."

Chloe gasped. Her eyes sparkled with malicious interest. "Are you saying her mother was a prostitute?"

"She may have called herself a laundress. All I'm sayin' is that she was hired help in a brothel. You can reach your own conclusions, surely."

"I see. And how old was Miss Adams when she left?"

"That'll cost you a bit more coin. Are you wantin' to know if the little girl was also used by the house?" His lascivious grin made Chloe ill.

She opened her reticule with shaking hands and slid two more coins onto the splintery wood. "Yes. I want to know."

He snaked out his hand and the money disappeared into his pocket in a wink. "That I can't tell you for fact."

Chloe opened her mouth to protest, but he leaned forward conspiratorially. "What I *can* tell you is that she was about eight or ten years old when she left the house. What they did with her before she left, who can say? But there are gentlemen who'll pay extra for a smaller dose of dessert." His gaping grin sickened her.

"Are you demanding money from her?"

"She told you so?"

"No, but I knew she was up to something, not telling anyone where she was off to," Chloe said in self-satisfaction. "Why else would she sneak out to meet you? Why else would you be approaching her? To ask for her hand?" This was accompanied by a smirk.

He raised his hand as if to backslap her and she jumped back in her chair. "Don't use your airs on me. You think I'm not good enough for her? Let me tell you, she'll pay me to keep her secret from that fancy lord she's plannin' to marry. Else I'll be goin' to himself to let him know what stains there will be in the family closet. And none on the wedding night sheets, eh? And when she's got nowhere to go but back to the school, I'll be waitin' to have her. One of these days my cousin will tire of Miss Adams's airs, and I'll be there to keep her from starvin'."

"What makes you think I won't go back and tell Miss Adams this minute?"

"Oh, I'm countin' on it." His wide grin showed black gums. "I'm hopin' you do let her know that I ain't leavin' yet. I think his lordship will be givin' his intended bride lots more of this to send my way." Simon reached into a torn pocket and pulled out a glittering gold chain. Though it was dark, the candle light cast was all that was needed to catch the scintillating pendulum of the perfect garnet, ringed by diamonds.

Chloe gasped when she saw Lady Croxton's necklace swinging from his grimy fist. "Where did you get that?"

"I told you she'd pay me to keep her secret. A nice little first payment, I think."

She could tell him Miss Adams would not be marrying Damion, that there would be no more treasures coming his way from the pretend fiancée. She could put a stop to this right now.

Instead, she smiled. Damion had been showing too much of an interest in Miss Adams, in spite of Ardis's near arrival. And Chloe now had the information she needed to force Miss Adams out of Damion's life forever. This disgusting creature sitting across from her would not see one farthing more.

She rose and left.

"In a military campaign, you must know your objective," rang out Lady Charlotte's deep, tuneful voice.

Alix looked up from her book. "I beg your pardon?"

It was late and Alix was curled up on a settee, warmed by the whimsical Jacobean fireplace in the corner of the sitting room.

Lady Charlotte stood inside the door, a maroon leather journal in her hand. "My Alfred was an expert at this. I can't believe I'd forgotten!" She came slowly into the room while shuffling through the pages.

Alix watched her approach, curious.

The older lady's eyes lit up, and she stopped, looking up at Miss Adams. "This is it! Oh, Alix, how could I have forgotten?"

Alix smiled and raised questioning eyebrows.

"Alfred, my former husband—Well, he wasn't a *former* husband, since I had none prior nor since. However, he's deceased, so I suppose I should simply say 'my husband?' But ignore my ramblings, dear. What I wanted to say is that this was his hobby. His passion, actually." She'd rushed through without taking a breath, but inhaled deeply now. "Alix, it's all here. Everything we need."

"Everything we need? For what?"

"For our campaign, dear." Lady Charlotte sat next to Miss Adams on the settee, and continued to flip through the pages.

"Lady Charlotte, I'm sorry to seem so dense. But I'm not sure I understand what you're talking about. What campaign?"

Lady Charlotte hiccupped, and her eyebrows flew up. "My! Excuse me. I think I drank my sherry too quickly. Jane brought a tiny glass to my room, as she usually does before I retire."

She closed the soft-covered book and placed a hand on Miss Adams's arm. "Our campaign is to get my grandson married. But to someone suitable, of course. *She* will not do."

Alix was too shocked to answer.

"As I was sipping my sherry by the fireplace in my room—I do love staring at the quaint little mantel, though I like this one too, don't you? As I said, I was thinking about Edmund. And you," she added pointedly, focusing her blue gaze on Miss Adams. "This whole engagement business is a fine ruse on his part, but it must be fulfilled. And not with his former fiancée.

This is a perfect opportunity to make Edmund see it is time he truly married, and not just anyone, but the proper person. Someone acceptable."

"Acceptable? Acceptable to whom?"

"Why, to me of course! Alix, have you been attending to anything I've said? This is all so very important. And then," she slapped the bundled manuscript, "I remembered what Alfred said to me. So many times, it's a shock I'd forgotten. He always insisted that every problem or dilemma in life was merely a small part of a larger campaign. I used to laugh at that, and he would always make me repeat it."

Her smile was soft in memory.

"You are saying that Damion's false engagement to me is a . . . a battle?" Alix's brow wrinkled.

"No, not a battle. Well, not yet. What I'm saying, Alix, is that if I want to see my grandson truly married—to a bride I will approve of—I must plan a strategy. Alfred studied military moves and patterns, you see, and he was convinced that if you want something, truly *want* it, you must plan a campaign. Or a skirmish, depending on . . . But never mind. We're going to think of this as a campaign."

"We?"

"Yes, of course. I'll need your help. So I remembered Alfred's words of advice, and then I remembered he used to keep notes of all the stratagems he read about." Lady Charlotte held the small, worn journal in the air. "And here it is. I cannot believe I was able to locate it so quickly. I'd tucked it away in the library. Between his maps. They do seem to go hand in hand, don't they?"

Alix nodded, since she wasn't sure what else to do.

"Look here. His whole first chapter is on Objectives." She turned the dusty journal so Miss Adams could read it with her. In a lecturing tone, she read, " 'Before engaging in any type of effort, one must know one's Objectives.' You see? He has underlined *objectives* and written it in a bold hand." She smoothed her fingertips over the page. "I loved Alfred's handwriting. Anyway—." She snapped the book shut. "Alix, I am going to study this, and we are going to mount a successful campaign."

Lady Charlotte rose, tucking the journal under her arm. She marched to the door, already in military mode. At the lintel, she spun.

"We are going to see Edmund married, Alix. To you." She gave one decisive nod and left the room.

"But . . ." Alix stared at the door, her grey eyes clouded. "But perhaps Lord Woodhurst doesn't wish to be married to me. And perhaps I don't wish to be married to him," she said to the empty room.

"Edwyn, I have the strangest letter from my mother."

Lord Nottingdale looked around his paper with annoyance. "What is strange about that, CoraLee? Have you ever known your mother to send a conventional letter?"

Lady Nottingdale sat down and fanned herself with the envelope. "I don't know what to make of it."

"Can you summarize, dear? I'd like to finish this article."

She looked down at the unfolded letter, then back at her husband. With pursed lips, she said, "She says we are not to come to visit. Not quite yet."

The earl ruffled his paper in annoyance and looked at his wife over his spectacles. "That *was* a brief summary. Now, would you care to elaborate a bit?"

The countess was shaking her head, perusing each line.

"CoraLee, it looks as if you'll keep me in suspense if I don't put down my paper and listen." He rustled it once more before setting it on his lap. "Proceed, please. Read the letter. It's only one page, I hope?"

"Yes, it's only one page," she said distractedly. She read aloud:

My dear CoraLee,

    I am writing to insist you do not leave London yet. Tactical events are unfolding here which I am not free to disclose, but the strategy is advancing, the objective is clear and the concentrated manoeuvres appear more secure each day."

"Edwyn? What do you make of it?"

"Simply that my opinion of your mother has not changed, CoraLee. She is an enigma." He returned to his paper.

CHAPTER TWENTY-FIVE

Three nights later, Damion once again returned to a quiet house. It was late, and as his butler lit the lamps on the library desk, Damion requested a plate of food be sent to him. "Are the others still up, Philbin?"

"Yes, sir. That is, Lady Croxton has retired, but I left the younger ladies and the youngest miss in the lavender parlor. Shall I have your supper sent there?"

"No." Damion looked askance at the neglected correspondence and ledgers stacked atop one another on his desk. "I'll be in here for a bit." He picked up a packet of mail.

"Very good, my Lord. I'll see to your meal, and a fire as well."

Damion grunted his approval and remained standing, leafing through the paper pile. A footman entered immediately to light the fire and had just closed the door behind him, when the wood echoed crisply with two firm knocks.

Damion spun toward the entrance in pleased anticipation. He remembered Miss Adams's sweet greeting on the last occasion he returned from Greeley Hall. The only prop missing from the delightful domestic scene had been the kiss of an anxious wife, and his imagination had Miss Adams crossing the room into his embrace.

He'd done a lot of thinking about the school miss during the last few days, and it was time for a serious talk about their sham engagement and the future.

One of the double doors swung open, and he schooled his face to a polite mask, hiding his disappointment as Lady Chloe slipped in and closed the door behind her.

"Damion, thank goodness you've arrived!" Chloe looked about to swoon, putting the back of her hand to her forehead. "And not a moment too soon. I asked your butler to let me know the instant you returned."

The wrong woman rushed across the room, clung to his arm. Theatrically, she whispered loudly, "Disaster is about to strike this house."

"What? Grandmother?" Damn, he should never have left Fern Crest for a second visit to the Greeley's farm. Well, with Sarah faring well, there should be no need to desert his grandmother, ever again.

"No," Chloe's nose wrinkled. "She's still the same. Still batty." She didn't seem to notice his look of chastisement.

"Then what?" He coldly ignored the touch of her hand on his arm.

"Damion, I'm sorry to be the one to tell you this, but . . . your family is being threatened with extortion."

"*What?*"

Chloe jumped. "It's all her fault. I told you nothing good would come of this the day you brought her to Fern Crest."

"Whose fault? Get to the point, Chloe."

"Miss Adams. This is all her doing. You should have listened to me." Chloe stepped closer; improperly close.

Damion put a hand on each of her upper arms, and moved her away, but didn't release her. "What are you talking about?"

"There is a man, in the village." She watched him and said, her eyes narrowed, "While you've been gone, she's been sneaking out to meet with him." At Damion's shocked look, she added, "Isn't it interesting, my Lord, that she wouldn't accompany *you* to town, but couldn't wait to hurry to her little assignations there?"

Damion tensed. "What does he look like?"

Chloe shuddered. "If he weren't so vile, I'd suspect him to be Elizabeth's father. I've never bought that sister story." She folded her arms across her chest and humphed.

Damion released her and paced briefly. Had he been truly duped by Miss Adams? If so, his earliest instincts had been right: Elizabeth's father was still around, and very much in her thoughts.

He turned back to Lady Chloe. "You mentioned extortion. Because of Miss Adams? What makes you think she's got something to hide?"

Chloe heaved an impatient sigh, and then spoke as if he were a simple schoolchild. "Damion, people don't demand money for no reason. Only a guilty party would fear an extortionist."

"Why would . . . even if he were . . ." He could not bring himself to name the man as husband or lover. "Why would he demand payment of a penniless school teacher?"

Chloe smirked. "Haven't you guessed, *my Lord?* Because he believes she'll soon be rich."

Good God, and he'd been thinking these last few days of making her his wife in truth. He struggled to think clearly. "And what if he *is* Elizabeth's father? Perhaps I wouldn't give a damn."

Chloe lifted an eyebrow at that. "A child out of wedlock? Oh, that's nothing compared to what our innocent little school-teacher is hiding, Damion. Trust me, that is not her deepest, darkest secret."

He waited, his jaw tightening.

Chloe continued. "Perhaps *innocent* is the wrong choice of words." When he didn't rise to the bait, she enunciated crisply, "Our Miss Adams came from a brothel."

Damion's mind worked furiously, denying her words. "She

couldn't have. She's been at the school since she was a young girl."

"She may have been young when she arrived at that school. But you can believe she wasn't innocent. She and her mother were both . . . Well, let's just say *already well educated,* since we're in polite company, and leave it at that. Of course, she'll claim they were both only laundresses while there. But I doubt any respectable person would believe it to be so."

"If that's what she said, I believe her."

Chloe shook her head sadly. "Poor Damion. She really does have you bewitched."

Damion continued pacing. "How do you know this, Chloe? What proof do you have?"

"I met with him."

This stopped Damion in his tracks. He turned his head and stared, open-mouthed. "I can't believe you took such a stupid risk."

Chloe flushed. "I did it for you. I expected to be thanked." She bit out each word in anger.

Neither spoke for half a minute.

"Chloe, I'm sorry, but I must confirm your story with Miss Adams. I made the mistake of listening to you last time, about the necklace Grandmother gave her. I swallowed your imaginative tale and made a fool of myself, besides offending our guest. This time, I'm not going to assume Miss Adams is guilty solely because you have a suspicion."

Lady Chloe's face turned a shade redder, and her twisted face lost its beauty. "A suspicion?" she hollered. She marched to the door and he saw her shoulders shaking. "Is that what you think this is?" she asked loudly of the door, and then turned to face him. Her fierce countenance fell away, leaving a mask of disgust. "God, you're so enamored with her, you're blind! If you think I'm imagining all of this, Damion, then why don't you ask your little pretend fiancée where the necklace is? Your *grandmother's* necklace. The one *he* showed me." Chloe slammed the door behind her.

Damion paced, running all of his previous conversations with Miss Adams through his mind. It was no use to think of denting the paperwork tonight.

And what would he do if Chloe were right? He knew what he'd do. Whether he believed Chloe's story or not, he'd find the bastard who threatened the young miss, and he'd make him stop. He owed this to her, as her employer and protector, for all she'd done for his grandmother.

Besides, the man thought he'd soon have access to the Woodhurst wealth, which infuriated Damion. No man who thought to profit from Damion's family would get away with this.

Did he believe the accusations to be true? It didn't matter, he told himself with a forced shrug.

But a weariness heavy as a paperweight tugged at his soul, and he left the library at a pallbearer's pace for the lavender parlor. As his butler had mentioned, Lady Croxton had retired. So, it seemed, had Lady Chloe. Only Elizabeth and Miss Adams sat near the fire. Miss Adams glanced up with a delighted look when he entered, but her smile dropped when she saw his solemn stare.

He moved to the couch facing them and caught Elizabeth in a hug as she ran into his arms, oblivious of his dark mood. "Do you wish me to read you a bedtime story?" he asked the little girl.

She climbed up next to him and stretched to retrieve a child's book from the end table. Without looking at Miss Adams, Damion focused on the story. Elizabeth leaned against his arm, and he lifted it to wrap around her. The longer he read, though, the more often he found himself glancing up at Miss Adams, whose auburn hair was bent over her needlework, reflecting the golds and russets of the fire.

If an artist painted a picture of innocence, it would look as Miss Adams did at this moment. He didn't want to believe Chloe; he'd made that mistake once.

But—he stumbled on the sentence he was reading aloud—no slender gold chain graced her neck.

He heard a soft snore as Elizabeth began to topple a bit to the side. He shifted her to a more comfortable position against his vest and closed the book. He reached to place it on the end table at his side, and glanced up to find Miss Adams's stormy grey eyes watching him.

Only the child's steady breathing and the occasional pop from the fireplace broke the night's silence.

Finally, Damion spoke. "Miss Adams . . ."

"Yes?" One syllable, quieter than her needle slipping through the unbleached canvas.

"Is there anything we need to talk about?"

The needle stilled. "No, I don't believe so, my Lord." Miss Adams looked hunted. "Why do you ask?"

He shook his head slightly. "I've been gone several days. Just making conversation, I suppose." His insides were heavy, leaden. He'd hoped Miss Adams would open up to him. He wanted Chloe to be wrong. Or he at least wanted Miss Adams to tell him the truth, to beg his forgiveness, to ask for his help. He would help her, if only she'd ask or speak about it.

But she didn't. He thought he detected a flush on her soft skin a moment before she dipped her head to study her embroidery.

Damion regarded her, once more disappointed. Well, he'd see to the extortionist tomorrow. Regardless, he would not leave Miss Adams helpless in the snare of a man who would threaten young women.

Miss Adams looked up again, finding herself the object of his brown study. "Yes, my Lord? Is there something on your mind?"

"Where is your necklace?" he asked in a gruff monotone.

"I . . ." She put a delicate hand to her throat, her eyes wide, like frightened foals he'd seen separated from their mothers.

Did her hand shake, or did he imagine it?

"Perhaps I left it in my room."

"Shall I send a maid up to look for you?" He sounded disinterested.

"No. On second thought, I don't recall seeing it there. I believe . . . I think I do remember clasping it this morning." She looked at the floral rug, as if expecting to see it lying there. "Perhaps . . . perhaps I misplaced it." With her hand still at her throat, she wouldn't meet his eyes.

"I see," Damion said with finality.

Still she did not meet his eyes.

He stood, carefully dislodging the sleeping child from his side. Bending over, he picked up Elizabeth with ease, cradling her head against his shoulder as he straightened. She never woke, continuing to breathe deeply. "I am going to take Miss Elizabeth up to her bedroom." He saw Miss Adams put her needlework aside. "No," he said firmly. "Don't bother. Just send one of the maids upstairs."

Miss Adams remained seated. She was white. "Lord Woodhurst," she spoke urgently, quietly, "Please. Perhaps we should talk later. Privately?"

He sighed loudly, moving Elizabeth up higher against his shoulder. "Miss Adams, I'm tired. It's been a long ride, a long day." He hesitated. But he couldn't face any more lies. Not tonight. "We'll talk further in the morning."

Carrying Elizabeth, he turned his back on her and left the room.

CHAPTER TWENTY-SIX

Alix hadn't slept well. Her stomach knotted when she thought of the lie she'd told Damion last night, and the way he'd looked at her. She rose and moved to the looking glass. Her hand went instinctively to her throat, but she found no warm pendant to touch as had become her habit. In the mirror, dark circles under her eyes reflected her haunted mood.

When Milly entered with a tray of hot chocolate, she asked if her mistress was feeling well. Alix said she was in fact not feeling ready to rise, and asked Milly to return later. After the maid left, Alix didn't touch her morning drink. She was afraid it would not stay down, with warships bobbing in battle in the hollows of her stomach.

She dressed herself before Milly returned, not wanting to be fussed over or engaged in conversation. Her fingers trembled as she buttoned up the long sleeves of the cerulean blue morning gown. She must face him today; she must tell him any remaining truths she'd not told. She'd tell him of her childhood home, working in the bowels of the brothel with her mother. She'd also tell him of the extortionist who stalked her. It would be a relief to confide in another about the nightmares, and her waking fears as well.

She hoped he would understand she'd had no choice but to give Simon Blackthorn the blood-red garnet on its golden chain, especially as it was only temporary.

Simon had threatened to follow her back to the mansion and

confront Lady Charlotte. Alix couldn't allow him to come to the manor while the women were alone, with Damion gone to Sarah Greeley's.

When Alix showed him the exquisite piece of jewelry to seal the bargain and keep him away from Fern Crest Hall, she'd carefully made him promise he would sell it back to her the next time she returned to the village. Just as soon as she received her wages from Lord Woodhurst, she would immediately retrieve the necklace and return it to Lady Charlotte or Lord Woodhurst. She'd explained to Simon that its absence would be noted, but she assured him that in a few weeks she'd have money to purchase it back, and he had readily agreed, anxious to snatch the fistful of gold twisted with its precious red gem and diamonds from her hand.

It was the only solution she could think of to protect Lady Charlotte from the evil intruder. Surely Damion would understand and approve of her quick thinking. He would still pay her, wouldn't he? Now that his fiancée was on her way to Fern Crest Hall, wouldn't he agree Alix had fulfilled her part of their bargain? The moment she received her payment, she'd hurry straight to Simon Blackthorn and retrieve Lady Charlotte's jewelry. Then she'd return the necklace here, to its owners, and then . . . she'd leave for the school.

She pictured Damion standing behind his bride-to-be, and lifting her hair to clasp the pendant. He'd whisper something in her ear and plant a kiss on her neck. He'd admire his future wife in the delicate red and golden heirloom. Alix wiped her eyes with the tips of her finger, and, taking a deep breath, left the room to find Lord Woodhurst.

At the bottom of the stairs, she straightened her shoulders as she moved down the hall, still clutching her waist to still the twisting ropes. But he wasn't in the breakfast room.

Alix quietly greeted Lady Chloe, the only guest at the table.

Perhaps a piece of dry toast would help settle her stomach and her nerves before she faced him, before he joined them to eat. Taking a seat, she bit on a toast point and forced herself to chew woodenly.

Chloe stirred her tea delicately, the spoon quietly swirling, never touching the thin china. Without looking up, she said, "I met a man in town yesterday."

Alix froze. "A man?"

"Yes. I believe his name was . . ." Chloe stopped stirring and studied Miss Adams, who was unable to look away. "I believe his name was Blackthorn?"

Alix set the toast on her plate. She forced herself to swallow the little bit that stuck to the roof of her dry mouth. "What did he want?" It came out as a whisper.

"I know all about you."

Alix put her shaking hands together on her lap where Lady Chloe could not see them. Looking down, she asked stiffly, "What do you mean?" But she didn't need to ask. She knew exactly what Lady Chloe meant.

Chloe sounded exasperated as she said, "You can't possibly stay here now, you know. If Damion finds out you lived in a bordello, it will disgrace him and his family. Especially his grandmother. Think of what the shock will do to her."

Alix nodded. "Yes. I realize that." She sighed and with the sigh let go the last of her tattered pride, forcing herself to ask, "Are you going to tell him?" She doubted Lady Chloe had any more compassion than a teacup.

Chloe studied her nails. "I haven't decided. I think if you were to leave Fern Crest Hall immediately, it would not be necessary. His real fiancée should be here by end of day. Will you agree to leave this morning?"

Alix hadn't known Lady Ardis was expected so soon. She didn't think her stomach could feel worse, but now the ships were firing heavy canon balls broadside, and she felt the first jolting blow of nausea. "He'll wonder why I've left so suddenly unless I tell him the truth."

Chloe shrugged one shoulder prettily. "I'm not sure he won't be relieved. This will all be so awkward, with Lady Ardis arriving and finding you here. And imagine, should our Mr. Blackthorn approach Damion . . . No, I think it wisest if you leave before Damion returns from his morning errands, Miss Adams."

Alix nodded mutely. Once again, she hadn't known of his plans, yet it appeared everyone else did. It no longer mattered, though. Putting a hand around her throat, she said, "I see. Yes, I will leave as soon as Elizabeth and I are packed."

"I counted on your being sensible. He always says you have such common sense."

Of course, thought Alix. He would say I have common sense. He would never say I am beautiful, as he would of Lady Chloe or Lady Ardis.

"Shall you need coach fare?"

Alix shook her head, in a daze. "No, Lord Woodhurst gave me some pin money. It should be adequate. I am not going to be travelling to London, after all. Just . . . just returning to the school."

She'd have to trust he would send her promised wages to the school, so she could pay the despicable Mr. Blackthorn, and return Lady Charlotte's necklace another day.

Chloe nodded as she said, "I think that is practical. Teaching does seem to be the best option for someone of your . . . station. Why don't I summon Philbin, and he can arrange for a coachman to take you there immediately in the family's carriage?" Chloe moved to the wall toward the bell.

"No. Please, not yet. I wish to say my goodbyes."

"To Lady Croxton?" Chloe tittered. "She's so batty she won't even notice you're gone, once we switch in the real fiancée. Why don't you let me explain to her? Gentlewoman to gentlewoman, that is."

"No." Alix's chin jutted firmly. "I insist I will make my own excuses to her Ladyship. And, I am capable of calling the coachman when I have packed. Good day, Lady Chloe." She stood. She should have added, "And thank you for all your help." But she couldn't. Or she wouldn't. The woman had made life difficult here.

The two ladies left the room, Chloe sweeping triumphantly out the door, and Alix much more slowly, as if she were sleepwalking.

One minute later, there was a soft scuffle behind the covered end table. Elizabeth squeezed out from her hiding place and wiped her eyes. She reached under the table and pulled out her duck.

"Don't cry, Mr. Fizziwig. You don't have to go back to that school with me. The other children will take you away, and they won't let me play with you. Maybe Grandmamma will let you stay here and live with her, if you promise to be good."

Elizabeth sniffed back a cry and squeezed the duck in a fierce hug.

"Let's go find Grandmamma. She'll know what to do."

CHAPTER TWENTY-SEVEN

"Yes? Come in." Lady Charlotte studied her husband's book, transferring occasional notes into the floral satin-covered journal at her elbow.

When no one answered, she swiveled toward the door. "Yes?" she repeated. She saw a small head of curls at about door handle height. "Lizzie?"

The little girl looked hesitantly around the corner.

"Elizabeth! Why, that's the saddest face I do believe I've ever seen, child. Come in and tell Grandmamma what's wrong."

Elizabeth hurried over to the waiting hug, and looked up with trembling lips. She'd been crying. "I don't want to leave you, Grandmamma."

The older woman hugged her closer, then bent her head to the child's. "And I don't want you to leave either, dear. What is all this about?"

"If Alix leaves today, then I have to go, too."

"Today!" Lady Charlotte's brows lowered in distress. "But . . . but why would she leave?"

"I heard her talking to Lady Chloe. Lady Chloe said Lord Woodhurst's real fiancée is coming to live here. Tonight."

"That girl couldn't possibly be arriving so soon. We haven't finished putting our plan in motion. Oh, dear. Are you sure that's what Lady Chloe said? Did she say anything more?"

Elizabeth sighed. "I think I can't tell you."

"Why not?"

"I made a promise. And I don't break promises."

"Of course you don't! And I would never want you to break a promise." She leaned her grey head on the little girl's. "Elizabeth, would it be all right if I were to ask you a question? This way, you are only answering my question. You're not telling me any secrets on your own, right?"

Elizabeth pulled away and looked up at her hopefully. "You mean I wouldn't be breaking my promise?"

"I don't think so. But if you think it's something you shouldn't answer, you can tell me so. Shall we try it?"

Elizabeth nodded so hard her curls bounced.

"Here's a question. Did you think Alix was truly going to marry my Edmund?"

Elizabeth shook her head back and forth slowly, her eyes sad and solemn.

"Well, see, I knew that secret too, dear, that they were both pretending. So you're not telling me anything you shouldn't. Do you know the name of the guest who will be arriving tonight?"

Elizabeth continued shaking her head. "They said her name, but I don't remember it."

"Was it Lady Ardis?"

"I think so. Maybe. I don't know. But Lady Chloe said she's already on her way here." Elizabeth started to wail. "And Alix and me have to leave before she gets here."

"Says who?" Damion's grandmother sounded as imperious as her namesake, the queen consort.

Elizabeth stopped crying. Soft whimpers escaped between hiccups of breath.

"I'm not angry at you, dear. But I *am* angry at whomever said you and Alix have to leave. Did Edmund say so?"

Elizabeth's shoulders hunched up to her ears. "I don't know. But Lady Chloe says so."

"Humph! She is not in charge here. Lizzie." Grandmother put her hands on Elizabeth's shoulders. "Do you think Alix wants to leave us? Is she upset?"

"She sounded very upset just now." Lizzie tipped her head so it rested on Lady Charlotte's hand.

"When? Where was this?" Lady Charlotte stroked the little girl's head.

"In the breakfast parlor. I was playing under the serving table, under its skirt, because I pretend it's a green cave, like the cave outside by the creek where the plants make a roof. And then I heard them come in, Lady Chloe and Alix, so I didn't make a peep." Elizabeth used her thumb and finger to squeeze her lips together.

Lady Charlotte would have laughed, but nothing seemed funny at the moment.

"Lady Chloe said, 'If he finds out you lived in a board . . .' A low board, I think she said, 'Then you will disgrace him and his parents.' Oh, and she said and you, too."

"A low board?"

"Maybe a board low. I don't know what that is."

Lady Charlotte's eyes flew open. "Heavens! Did she say a bordello?"

"That was it!" Elizabeth nodded her approval. "What does it mean?"

"Let's just forget about it for now, dear. It's not a nice place for *anybody* to have to live."

"Is it worse than the school where me and Alix have to go back to?"

Lady Charlotte pulled her close. "I don't want you to go back, Elizabeth. And, yes, it is worse."

Elizabeth's eyes started tearing again. "Then I don't want Alix to have to go back there neither."

"No, she won't. We won't let her, will we?"

Elizabeth shook her head.

"What else did they say, Lady Chloe and Alix?"

"Lady Chloe said Lord Woodhurst was running some errands, and Alix should be gone before he comes home. Lady Chloe said she would call the carriage man for her."

"I'll bet she did."

"Alix said she won't leave until she packs and says goodbye to you." Elizabeth reached her arms as far as she could around Lady Charlotte. "I don't want to say goodbye to you, Grandmamma."

"No, dear, of course we don't want to have to say goodbye."

"Lady Chloe said we have to leave before that man from the village—" Elizabeth stopped in mortification.

"What man?"

Elizabeth's round eyes looked haunted. "I can't talk about it. You said I didn't have to talk about my secrets or my promise." She pressed her lips closed. "I have to go." She turned and ran toward the door.

"Wait! Wait, Elizabeth."

But the little girl didn't stop. She kept running.

"Are you busy?"

Alix glanced up from her packing to see Lady Chloe standing at the door. She wanted to snap, "Of course I am. Can't you see I'm packing?" Instead, she answered in a flat voice, "No. What did you want?"

"I want to introduce you to someone. She's waiting in the parlor."

"Who is—" Alix realized the answer.

"Well," said Chloe, "I didn't want to shock you."

"It's she? She's already here? Lord Woodhurst's . . . fiancée?"

"Yes." Chloe studied her, as if waiting to see if she would faint or scream.

"I . . . I didn't expect her to arrive so soon." Alix's lips trembled a bit as she said, "I'm happy for his lordship, of course."

An awkward silence descended.

"Come along, then, Miss Adams, since you're still here, and meet her. You'll like her." Chloe didn't sound interested either way as she added, "I'm sure you will."

Alix placed one foot in front of the other as she forced herself to walk down the long hallway. She'd been picturing the mysterious fiancée forever, it seemed. What would she look like? Damion was so handsome; surely his fiancée would be beautiful. Petite. Feminine. Blonde. Large eyes with thick eyelashes. Curls.

She turned the corner and entered the parlor. A young lady rose from the sofa, her manner cool and imperial. A young blond lady. A portrait of femininity. With large aquamarine eyes and curly hair. Beautiful. Of course.

Alix continued across the room, drawn to her like a magnet that repels when it gets too close.

"Lady Ardis, this is Miss Adams." Chloe stood aside, with arms folded, as if in anticipation of an entertaining Drury Lane farce.

"I'm pleased to meet you," mumbled Alix, wondering if they knew it was a lie. She didn't hold out her hand. Didn't curtsy.

The pretty young lady nodded, but her eyes darted to Chloe.

"I already told Lady Ardis who you are," said Chloe to Miss Adams. "She knows you've been pretending to be Damion's intended. She's not the least bit angry with you. In fact, she believes it conveniently opened the door for her return, and thanks you for standing in."

Alix wondered why Lady Chloe did all the talking.

The young woman finally spoke. Still not looking Miss Adams in the eye, she appeared to study the desk as she said, "Miss Adams, let me be blunt. You do understand how very awkward it would be for Lord Woodhurst were he to find you in the house now that I have arrived?"

Her voice was a flute, high and musical. Alix knew it would be beautiful, to match everything else about her. A perfect counterpoint to Damion's deep rumbling bass that sent thrills through Alix when he spoke.

Alix nodded dully. She was leaving this house. Leaving Damion. She would not let herself cry in front of these women. "Of course."

"I am glad we understand one another. In that case . . ."

"I am almost packed." Alix turned to Chloe, her body stiff. "I'll say my goodbyes, and I'll be gone." Her voice was as wooden as her stance. "I should thank you for all you've done these past weeks." *I should, but I won't.*

Chloe didn't meet her eyes either. "It was nothing," she murmured.

The three ladies stood, an awkward tableau in the middle of the room. Alix was the first to move. She almost curtsied, but stopped herself in time. She might be a lowly teacher of lowly beginnings, but she'd be damned if she'd curtsy to either of these ladies.

She turned at the door to close it behind her, and noted the other two women stood frozen where she'd left them, staring at her. She didn't bother to smile. She couldn't.

She practically ran along the hallway, determined to hold back the tears until she was alone. Turning a corner, she ran into Philbin, who was escorting a male guest to the parlor.

"Forgive me, Philbin," she stuttered. She inclined her bent head, and moved to the side to pass them.

"Whoa! I beg your pardon. It's Miss Adams, is it not?" Myles's tall frame filled the hall, as he stepped beside Philbin and looked at Miss Adams with appreciation in his eyes. "I can see why Woodhurst found you perfect for the part. Forgive me."

He bowed. "I am Cantwell, a friend of Lord Woodhurst."

"Please," she said in a strained voice. She did not look up, but felt her eyes filling with moisture. She waited for them to move so she could slip by. But Lord Cantwell didn't budge.

"Miss Adams, is everything all right?" He touched her gently on the arm.

Alix nodded mutely, and insistently squeezed past him to continue down the hallway.

"Miss Adams?"

She didn't answer him. She'd already reached the stairs and could see the path clear to escape to her room.

Myles caught up to Philbin, who waited taciturnly at the parlor door. As the butler opened it, Myles strode past him, not waiting to be announced.

"Chloe, what is the—" Myles stopped short when he saw his sister's guest.

"Myles! What a delightful surprise. And wonderful timing." Chloe took Lady Ardis's elbow and they floated gracefully toward Myles. "Lady Ardis, may I present my brother, Myles Grisham, Earl of Cantwell? Myles, Lady Ardis Pinster." Chloe tilted her face, her cat's eyes coyly admiring her friend. "Lady Ardis is one of my dearest friends from school," she purred.

Myles executed a perfect bow, mirroring Ardis's perfect curtsy. Both studied one another without embarrassment.

"Welcome, Lady Pinster. Your name is familiar, but we cannot have met. I'd certainly have remembered you." His eyes held hers in mutual interest. "Will you be staying long?"

Lady Ardis tittered, two musical notes. "I suppose I must, at least until I meet my fiancé."

"Ardis," warned Chloe, shaking her head in the barest warning. Briskly, she said to Myles, "She'll be staying a bit with us, brother, to keep Lord Woodhurst and his grandmother company."

"Ah, that's it. I knew the name was familiar. You and Woodhurst were engaged at one time."

"How did we never meet, my Lord, if you and Lord Woodhurst are friends?"

"I was travelling. My loss." Myles smiled engagingly, and then remembered why he'd entered the room. "Chloe, I've come to ask you about Miss Adams. I passed her on the stairs a moment ago, and she seemed upset. Is anything amiss?"

Chloe shrugged. "Really? What did she say?"

"That's just it. She didn't say anything when I introduced myself. Truth be told, she looked about to cry."

Chloe tsk-tsk'd.

"Well, I shall leave you two ladies until Woodhurst returns. Lady Ardis, I look forward to seeing you again." Myles bowed and exited.

Lady Ardis walked over to the door, peeked out, and then closed it. She leaned against it with a sigh. "Your brother is the handsomest of men. I find myself enthralled."

Chloe followed her to the door, and pulled her by the arm. "And you find yourself engaged. Don't forget that."

Ardis pouted. "I'm not sure I still want Damion. I think I'd prefer to be engaged to *him* instead."

"Ardis, you've got to make up your mind. Listen, as soon as Miss Adams leaves, if you're no longer interested in Damion, you're free to pursue my brother." Chloe looked disgusted. "Though why someone would want to is beyond me. But remember, dear, I've been behaving with perfect innocence around your ex-fiancé out of respect for our friendship. However, if *you're* no longer interested in Damion, then he's mine."

CHAPTER TWENTY-EIGHT

Elizabeth tugged on the fabric, pulling it over the little duck's head. "Mr. Fizziwig, you must sit still. I can't button your cloak."

With one glassy eye on the side facing his mistress, the duck stared at the little girl.

"And you have to be the best secret keeper. Exactly like me. All right?" She put a pudgy hand on each side of his face, turning him so his beak faced straight toward her. "All right?" She gave the hood another good tug, and the ivory button popped off. Elizabeth exclaimed, and chased it to where it rolled under the bed. Lying on her stomach, she crawled under just far enough that her little fist could grab it. She scooted backward and stood next to the counterpane, where her duck lay on its side.

"Ohhh. Look. You've lost your button."

She tried putting the button through its hole, but it fell through every time. "It's all right, Mr. Fizziwig. I think you'll be warm enough without your button. You can share my coat."

Elizabeth stuffed the duck inside the warm safety of her own cloak and headed downstairs.

Alix was packed and ready to leave. There hadn't been much to do, as she left the new clothes hanging in her wardrobe.

She sent the maid to pack Elizabeth's clothes. Alix wasn't sure whether to allow the little girl to take her new dresses and dolls. What would the headmistress say? Would it be more devastating to the child to leave them behind or to risk having them taken away when they reached Widpole Manor?

All that remained was to say her goodbyes to Lady Charlotte. Sighing, she looked around the room, tinted in apricots by the morning sun. Gliding over to the window, she took one last look at the scene below. The rose beds saluted her with fistfuls of violent colors at the tips of their branches. And the ducks quacked loudly, as if in admonishment of her desertion. A bittersweet smile touched her lips, as she remembered running out her door to rescue them the morning she'd believed they were drowning.

But that made her think of Damion, and the first time he'd touched her, on the stairs. She could still feel the lingering trace of his warm fingers as they'd outlined the curve of her shoulder. She could feel the touch of his lips on her cheek. She put a hand there now.

This would not do. She must not let these sweet memories depart with her. They must stay trapped here at Fern Crest Hall where they belonged. If they followed her to the school, she'd have no peace. No. When she closed the bedroom door—firmly—these memories of Lord Woodhurst must stay locked inside to haunt the next guest. Would this be *her* room, his fiancée's?

Alix turned away from the window to leave. And saw Lady Charlotte standing in the doorway.

"Alix, you can't be leaving." Lady Charlotte looked Miss Adams up and down.

Alix was sure the dowager countess wondered why she was dressed in the drab grey outfit, with her hair pulled severely back into tight auburn braids coiled primly around her head.

Alix turned her tear-stained face from the countess's close scrutiny. "These are my teacher's clothes." Alix smoothed the coarse fabric with her hand. "I'm returning to the school, my Lady."

"But what of your other . . ." Lady Charlotte's voice trailed off. "And what of our strategy? It's not fair. We never even had a chance to put our plans in place."

"We lost." Alix spoke softly. "It's too late, Lady Charlotte." Shaking her head, she said, "Did your husband never mention the Battle of Adrianople? Emperor Valens arrived too late. His strategy was all for naught. He was too late, and that one battle with the Goths led to the fall of the Roman Empire.

"But perhaps *we're* the Goths!" Lady Charlotte was animated as she moved farther into the room. "Don't you see? The Goths were *asked* to settle in Roman territory. And then they defeated the Romans. And you and I shall—"

"No." Alix smiled, but couldn't laugh. "We lost. The battle, the war . . . It's over, Lady Charlotte." Alix shrugged. "It's over."

The older lady appeared deflated. Looking around the room distractedly, she asked, "Where is your luggage?" Only one large, battered travel bag stood near the bed.

"There is nothing here for me to take with me. I don't mean to sound ungrateful, my Lady, but I cannot use the fine clothes you bought for me. Not where I am going." *And I can't even allow myself to take the memories of your grandson with me.*

"You do have something, you silly girl." Lady Charlotte crossed the remaining space and hugged Miss Adams. "You have my friendship," she said as she held Miss Adams in her embrace. Releasing her, she said briskly, "Promise me we shall write to one another and remain friends."

"I shall miss you terribly," said Alix. "More than you shall know," she managed in a choked voice.

"I shall miss you too, Alix. But that is not an answer to my request for correspondence."

"All right, I promise," she said. "Oh, Lady Charlotte—" Alix remembered. "About the pendant from your hus—"

"No! That necklace is yours, Alix, and I tell you I shall not accept it, nor shall I hear another word of it, else I shall become quite irritable. And I do not wish to be irritable as we say our goodbyes." She swiped her eyes with a silk handkerchief. "Why will you not wait until Edmund returns?"

"Did you not know? Lady Ardis has arrived."

"What? She cannot already be here. I am so upset, the last thing I need is to have guests."

"Lady Chloe's brother has arrived as well," said Alix. With chagrin, she said, "Perhaps they were afraid it would take several adults to evict me."

"If so, I shall be the one evicting them!" Lady Charlotte sputtered. "I don't want that cat-eyed Lady Chloe here another day, and she can take her brother and that . . . that . . . Oh, botheration! I shall refuse to refer to her as Edmund's fiancée."

This lightened Alix's mood, and she chuckled. "And what shall you call her when she is his wife?" But the small laugh died at the thought of another becoming his wife. "I must take my leave, my Lady, before your grandson returns."

"Alix, at least allow me to accompany you on the ride." When Miss Adams began to shake her head, Lady Charlotte added, "Please. It would mean so much to me. And you would be doing me a favor, because otherwise I'll have nothing to occupy me, and I might strangle the two ladies in the parlor."

"All right," Alix said with a laugh. "You've made me feel better already, and I am determined not to be so solemn. There is no use going to the school in a funereal coach. Let's enjoy ourselves, as we always have." She smiled. "What I mean to say is yes, I would treasure your company this one last time. I'll just fetch Elizabeth, and—"

"No!" Lady Charlotte moved to the bed, and sank down to

sit on it, the handkerchief clutched closely near her eyes. "Dear me, I shall try not to start crying, Alix, but please. Please tell me I may keep Lizzie with me. As my own." At Miss Adams's shocked look, the countess continued. "I realize that though the two of you are not related, you have the deepest love for one another. But . . . I think this would be best for her, to grow up as my ward. I wish to adopt her. Is that selfish of me? I can't bear the thought of losing her. No more than I can bear the thought of losing you."

Alix bit her lip. "No. That's not selfish at all. It's most generous of you. And . . ." Alix took a deep breath. "As hard as it is for me to say this, I must agree. Living with you *would* be best for Elizabeth. There is nothing for her at the school but training for a life of servitude. I'll miss her terribly, but at least I'll know—"

"My lady!" Milly burst into the room. She stopped short, and noticing the countess, said, "My Lady." She curtsied quickly, then turned to Miss Adams. "I can't find Elizabeth." The maid was pale and shaking. "I can't find her anywhere. I went to pack her clothes, as you requested, and sent the footman to bring her to me. But none of us could find her. We don't know where she's gone. And it's not like Elizabeth to hide, but we've looked everywhere, and—"

"Elizabeth!" exclaimed Lady Charlotte. "Oh, Alix, she was so upset."

"What? When? What about?" asked Alix.

"She overheard you and Lady Chloe talking, and she came to me—"

"She heard us? Everything?" Alix put her hands to her mouth. "She was in the room? I had no idea! Perhaps she's gone back to . . . I must go look for her."

"She'd been crying. She knew you were leaving. Oh, dear, where do you suppose—"

"I'll help. We'll find her." Alix rushed to where Lady Charlotte sat on the bed and put her hands on the woman's shoulders. "I won't leave until we find her. I'm sure she's fine. I'll check the schoolroom and the attic. She likes to play there." Alix moved quickly to the door.

"I'll have the servants turn the basement floor upside down," volunteered Milly as she hurried out behind the ladies.

Everyone exited in a hurry, spinning off like tops in different directions.

Lady Charlotte should have walked more slowly, as she'd been too upset to remember her cane.

She tramped along the muddy path by the stream, her heart in her throat. She knew this was Elizabeth's favorite hiding den, among the plants arching over the creek. What if Elizabeth had been so upset she'd slipped on the bank and fallen into the water?

The creek, which had always seemed bubbly and friendly, looked sinister. Dark fern fronds hung over its edge. The path was slippery; recent rains had made it as slick as an otter's pelt. The countess ducked through tunnels of honeysuckle vines, which met above her to form a dark cave.

She was almost there. What would she do if she couldn't find Elizabeth? She was afraid to look at the water, but she made herself scan it for bits of floating cloth.

Lady Charlotte cried out. Ahead, she spied something lying on the side of the path. Something familiar.

She stooped and touched the green fabric mound. Mr. Fizziwig was sitting in the grass, facing the water. Turning him around, she saw he was missing the button on his cloak. She picked him up and scanned the creek again. Nothing floated in the water. Her eyes closed in relief.

She walked more slowly, alert for clues or noises. And she

heard a sound. Was it the water gurgling over the pebbles? She turned her head, listening with both ears. There. Yes, a sound that was distinct from the water.

Lady Charlotte took several more steps and stopped. She heard it again, more clearly. A singing?

She moved forward. No. It wasn't a song: it was soft crying.

She hurried through the brambles, and a thorny vine caught and bit her forearm. She ignored the red welt and pushed on ahead.

"Lizzie? Elizabeth?"

The crying stopped. "Grandmamma?"

"Lizzie!" Lady Charlotte saw a patch of yellow through the bushes and hurried around the curve in the path. She couldn't stop the tears spilling from her eyes as she rounded and saw Elizabeth huddled in a small cave of laurel bushes, clutching a soft woolen cloak in her fists. Elizabeth's eyes were swollen.

"Darling, Grandmamma is here. Everything is all right, Lizzie."

Lady Charlotte held her arms open, and Elizabeth flew to her, wrapping small arms about the older woman's waist. Her small eyes were squeezed tightly shut.

"Grandmamma! It's *not* all right. I have to go away, and I can't be with you anymore." This brought fresh tears to both of them.

"Lizzie, Lizzie," Lady Charlotte crooned, rocking back and forth soothingly with Lizzie captured in her arms. "Everything will be fine." Lady Charlotte wiped away her own tears, and then Elizabeth's. "And look," she held out the duck. "I found Mr. Fizziwig. Did you know he was lying in the path back there, all alone?"

Elizabeth nodded, but didn't reach for her pet. "He asked me to leave him there."

"He asked you? But why?"

"He knew I was going to run away, and he said he didn't want to go back to the school." Elizabeth's eyes were pleading as she looked up at Lady Charlotte. "Jenny Noelle is mean, Grandmamma. She will take Mr. Fizziwig away from me. She takes all the dolls away from me. And she'll take his handsome cloak from him. Mr. Fizziwig wants to stay here at Fern Crest Hall so he can be safe, near you, Grandmamma. I told him it was a good decision."

Lady Charlotte made herself talk past the catch in her throat. "I think it's a very good decision. For *both* of you. I want you both to stay near me, Lizzie, where it's safe. I'm not going to let you go away. Do you believe me?"

Elizabeth buried her face and nodded against Lady Charlotte's dress.

"Good!" said the older woman. "Now, let's get you and Mr. Fizziwig cleaned up, and we'll sew a new button on his cloak as well. Do you think he would like that?"

Elizabeth nodded and took the duck from Lady Charlotte's hands. Holding him close to her young face, she said, "Mr. Fizziwig, did you hear? We're going to clean your feathers, and me and Grandmamma are going to fix your button. And Jenny Noelle won't be able to hurt you or take you away. And you get to live with me and Grandmamma." She glanced up. "Forever?"

Lady Charlotte nodded.

"Forever," Elizabeth repeated. She leaned back into her grandmother's arms, holding up the wooden duck. "See? He's smiling."

CHAPTER TWENTY-NINE

Damion Templeton, Viscount Woodhurst, lusted to kill. There was no magic sword at hand to slay the bloodthirsty dragon usurping his mind, body, and soul. The coming settlement with Simon Blackthorn consumed him with a fever he'd never experienced in his life.

He fought to harness his rampant anger as he rode through the village, approaching the inn. He wasn't afraid of confronting the extortionist. He was afraid of killing him too quickly.

Always in command of his passions, Damion was shocked by the blood drumming through his veins, so loud he could hear it carving a channel. His hands shook, curling into choking machines without his notice. He forced himself to a cool calmness by focusing on the various ways he could destroy Simon Blackthorn. It was important to Damion that he be in control of himself during this meeting.

Breathing deeply, he entered the noisy tavern. He'd had to stoop at the low lintel like a nocturnal bat swooping into the darkness, the collars of his great coat turned up, and his brow half-concealed by a hat pulled low.

He found the man matching Simon's description holed up in an even darker corner.

"Blackthorn?"

Simon worked to focus his eyes, rheumy with beer. With unconcealed belligerence, he said, "Mayhap. Who are you?"

"Someone who needs . . . a favor." The flash of gold as Damion opened and closed his hand revived the man, who sat up, blinking, ready for business. Damion sat down on the bench facing Simon Blackthorn. "Your Christian name?"

"Simon." This said with a slight slur. "What kind of a favor are you needin'?"

"Perhaps advice from an expert such as yourself is all I need."

"You'll pay for advice as well." Simon watched Damion's large fist, salivating for another peek of five-guinea pieces.

"That's not a problem," said Damion, sliding his hand back into his pocket.

"I'll have the money first," demanded Simon gruffly.

"I think not." Damion stared coldly, waiting until Simon broke eye contact briefly.

"Well, then, out with it." Simon looked petulantly at his empty earthenware mug. He raised it toward Damion, one eyebrow quirked, but was ignored.

"I have a friend," said Damion.

"Sure you do." This was accompanied by a guffaw. "Tha's what they all say." Simon held the empty mug toward the nearest barmaid. "And what's your *friend's* problem?"

Damion was pleased the fever in his veins had been replaced by cool water; he felt calmly in control of himself with this human scurf. "This *friend* is being threatened."

"Does he know who's threatenin' him?"

Damion let Simon believe it was a man they discussed. "We do."

"Then, if you know who it is . . ."

Damion nodded. "Yes, and now I must do . . . whatever it takes to end this."

"Despicable deeds, you mean, which fine-sleeved gentlemen prefer not to be associated with." Simon winked at the maid as she set down the slopping mug.

Damion was hit with nauseating disgust that a man such as

Simon might have fathered Elizabeth, if Lady Chloe was correct. "I wish to discuss and explore some options," said Damion. "Through business acquaintances, I know the captain of a merchantman that trades to the Indies. He happens to be in port. Quite tyrannical, from what I hear, but I think he'd be more than willing to impress a man found on the wharf, drenched with liquor, unconscious."

Simon chewed on the idea. "Aye. But what if the man makes it back? It's a quick solution, I agree, but in a few years . . ."

"Another option," said Damion, "might be to have him badly roughed up. A warning."

Simon liked this better. Nodding, he said, "Sure. But you'd need to break some bones, or it don't scare 'em badly enough. Maybe slice off a finger, you know? Nice and slow. Put the fear in 'em. Do you need someone to do it for you?" He'd sobered; appeared eager.

"But that's not a guaranty, either," said Damion, ignoring the offer.

Simon shrugged one beefy shoulder toward his chin. He had no neck to speak of. "Well, unless you're lookin' to murder the man and be done with it."

"How would *you* do it, Blackthorn?"

Simon sounded bored. "Slit throat's preferable to the gun. Less noisy. Easier to escape the notice of witnesses."

"Messy," commented Damion. "It might get traced back to me. I don't want to hang for murder."

Simon sneered. "Your hands would stay snow-clean, guv. You wouldn't be doin' the murderin'. And I'd swear on the saints and my soul that no one would ever know."

"I'm not asking you to do it, Blackthorn." Damion wore an unfathomable mask. "I'm more than willing to kill the bastard myself."

Simon looked confused. "Well, I gave you your advice. Let's

have my payment."

"But there's one other option we didn't explore: beating him at his own game."

"And what game is that?"

"Extortion," said Damion. When Simon didn't answer, he continued, "What do you think of this? I frame him for a crime. I must make certain it is a hanging crime, but nowadays, what isn't?" Damion's teeth gleamed in the dark cavern. "This way, the courts hang him, and I remain innocent. Yes, I believe I could frame him for a theft. Make sure he gets caught."

"How would you seed the goods?" Simon looked wary, as if Damion were slightly mad.

It was Damion's turn to shrug. "I'm not too concerned. We'll find it in his room. Or perhaps we'll find it on his person." He watched Simon closely. "Something so valuable, I don't think he'd hide it anywhere else." Damion sat back. "Anyway, all that remains is to find it in his possession, and he'll hang as a thief." He grinned. "Extortionists, thieves, they all swing from the neck in the same direction." Damion nodded to himself in satisfaction. "Yes, that should do it. The man is found with a very expensive piece of stolen jewelry, perhaps a family heirloom. A large garnet. Diamonds. That should—"

Simon started, and made to rise.

"Don't move, Blackthorn! I have a gun pointed at you under the table. If you move one inch from your seat, I'll have to shoot you. In truth, though, I'm a terribly bad shot. I *think* it's pointed at your stomach, but it could well be aimed several inches lower."

Perspiration glistened on Blackthorn's swarthy skin. "I didn't steal it! She gave me the necklace."

"Did I say it was a necklace? I don't recall saying that, Blackthorn."

Simon's face was dark, livid. "What is this? What is it you

want from me?"

"I want you to leave Miss Adams alone."

"I'm tellin' you, the bitch gave me the necklace of her own free will."

Damion's finger tightened on the trigger. Had this man forced himself on Miss Adams? Damion was sweating, fighting the blood fever again threatening to take over his vision, his sanity, his hand. One jerk of his finger, and Blackthorn could never hurt Miss Adams again.

"Is this the man, my Lord?"

Damion took a deep breath before he looked up at the Bow Street runner standing near the table, his weapon trained on Blackthorn.

"Yes," exhaled Damion.

Simon's mouth twisted violently as he looked at the stranger, pointing a burly arm at Damion. "I tell you, he's tryin' to frame me for somethin' I didn't do!"

The stout, muscular man in tight vest and jacket spoke to Damion as if Simon hadn't spoken, as if Simon didn't exist. "We found it in his lodgings, my Lord, as we guessed." He dug his other hand in his pocket and held an open palm toward Damion.

Even in the dusky, smoke-filled tavern, the diamonds sparkled brilliantly around the perfect crimson garnet. The delicately roped gold glinted in candlelight.

"She gave me that necklace!" yelled Simon. "I didn't steal it!"

"Yes," drawled the runner. "I'm sure she did. A family heirloom. And exactly why would she give it to a scurvy mate such as you?"

Damion noted Simon's hesitancy. It appeared Blackthorn was debating whether extortion was as serious an offense as theft. "You'll hang regardless, Blackthorn." As Damion rose, his gun still pointing at Simon, he added, "Unless, that is, you favor that working crew to the Indies? I know for a fact Mr. Potter here would be more than willing to oblige. Of course, you won't be able to show your ugly face in England again."

Damion stood next to Potter, who held his fist to Damion and tipped the handful of gems over to the viscount.

Damion pocketed the necklace, and both men stepped back, motioning for Blackthorn to rise.

CHAPTER THIRTY

The coach swayed with a gentle lullaby rhythm, and Elizabeth snored softly, curled next to Lady Charlotte. The countess took this opportunity to reach across and touch Miss Adams on the knee.

"Alix, you haven't said anything, but I know you must wonder how I can adopt a child at my age."

Alix smiled. "No, I don't, Lady Charlotte. I don't doubt there is anything you cannot do, at this age or in another twenty years."

"Well, thank you, but I must tell you I've thought hard about the silliness of an old woman adopting."

"You are hardly old!"

"You know what I am saying. I've been thinking, Alix. I shall need a governess for Elizabeth. I'd prefer you come with me."

Alix shook her head. "I appreciate the generous offer. And I wish I could."

"But of course you can. And I was about to say it would not be merely a governess position. I'd want you to be my companion, Alix. In truth, I would consider you a member of the family, as dear to me as Elizabeth."

"I am touched, my Lady. More deeply than you know. But I cannot."

"Why? What other plans do you have other than teaching at the school? And I'd feel terrible knowing I've deprived you of Lizzie's company."

"It would be selfish of me to deny Elizabeth a loving home, and a loving guardian," said Alix. "I am so happy for Elizabeth. I prefer this to her returning to the school."

"I don't understand, Alix. I know in my heart we are more than fond of one another. And Elizabeth will be with us. What reason could you have for turning your back on us and returning to that school?"

Alix twisted her hands as she composed her thoughts. When she looked up at Lady Charlotte, her eyes were moist. "Forgive me. It seems all I've done lately is cry. Lady Charlotte, I do love both you and Elizabeth. But . . ." She looked down again, shaking her head sadly. "I also love your grandson. I know now I should never have allowed this to happen." With wonder, she looked out the window and added, "I don't even know when it did happen." Her eyes sought the older woman again. "I only know it is true. Can't you see? If I were to come and live with you—his family—I would be tortured by his visits, and by the sight of him. I should be the spinster companion, watching him marry another woman. I would see him kissing his wife beneath the mistletoe on holidays, and I would see him watching his wife grow plump with his children—I can't." She stumbled on the last phrase and stopped talking.

Lady Charlotte patted Miss Adams's knee. She left her hand there and didn't say anything more.

Alix placed her hand atop the older woman's, and again stared out the carriage window. Lady Charlotte sat back, sliding her hand out, and turned to look solemnly out her own window.

After a few minutes of silence, Lady Charlotte spoke. "Before the child wakes up, Alix, I would ask a favor of you."

"Any favor, my Lady, other than . . . other than that." Alix gave her full attention.

"Listen before you decide," said the dowager countess. She looked at the child to make sure she slept, and lowered her voice further. "In my will, I shall leave a trust for Elizabeth. Part of that trust will be for someone to care for her, and for her inheritance, should . . . should I not be able to, until she is an adult. I wish to name you as that person." When Miss Adams opened her mouth to protest, Lady Charlotte said, "You would not have to live in my home, or even near my family. You would have the money to take Elizabeth to wherever *you* are. It would be a very generous settlement, Alix."

"I am sure it would be." Alix did not hesitate. "You are a most generous person, Lady Charlotte. And even if Elizabeth came without a penny to her name, she shall always have a safe home with me."

"Thank you, dear."

The two women continued the journey in companionable silence, each staring at the passing countryside without seeing it.

Damion strode impatiently into the library.

"What's this about, Chloe? Philbin insisted I stop in here to see you at once. I'm extremely busy. I need to see—" His impatience turned to concern. "Is my Grandmother well?"

"Yes, yes, your grandmother is fine. Or, at least as fine as a woman in her condition can be. She appears the same as yesterday. No, this is not about her."

"Is it Miss Adams? Or Elizabeth?" Damion was white.

"They are fine as well. At least, all is fine *now*. I wanted to inform you we have guests."

"My parents are here?" Damion, again impatient, turned to leave.

"No, not your parents, Damion. My brother Myles is here—"

"Wonderful!" He turned back in pleasant surprise to Chloe. "Why didn't you have Philbin inform me himself? Where is your brother?" Damion looked impatiently toward the door again.

"That's not what I wanted to tell you, Damion," said Chloe with an exasperated sigh of pettiness. "If you will only attend me, I have some delightfully good news I am anxious to share."

Damion made a polite effort to give her his attention. "What news?"

Chloe stepped closer to Damion, close enough to trace a finger delicately along his arm. "I think you'll be happy to know we've solved several of your problems, Damion. I know how upset you were about the pending embarrassment of the extortionist. Well, that problem is solved."

"Solved?" Damion lifted a brow as he looked down at Lady Chloe, whose hand still lingered on his sleeve. How would Chloe have known about his successful errand in the village?

Chloe beamed up at him. "Yes, I've taken care of everything for you. For one, Miss Adams and Elizabeth are gone."

"What?"

Chloe jumped back, startled at his tone. "Don't worry, the details have all been thought through. You'll still have a fiancée to please your grandmother. And your parents. *Especially* your parents," she added smugly. "You'll be quite pleased with what I've orchestrated, Damion. I told you I would make a perfect—"

"What have you orchestrated?" It was a fierce whisper, as Damion grabbed her arms.

She looked at the clamps of his hands, and spoke quickly. "I found you a proper fiancée, Damion. A *very* proper fiancée." When he didn't release the viselike grip, she pulled free and stepped around his desk, putting a few feet between them, rubbing her arms. "Knowing our little Miss Adams has quite the scandalous skeleton just waiting to fall out of her closet, and the extortionist on her trail—"

"I told you I don't give a damn about the extortionist.

Besides, the man's been taken care of." Damion looked toward the window, then the door, ready to be back in the dust of the road again, immediately. "Where is she? When did they leave? Are you sure they've gone?" He took a step backwards.

"Wait!" Chloe hurried back around the desk toward him. "She wanted to leave, Damion. There's no point going after her. She won't return, especially since I told her your real fiancée was waiting to step into her shoes."

He looked through Lady Chloe. He didn't say anything. He didn't move. If he moved, he'd walk over to her and choke her, he was sure.

"You told her *what?*"

"I explained to her that Lady Ardis was your true fiancée. And that Lady Ardis has only recently returned to England, professing her interest in renewing the engagement."

Damion was too stunned to speak for a moment. "Please tell me you did not say that Miss Adams thinks Lady Ardis is still my fiancée. Last month I had *no* fiancées. This week they are coming out of the corners."

Chloe pulled out a handkerchief and sniffed, dabbing at her eyes. "I thought I was doing you a favor!"

Damion ran his hand through his hair. "I cannot believe this."

Chloe dropped the handkerchief faster than her pretense of tears. "Damion, you don't need Miss Adams."

"Yes, I do, Chloe. More than you know."

She moved closer and put her hand on his arm possessively. "But you have me."

"The last thing I need at this moment is another fiancée. You *or* Lady Ardis. That debacle of a betrothal is finished, thank goodness. And *this* farce has gotten out of hand."

"Then make it more than a farce," she pleaded, her face upturned to his. "Propose to me, Damion. Make it real."

His lip curled. "Please, Chloe. You're the last woman in

England I'd want for a wife. Especially right at this moment." He spun on his heel. "Perhaps I can still catch her."

After he exited, Chloe clenched her fists. "I hate you, Damion Templeton. And I would be the perfect wife for you." She crossed her arms peevishly. "But perhaps now I won't even consider it, until you beg me to."

After standing in petulant silence a minute, she realized she'd better find Ardis and let her know Lord Woodhurst might not be the smitten lover waiting to embrace his ex-fiancée tenderly.

"I will ensure the school has the proper papers drawn up with greatest haste, Lady Croxton." Headmistress Staunton leaned forward obsequiously, as if bowing.

"I shall have my counselor review them as well, Madam Headmistress. Thank you for accommodating my request so quickly." Lady Charlotte glanced, smiling, at the little girl at her side who clasped her hand tightly, as if afraid she'd be sucked away through the ominous walls of the office.

"So, Elizabeth," said the headmistress. "You have a new home." The woman smiled her sharp-toothed little smile, and Elizabeth stepped behind Grandmother's skirts.

"Yes, mum," she mumbled.

"Elizabeth." Lady Charlotte prodded her forward gently. "Will you curtsy and say your goodbyes to Madam Headmistress? Then we may be on our way back to Fern Crest Hall."

Elizabeth looked up at Lady Charlotte with starry eyes. "It's really true? I'm to leave with you, Grandmamma? Today?"

"Today," said Lady Charlotte firmly. She glanced up at the headmistress. "Are there any belongings I need to gather of Elizabeth's before we leave?"

The headmistress appeared embarrassed. "No. No, I don't believe so. Elizabeth?"

Elizabeth shook her head. "I don't have nothing, Grandmamma."

"Do you mean, 'I don't have anything,' Elizabeth?" asked Lady Charlotte.

"I don't know what *you* have, Grandmamma. I meant *I* don't have nothing."

Lady Charlotte placed a ringed hand on the little girl's head. "But now we have each other, don't we?"

Elizabeth nodded in awe.

CHAPTER THIRTY-ONE

The sunny yellow coach wheels matched the lustrous canary varnish on the lower half of the travelling coach. Above the elbow line, the upper door and sashes wore a mirror of black lacquer. A matched team of blacks snorted their impatience, ready to trade their satin coats for a fine sheen of sweat. Soon, both animals and coach would be dulled by the fine highway dust.

The sunny yellow coach wheels did *not* match the mood of any of its occupants.

Myles Grisham, earl of Cantwell, slumped in one corner of the coach, arms folded across his chest. At Lord Woodhurst's insistence, Myles was to see the two ladies escorted back to London. Apparently, for some reason Myles did not fathom—or appreciate—Damion blamed his friend for all of the present problems at the manor, and in particular for Chloe's presence at Fern Crest Hall. Damion had further insisted Myles would not be welcomed back unless he could swear on a holy book that he had witnessed both women deposited in London—*did he think they'd escape on the way,* wondered Myles—Did he really think they'd wish to return to this hall of wrath, solely for the fun of enduring Woodhurst's sour temper? Myles puffed his lips out with an expulsion of disgust.

Lady Chloe sat across from her brother, brooding on the many reasons she hated Lord Woodhurst. Unfortunately, she only had ten fingers. She also hated her brother, for she *was* sure it was his fault she had wasted several parties' worth of weeks at Fern Crest Hall. And all for naught, as Damion had been intolerably rude as he'd escorted her just now, her elbow pinched tightly in his brutish hand, all the way down the manor steps as he rushed her out to the gravel sweep and into the coach. In full view of the staff! She rubbed her elbow tenderly through the fine muslin, certain the lout had bruised her delicate skin.

All those weeks wasted companioning a batty, dying woman and a scheming, penniless prostitute. And this was the thanks she received! Then she recalled the promise of a trinket from Rundell and Bridge. Very well, she'd make him pay. Perhaps her brother would agree to a quick shopping detour once they reached the city? She opened her mouth to ask, but snapped it shut when she found Myles scowling deeply at her. Well, there'd be plenty of time to cajole him on the long ride to London. She looked impatiently out the window, where Lady Ardis and Lord Woodhurst stood next to the coach, nose-to-nose.

"You'll be sorry, Woodhurst!" The occupants in the coach could hear every word Lady Ardis threw at him, could practically see the venom riding each word through the air. "You could have had me. *Me!* I can't believe you are choosing that pasty-faced church mouse. You must be more desperate than even I thought you were all these years."

She yanked her glove on. Everyone heard the delicate seam rip at her violent wrench. She screeched, and pulled off the torn glove.

"This is your fault." She threw the lacey glove onto the ground. Yanking off its mate, she shook it in his face. "And don't expect to come crawling back to me. Because I won't be there for you this time." She threw it down in the dirt with its mate, furiously, without a glance where it fell, holding his gaze all the while in a glare.

Unlike Ardis, Damion's voice was calmly dispassionate. "I never expected you to wait for me, Lady Ardis. And well you know it. We ended our relationship, thankfully, and what you do with your life now or in the future does not interest me in the least."

Her eyes narrowed further at his words. It was quiet of a sudden. After a calming deep breath, Lady Ardis said slowly, "It's your loss then. Because you could have had me if you wanted, my Lord." She stepped closer, her voice a throaty intimacy. "Do you know, other men *pant* for me?" She looked up at him through thickly blackened lashes, her ample chest almost touching his. In a sensual voice, she said, "I'll have you know I can have any man in the *ton* that I want."

His reply was cold. "Yes, I believe it. And from what I've heard, you already have."

Her bare hand cracked across his cheek. "I'll ruin you for that, Woodhurst. And don't think I won't." She stepped smartly into the coach, taking the seat next to Chloe.

Damion didn't lift a hand to help her, didn't close the carriage door. Didn't touch his cheek, didn't move.

Lady Ardis leaned out, her feathered hat getting caught on the top of the window. Impatiently she shook it free. "You won't be able to show your face in London, my Lord." She drawled the honorific. "Not after I tell them your precious little bride-to-be grew up in a brothel." Her lips curled as she spat out the word.

He moved into full view of the occupants of the carriage. His eyes bored into hers. "You do that, Lady Ardis. And after you do, all the *ton* will soon find out the real reason our engagement was ended."

This stopped her. "You wouldn't!"

"Oh, but I would. I think they'd be utterly fascinated to know I discovered you in Knightbridge's garden the night of his party.

Lying on your back atop a marble bench. With your skirts flung up over your face, and Sir Roderick hovering above you."

She slammed the carriage door shut, making the horses skitter. The window was still lowered, and Damion put his hand on the sill.

"And may I give you a word of advice, Lady Ardis?" He didn't wait for her answer. "Next time, at least find a man who wants to look at your face as he makes love to you."

She was still screeching as the coach rolled forward at Damion's signal.

Damion was questioning Philbin, hoping the butler might know where Miss Adams could be located, when they were interrupted by his grandmother's arrival.

"Edmund, we must talk. Before it is too late." Lady Charlotte swept into the room with a determined stride.

Damion signaled his manservant to leave. "We'll continue our discussion shortly, Philbin." By time the door closed, he was already at his grandmother's side. "Please. Sit down, Grandmother." He handed her onto a long, comfortably-padded sofa. "Shall I call for the doctor?"

"The doctor! No. Whatever are you talking about?"

Damion straightened. "You said before it is too late. Too late for what, Grandmother?"

"Too late to stop your plans for marriage! Edmund, I want to talk about your choice of spouse."

His jaw tightened. "And that is why it is called a *choice*. Forgive me, Grandmother, but it is *my* choice. Not mother's. Not father's. Not yours."

"But your choice affects the entire family. And your entire life. Edmund, you must *not* marry that girl."

Damion paced, choosing his words as he re-crossed to the sofa. "Grandmother, all these years you have hounded me to marry. Finally I tell you I shall marry, and now you do not want me to?"

"Of course I want you to marry. I simply don't want you to marry *her.*"

His lips pressed together; it took him a moment to answer. "I find her above reproach. Is it her lineage that concerns you? It cannot be her manners. And I thought you both had such high regard for one another. I know she considers you an angel."

"How on earth—? Why, that's absurd. We barely know one another." She sniffed; pointed her lorgnette at him. "Your mother and father may approve of her, but I do not."

"Mother and father have never met her. And it's inconsequential to me—"

"What?"

"I said it's inconse—"

"No. Before that. You said your mother and father have never met her. How can this be?"

"They haven't. She—"

"Your mother could not stop talking about her." She remembered what Miss Adams had told her. "Even Lady Chloe admits your parents are enthralled with this gel."

He shook his head firmly. "I tell you they've never met her. And *I* never set eyes on her until a few days before your arrival."

"Edmund . . . I am so confused." She put her hands to her brow, then placed them back on her lap, and looked up at her grandson. "May we begin again? And may we promise to be honest with one another?"

He opened his mouth to speak; shut it. "Grandmother," he said after a moment's hesitation. "There are certain things I'm not sure I want to hear your honesty on."

"Please, Edmund? To amuse an old woman?"

Damion looked toward the door, as if he could see Miss Adams's whereabouts through the wooden panels. He sighed; nodded to his grandmother.

"Sit, dear. Here. Next to me. Oh, could you pour a drink for me first? I fear I may need it."

She waited to speak until he returned from the cabinet with two drinks. He took a seat next to her as he handed her a glass of rattafia.

"Edmund." She reached for his hand. "I could always talk to you so easily. I always treasured the fact we were honest with one another."

He squeezed her hand in return. "We were, Grandmother. When I was young, I knew if I asked you for an honest answer, you would always tell me the truth."

She smiled.

"But," he continued, "that's when I was a boy. The man I've become may be too . . . stubborn . . . to want to hear an honest answer."

"I see," she said. "Young lads may endure advice, but a grown man might not?"

"Precisely."

"And are most men like that?"

Damion grinned. "Was my grandfather like that?"

"*Touché*, Edmund. Yes. He was . . . stubborn." Her eyes twinkled. "But he was his own man. And I loved him for it."

"Shall you love me for that as well?" He put a hand on her arm.

"No. Because I couldn't argue with *him*. But I believe I can get away with it with you."

He laughed. "How charmingly honest of you, Grandmother." He raised his glass in salute. "Very well. I shall try to keep an open mind, but my first reaction is to become defensive."

"I appreciate your honesty as well." She raised her own glass in salute, and they shared a smile.

"Let's begin again," he said. "My fiancée—"

"No," said Lady Charlotte. She saw his surprise at her interruption. "Edmund, we must begin several weeks ago. Before I arrived at Fern Crest Hall."

He waited politely for her to continue; took a sip.

"It starts with my friend, Lady Elderberry. She was my dearest, my closest friend. It starts the week I lost her."

"I am so sorry. I didn't know."

"I wanted to tell you, to share it with someone. She was on my mind, you see. Behind every sorrowful, bittersweet word flowing from my pen to paper . . . Do you recall my note to you? About dying?"

He looked down at his glass. "How could I forget it? It brought great sadness to me."

"You felt *my* sadness, Edmund. Coming through the paper."

Damion looked up. "But you never mentioned *her* death."

"Didn't I? But every word I wrote was because of her death. I remember sitting by the fire, pen in hand, thinking about everyone I loved. Especially you. You and Lady Elderberry have always been the two persons closest to the center of my heart." She wiped a tear from the corner of her eye, and her grandson took her hand again. "And I no longer have her. I thought about how little I've seen you recently, Edmund. And how much I've nagged you. All I wanted was to see you again. Not to see you wed, but solely to see *you.*" She twined her fingers in his. "And, I'd decided to take that trip Lady Elderberry and I always said we'd take together. To Wales. I'm going to Wales, Edmund."

"But—How can you? Your health . . ."

"I am in perfect health, dear. Well, perhaps not perfect, at this age." She chuckled.

"Your letter said—"

"It was a mistake in wording. As I told you, I was quite distressed that week. And distracted. It was Lady Elderberry's death I referred to, not my own. My letter said I would not be here, and that I wanted to see you before I left. I realize I did say I would be leaving, but I meant on a trip. A trip to Wales."

"I thought . . ." He was embarrassed to put it so bluntly.

"I know, and I am sorry." She squeezed his hand. "I never meant for you to think that. It was not intentional. And I should have corrected it immediately, I know. But then your mother rushed over to visit, and . . . I can see now, in hindsight, of course, how maudlin and fatalistic my letter must have sounded. But all I wanted to tell you, from my heart, was that I was going to go away—to Wales—and I felt such a strong need to see you before I left. That was all. But when we realized you meant to marry so soon, and we guessed it was my letter that was the cause . . ."

He shook his head.

"Oh dear, please don't be angry at me. Please."

He looked up at his grandmother with tears in his eyes. "Angry? Because you are not ill? Because you are not dying? I am unspeakably happy." He leaned over and gave her a hug, holding her.

When he sat back, she pulled out a handkerchief and dabbed her own tears away. "I have so enjoyed our time here together. It's been . . ." She sniffed. "Magical."

"I agree. And we must see each other more often in the future. But why didn't you tell me the truth right away? When you arrived?"

She looked askance. "Well, that. Though misleading you with my letter was never my intent—of that I am innocent—I must admit I took shameless advantage of the situation. I even forbade your mother to write and correct the misunderstanding."

"I am amazed my father allowed her to go along with it."

"Yes. Him. Well, I had to promise that after he arrived I would confess all. Or rather, I'd not stop him from telling you the truth."

"But what if he'd written me sooner?"

She raised an eyebrow. "Your father? Put pen to paper?"

"Ah."

"Yes. As you see, I was not in fear of *that* happening."

They sat a moment in silence.

"So," said Damion. "This was quite a misunderstanding."

"I wanted that misunderstanding laid open between us. I feel better now."

Damion rubbed his large hand across his face and sighed.

"What is it?" Lady Charlotte asked.

"I think it is my turn to speak the truth."

"About . . . ?"

"My fiancée."

"Oh, thank goodness! You will now tell me you are not truly engaged to that young lady."

He stood and was soon pacing. "No. I wasn't. I mean, I am not." He turned to face her. "When I thought you were . . . not going to be with us much longer . . . I decided to make you happy. But I never intended to go through with it."

Her brows were almost touching her hairline. "I must again be truthful, and tell you I am relieved. I—"

His own brows lowered. "No. Say no more."

"But why?"

"Because I intend to soon change the situation."

"To send her home?"

"No."

Lady Charlotte put her hand to her throat. "Edmund. Don't. You are making a mistake."

"Grandmother," he warned softly, "do not say anything we shall both regret. I plan to ask her to be my wife in truth."

"Oh! This is all my fault. If I'd foreseen this . . ." She looked at him. "You love her?"

"Yes."

"And you think she truly loves you?"

"I don't know. I hope so. If not now, I shall do my best to win her love." Damion seated himself close to his grandmother's side. "She deserves to be happy. She has not had a happy life."

"Then why did you two break the engagement before?"

"What do you mean?"

"You were engaged to this young woman a year or so ago. Why—"

"Not *this* woman. I was engaged to Lady Ardis." As he said her name his lips curled slightly, as if smelling spoilt egg.

"Edmund. What are you saying? What woman are we speaking of? If not—" His grandmother's eyes lit up. "Do you mean . . . Can you mean . . . Edmund," she demanded loudly in haste, "exactly which young lady do you plan to marry?"

"Miss Adams, of course." He shook his head in confusion. "Grandmother, whom else could I mean?"

"But Alix said that Lady Chloe said . . . and Lady Ardis arrived, and . . . Oh, dear! Edmund! I thought you were going to marry that horrid Lady Ardis."

His silence bespoke his shock.

"When she arrived here, I was sure of it. And she's . . . well, she is so like Lady Chloe. They are two halves of a rotten walnut." She grabbed his arm and rose, pulling as if to pull him up with her, but it was a useless effort, as she was not strong and he was solid. "You must go to Miss Adams, and tell her!"

Damion rose. "Lady Chloe told me she'd already left. But she can't have gone. I had Milly look, and all of her dresses are in her cupboard. And Milly says her other . . ."

He hesitated, but didn't blush, Lady Charlotte noticed. Of course; she was certain her grandson could name more ladies undergarments than she could, if it came to a contest.

"Unmentionables?" she suggested dryly.

He nodded. "Her other unmentionables are in place as well."

"So, therefore you have concluded she is still here," she said with a tinge of asperity. "Yet you cannot locate her. Perhaps she is wandering the farthest pasture, as I'm sure she's wont to do." She waved behind them. "Perhaps she is hiding under a table."

Damion, lost in thought, did not appear to hear. "She must still be here on the estate. Else why would her clothes be here?" He looked at his grandmother.

With deliberateness, she said, "Perhaps she went someplace where such fancy dresses are not needed."

"Not only ball gowns. Her walking dresses are here as well."

"All right. Let me restate, with less ambiguity, Edmund. Perhaps she went someplace where walking dresses are not needed either."

She watched her grandson; knew the precise moment he realized what she was saying. He looked sharply at her, probably wondering what else she knew.

"Oh God, I've been such a fool," he said.

"Yes. We've already established that, Edmund. Now, what do you plan to do to rectify it?"

"Pardon me, grandmother. I need to educate myself, obviously. And, I know just the school."

"I can only hope you will not find you've learned your lesson too late, grandson."

He bowed, and began toward the door. Spinning around, he walked quickly across the floor, and placing his hands on his grandmother's shoulders, he kissed her softly on the cheek.

"Thank you, Grandmother. I love you." He grabbed her in a quick, fierce hug, then strode across the room again.

"Edmund."

"Yes?" He turned impatiently at the door.

"She *is* the wife for you, Edmund."

"Yes. I know." He smiled grimly, then hurried out.

CHAPTER THIRTY-TWO

Georgie's hand shot into the air. "I know, I know! Miss Adams, I know the answer." In his exuberance, he knocked his hornbook from his desk.

Alix waited until he retrieved it, then smiled and nodded at him. She sat at her desk facing the class, watching dust motes slant down sunbeams in the familiar old schoolroom. Lucy had welcomed the break from teaching today's class, and Alix needed to move quickly back into a routine. It wasn't as easy as she'd expected, though, to engage her attention.

Georgie stood, his arms straight as rulers along his sides. As he recited, Alix found herself glancing out the window. It seemed both familiar and odd to be back here so suddenly. She rose from her chair and glanced at Georgie, and then her concentration drifted as she moved toward the irregular window panes.

This morning she'd looked out her bedroom window. No. She'd looked out the bedroom window at Fern Crest Hall, no longer hers. She'd looked out on rose gardens and bobbing ducks, and the silver ribbon of a faraway river. Here . . . The school yard came into focus. She looked at an old horse-chestnut tree with a knotted rope swing and some dry islands of straw-colored grass that survived in the trampled dirt yard. Only the hardy dandelions still wore green.

Fine. She was happy to be back at the school, happy to be helping the children once more. She folded her arms across her chest and glanced over at the third row, fifth seat. Vivian sat there by herself. Normally, the little girl shared that seat with Elizabeth.

There was an Elizabeth-shaped hole in Alix's heart as well.

She sighed, and then realized the young boy was silent. Still standing, he looked at her expectantly.

"That was very good. Thank you, Georgie. You may sit."

Georgie stayed at attention, his eyes large. He was looking past Miss Adams, where a tall, dark-haired stranger lounged in the doorway, a finger placed conspiratorially over his lips. Several children giggled.

Alix's eyebrows lifted. "Georgie," she said kindly, "I said you may take your seat now."

"Yes, Miss Adams."

Georgie looked around at the other children as he sat. They were all aware of the man who filled the entrance to the small schoolroom. One little girl could stand it no longer. "Miss Adams!" She pointed her tiny finger to the classroom doorway.

Without turning, Alix knew who it was: Headmistress Staunton.

The woman would assume Lady Charlotte had died, of course. Like a vulture, she'd descended to feast upon the grisly details. Alix was exasperated. Her spirits were not up to the woman's interrogations. And couldn't she see Alix was in the middle of a lesson? Sighing, Alix did not turn to acknowledge the headmistress. She merely looked over her shoulder. And gasped.

Damion rapped on the door frame with his knuckles. "May I come in, Miss Adams?"

She turned to face him, conscious of her drab schoolteacher's dress. With an ineffective gesture, she smoothed the rough homespun skirt, then lifted a hand to touch a curl that had pulled loose from her severely twisted braids. Her face was hot with embarrassment that he should see her like this.

Alix glanced hurriedly at the children. "Please practice your letters."

They buried their heads over their desks, peeking up through strands of hair, as if that made them safe from detection. Alix stared at Damion without moving, half believing she beheld an illusion, as the viscount was outlined in the same bright sunlight throwing fairy beams across the classroom floor.

"May I?" he repeated.

She nodded mutely.

Damion stepped across the threshold, one arm behind his back.

Alix moved a few steps toward the door; stopped a safe distance from him. "Why are you here, my Lord?"

Of course. He was here to recompense her per their agreement. She was afraid if he came any closer, he would hear the thundering of her heart.

Sadly, but with a smile to belie his words, he repeated, "Why am I here? Not 'I am so happy to see you again, my Lord?' "

Alix ignored that. "And why is your hand behind your back?"

He took another step into the room, a step closer to her, and brought his arm from its hiding. The snowy sleeve of his immaculate jacket ended in a massive bouquet of bluebells. On tall, grassy stalks, masses of elongated bells crowded together.

Alix sucked in her breath. "They are beautiful! Where did you find so many?"

Damion studied her as he said, "I found them on the other side of the wall. Where you told Tommy they grew."

She smiled. Had it been only a matter of weeks since she'd first met this man riding by the school wall? This man who had turned her world upside down?

The other side of the wall. She'd never known before what was there, and now that she knew, she could never have it. In the future, if ever she looked, she'd see only barren ground along the lonely road . . . like the school yard and her life on this side of the wall.

"There's nothing there, and you know it," she chided softly.

"That's not true. It's where the best treasures are to be found."

"Treasures?" Her throat was dry.

"Bluebells, charming schoolteachers who fall from the sky . . ."

"My Lord," she whispered, her hand at her throat. "Please. Don't make me cry in front of the children." Alix glanced down to hide her trembling lip.

Folding her hands primly against her skirt, she cleared her throat. It would be best to be businesslike, formal. Alix looked up at Damion with determination. "Besides, this conversation is most inappropriate." *The man was engaged.* "How is your fiancée?" she asked, too brightly.

When he did not answer, she continued. "And why are you here, my Lord?"

"Why do you suppose I am here, Miss Adams?" he asked with the hint of a smile.

She did not see any humor in their situation. With a hint of annoyance, she stated, "You are here to pay me my wages, I hope. Per our agreement."

Damion lowered one eyebrow aristocratically. "Unfortunately, I don't believe you kept your part of the bargain, Madam."

"What?" She glanced around at the children. "Carry on, please," she told them.

Caught staring, they snapped their faces down with great concentration.

Alix spun back and whispered fiercely, "We made a bargain. You shook on it."

"We did make a bargain: Fifty pounds if you remained until

my family departed. And you must admit they cannot have departed, since my parents have not yet even arrived."

"But—"

"One hundred if you could convince them. However, prior to their arrival, I find myself without your presence as my fiancée, so they obviously will not be convinced."

"But," she sputtered, "that's not fair. You *have* a fiancée. And I couldn't possibly stay once she arrived. You can't have *two* fiancées running around the manor when your parents arrive!" Her voice became louder, inflamed by the injustice of her situation.

"Shh, Miss Adams," he counseled her, with a brief nod behind her.

Alix looked slowly around. Fifteen pairs of eyes watched them. Over half of the small mouths hung open.

"May we step outside?" Damion asked.

She turned back to him. "I . . . I don't know."

"Just for a few minutes. I promise you will receive your one hundred pounds, if that is all you are concerned—"

"Shh!" Her eyes flew wide. "Don't speak of giving me money. What will the children think?"

This seemed to resolve her. She moved toward the door, and Damion followed closely. They walked to an outdoor bench, not too far from the classroom's window. From here she could keep an eye on her students.

"I was teasing you about the money. It is yours, as we agreed." Damion sat next to her, and she scooted to the farthest edge of the rough plank, frowning. "Miss Adams, these are for you." He held out the armful of scented flowers.

Alix shook her head, her hands locked together on her lap. "This is not proper. You must know I cannot accept a gift from a man who is betrothed to another."

She pictured the cool Lady Ardis accepting this bouquet

from him; the flowers matched the exquisite lady's eyes. Perhaps their hands would touch as they exchanged the precious gift. Alix looked at Damion's large hand. The thought of another woman feeling his warm touch tortured her and she blinked back a tear, reaching out a finger to wistfully touch one perfect bell-shaped bloom.

"Please. I want you to have these. It's a very small token, just a bouquet of wildflowers."

Alix knew she should not accept, but her hand reached for the stalks. She already pictured them hanging upside down from a rafter in her small bedroom, cheering its drabness as they dried. She would treasure this simple gift from him forever.

She buried her nose in the bouquet, her eyes closed, inhaling.

Something tickled her hand. She held the flowers away, and saw they were tied with several twined strings. And . . . another string. A shiny string. She turned the stalks up for a better view, as the bluebells nodded to the side.

The garnet pendant swung from the twined bundle.

Alix's gaze flew to Damion's. "How did you . . . ? Where . . . ?"

"You're safe from Simon Blackthorn. Forever." And he did place his hand upon hers.

Her heart thundered at the touch she craved, wrongly. Tears of confusion filled her eyes. "He came to Fern Crest Hall?" she whispered in mortification, picturing Lady Charlotte's discomfort and shock. "Oh, I am so very, very sorry!"

"No, he did not."

"But, then how . . . ?"

"I tracked him down, Miss Adams, and confronted him in the village."

Alix looked down in shame. "I . . . I was afraid to tell you. Though I wished many times that I could. But he wasn't your problem. And I was going to return it." She handled the necklace chain delicately, and then looked up into his eyes. "Please believe me, my Lord. I was going to return it, just as soon as you paid me my wages. He—Simon Blackthorn—he promised to give it back to me, in exchange for the money."

Damion shook his head. "He wouldn't have."

She opened her mouth to protest.

"Miss Adams," he said, "I *do* believe you had every intention of buying it back from him. And I believe that you had every intention of returning it to my family. But I believe just as firmly that Blackthorn merely agreed to appease you at the time. This necklace . . ." He held up the end that dangled. ". . . is worth more than five times the wages I would have paid you. Simon Blackthorn was not about to give it up in exchange for your one hundred pounds."

Alix looked about to faint, but quickly revived, angry now. "That blackguard! I've half a mind to—"

"No." It was a command.

She put a hand on her hip, ready to argue with him.

"He's gone," said Damion. "You'd never find him. Well, perhaps *removed* is a better word. Removed, as one would remove vermin from the house. Or," Damion said, smiling with satisfaction, "perhaps this vermin has gone to join the other lice on a ship."

As she comprehended, Alix's body sagged with relief. "I don't know how to thank you," she said softly, wiping warm tears from her cheeks with the back of her hand.

"Escape with me," he whispered as quietly. "I know you wish to escape from here."

Alix looked toward the classroom. Several heads quickly ducked to the side and out of view.

"How can I?" She did not even deliberate. "No, my Lord. I won't come to work for you at Fern Crest Hall. Nor for your grandmother."

"I'm not asking you to come back as an employee."

Alix's brow wrinkled. "Then I don't understand. Your wife . . ."

"Miss Adams, I have no wife," Damion said impatiently.

"Well, that's a matter of time. Your fiancée, then—"

"Listen to me." He laughed. "Good God, if you were any other lady of my acquaintance, I'd know you were being purposely coy. Miss Adams, please, listen carefully. Lady Ardis will *never* be my wife. Never. And she is *not* my fiancée, in spite of what she or Lady Chloe told you. Nor will she *ever* become my fiancée. Again," he added sheepishly.

Her heart skipped one beat before it turned over.

"Furthermore," he continued, "Since you made a promise to pose as my fiancée and then ran away, refusing to continue thus before my parents have arrived . . . Well, I see I shall have to use my best powers of persuasion to convince you to become my fiancée in truth."

Alix blinked, but couldn't respond.

"We'll return to Fern Crest Hall," Damion continued, "and we'll announce our engagement. After my grandmother departs—on her *trip*," he added dryly, "we shall depart for our own honeymoon. I do believe you knew about my grandmother's little secret?"

"I wanted to tell you!" Alix felt her cheeks turning pink. "Truly, I wanted to confide in you, but I thought she should be the one—" She gasped. "Did you say honeymoon?"

"I did."

"Would we go—"

"To Bath?" he said. "Yes, I believe that was the agreement."

Alix was overcome with happiness. Everything in the world seemed impossibly wonderful. Lady Charlotte would live. Elizabeth had found a happy home. She, Alix, would become Damion's wife.

"Miss Adams," he interrupted her rapture with a dimpled grin. "Are you more excited about a honeymoon trip to Bath than you are about becoming my viscountess?"

Alix laughed through more tears. "Only if you'll show me the bridge."

Damion sighed dramatically. "Yes, I suppose I must, if that's what it will take to convince you to marry me."

Alix smiled slowly. "But you haven't asked me properly, my Lord."

To her shock, Damion came off the bench swiftly, and planted one knee in front of her, in the powdery dirt. He took one of her hands in his. His touch felt as warm and as solidly right as she knew it would. "Miss Adams, I would be honored if you would become my wife. Will you?"

Alix could not contain her teasing smile. "And we shall walk together at Prior Park, down the path you described, to the bridge: your favorite spot?"

"We will. And, when we return, I shall build the same bridge for you at Fern Crest Hall. Over Drowning Duck Pond."

She chuckled, but it bubbled out through the tears as a happy sob.

"Now, Miss Adams: Will you marry me?"

"Oh, yes. Yes!" Alix wrapped both hands around his.

Damion, capturing her hands, rose from where he kneeled and pulled her up from the bench. They stood close, facing one another. He pulled her even closer until they were thigh-to-thigh, and only then did he kiss her.

Alix and Damion broke apart at the sound of cheering and laughter, turning as one to the classroom window. Its panes were covered by a bevy of hands and noses pressed against the glass, and mischievous grins and laughing faces.

"Oh, dear, I do believe we've shocked the students." Alix laughed, her delight bubbling over.

"Then I plan to thoroughly scandalize them and kiss you again."

"Is it on the curriculum, my Lord?"

"It is now, my love." And he did kiss her again.

ABOUT THE AUTHOR

Sharol Louise and her husband live in the Pacific Northwest, where her psyche was born. However, her body was born in Los Angeles, so it took about 25 years for the two to catch up. As a youngster, she thought people were referring to the dictionary when they said "the good book," as she grew up in the library reading Edgar Rice Burroughs, Mary Stewart, and Sir Arthur Conan Doyle. Sharol is a docent with The Seattle Public Library.